CW00499287

NO MEMORY LOST

VALERIE KEOGH

BLOODHOUND
— BOOKS —

Copyright © 2020 Valerie Keogh
The right of Valerie Keogh to be identified as the Author of the Work has been
asserted by her in
accordance to the Copyright, Designs and Patents Act 1988.
First published in 2020 by Bloodhound Books
Apart from any use permitted under UK copyright law, this publication may
only be
reproduced, stored, or transmitted, in any form, or by any means, with prior
permission in
writing of the publisher or, in the case of reprographic production, in
accordance with the
terms of licences issued by the Copyright Licensing Agency.
All characters in this publication are fictitious and any resemblance to real
persons, living
or dead, is purely coincidental.
www.bloodhoundbooks.com

ALSO BY VALERIE KEOGH

For my sister, Patricia Hudson.
This is your reward for reading all those rough drafts.

An Garda Síochána: the police service of the Republic of Ireland.

Garda, or gardaí in the plural.

Commonly referred to as *the guards* or *the gardaí.*

Direct translation: "the Guardian of the Peace."

1

The high hedge around the abandoned house dulled the sound of traffic and shielded the group from the curious eyes of the crowd that had already started to gather. Soon they'd be joined by news cameras and journalists and the questions would start.

But for now, Detective Garda Sergeant West stood quietly, unable to take his eyes from the battered brown suitcase that lay open among the weeds. He couldn't see the contents from where he stood, but the case was small. If there was a body inside, it had to be smaller still. With a deep breath, he moved closer, taking careful steps through the undergrowth with his bootee-covered feet until he was close enough to see, breathing slowly in and out to calm the sudden painful grip he felt in his belly, moving closer still to be within touching distance. Squatting down, his eyes focused on the small, skeletonised body curled up inside.

'Female,' the man already squatting opposite said quietly.

Detective Garda Andrews wasn't a man given to taking uneducated guesses. West examined the small body more carefully. The child's hair was long, but he wouldn't have been able to say, with certainty, which sex it was. Then he saw it. A small hair slide almost lost in the tangle of unkempt hair. 'That's probably as much as we're going to learn from her clothes,' he said, eyeing the remnants of fabric that partially covered the small bones.

He sat back on his haunches. Had the child died here, curled up and alone? Or was she killed and tossed away like garbage? Either way, it was grim. 'She's so small,' he said. 'How old d'y'- think? Three or four?'

Andrews, picturing his five-year-old son, Petey, shook his head. 'Maybe not that old.'

West stood and looked around. The front garden was long, the house barely visible behind overgrown shrubs and trees. It looked abandoned. 'You know anything about this place?'

Andrews pushed to his feet and stood beside him. 'No, I don't, maybe one of the uniforms will.' Turning, he looked back toward the gate where a number of uniformed gardaí were unrolling crime-scene tape. 'Garda Mackin,' he called, raising his hand at the same time to beckon him over. 'Do you know anything about this place?' he asked when the garda hurried to his side.

Garda Mackin was young but eager to impress. 'The owner died a couple of years ago,' he said promptly. 'The new owner, a nephew I think, put it up for sale almost immediately, but then the housing market crashed and he withdrew it. I guess he's waiting for the market to recover again. There was a problem with squatters about a year ago. It took a while to get them out and he boarded up the downstairs windows afterwards. I don't know the exact date,' he blushed and added hurriedly, 'but I can get it for you.'

Andrews shook his head. That kind of information would be easy to find once they were back in the station. 'Anything else?'

Mackin, wishing he had something exciting to add, shook his head regretfully. 'No, we kept a close eye on it for a while, but there were no reports of anything suspicious.' He waved a hand toward the street behind. 'It's a quiet road. The neighbours are quick to pick up a phone if anything fishy is going on.'

Andrews dismissed him with a nod and turned to West. 'So, it's been pretty much left alone for the last year. I'll get the dates when we get back.'

West pointed toward the brambles and nettles that had invaded what had once been an orderly hedge. 'They're a good deterrent, Peter.'

'And there's usually a chain around the gate,' Andrews told him. 'The uniforms that answered the call used bolt cutters to get it off.'

Raised voices alerted them to the arrival of Niall Kennedy, the pathologist. With a wave, he headed in their direction. He was wearing the biggest Wellington boots either man had ever seen, lifting his feet with exaggerated effort that made both men smile and shake their heads. Kennedy was a short man, not above five-five, and the boots, designed for a much taller person, made him look ridiculous.

'We've a new supplies officer,' he explained, stopping in front of them, 'he must think we're all giants. I'll have to drop in on him and explain that it's my personality that's oversized, not my feet. But never mind that,' he said, waving it away like an irritating fly. 'Sorry, I'm late. The traffic was stop-go the whole blasted way. A most inconvenient time to find a dead body,' he joked before his eyes looked past the two men and saw the victim. 'Ah, God,' he said, his face falling.

West wanted to snap that God wasn't very much in evidence at the scene, but he bit his tongue. They all had their own way of dealing with what they faced. If a prayer, to the god that West wasn't sure he believed in anymore, helped the pathologist, who was he to criticise?

He stepped away from the immediate scene, Andrews following behind, and they waited silently.

They weren't waiting long. 'There's not much to tell you,' Kennedy said, joining them, his face unusually grave. 'There's no obvious sign of injury, no broken bones.' Pulling his gloves off, he rolled them up and shoved them into his pocket. 'Based on ornamentation, it's likely to be female, but that's all I can say until I get everything back to the morgue.'

'Any idea how long she's been there?' West asked.

The pathologist shrugged. 'At a very rough guess, I'd say several months. I'll have a better idea after the post-mortem.'

'Wouldn't being closed up in the case have slowed decomposition down? Could we be looking at a longer time period?' West asked.

Kennedy shook his head. 'It would have slowed the initial decomp, certainly, but once those insects got in, the interior of the case would have become wet and warm and the process would have been accelerated.' He sighed heavily. 'We're really busy thanks to that car smash in Bray yesterday, but I'll bump this poor scrap to the head of the queue. It's not going to take very long.'

And with that, he left, his gait less exaggerated but still enough to raise an automatic smile on everyone he passed.

His departure was a nod to the garda technical team to move in. Normally, they were a noisy bunch, shouting directions, commenting on the scene, calling for various pieces of equipment. But this time, their silence was unsettling. Even these veterans of multiple crime scenes were silenced by the tiny body so carelessly abandoned.

The boy who'd found the suitcase was standing quietly near the gate. Already unnaturally pale, his lower lip trembled and his eyes grew larger as the two six-foot tall men approached.

With a hand on his arm, West drew Andrews to a halt.

'Maybe you'd better have a word with the uniforms to see if they've organised a house-to-house yet. If the two of us get any closer to that boy, he's going to pass out.'

The boy looked relieved when Andrews moved away, but his lower lip still trembled.

West gave the boy a reassuring smile. 'What's your name?' he asked.

The boy gulped and looked at him from the corner of his eye. 'Toby Ferguson.'

'I know you've already told the other gardaí, Toby,' he said, 'but can you tell *me* what happened?'

It was a simple story. The boy was walking to school with friends when one of them, for a prank, threw his backpack over the hedge into the garden. 'They ran off and left me,' he said. 'I had to climb over the gate to get in. My bag was lying among the nettles.' He held up his hands to show the distinct raised lesions he'd suffered as a result. 'When I picked it up, it disturbed some of those bigger weeds. That's when I saw the suitcase.' He blinked and looked even younger. 'I didn't mean any harm; I just wanted to see what was inside.' His gulp was louder this time. 'When I saw what it was, I came away and rang the guards.' The smile he tried was forced, shaky, and didn't last long. 'Then I rang my mum,' he said. 'She's coming to take me home.'

Before West could answer, a woman rushed through the gate, hair askew, forehead lined with worry. 'Toby!' The cry was part relief, part terror. She pulled the boy into her arms and held him tightly. Her eyes closed for a second and when they opened, they were fixed on West in indignation. 'What the hell is going on here?'

West explained briefly. 'We'll need Toby to sign a statement of what happened. I'll send someone to your home, if that's acceptable.'

Mrs Ferguson kept her arms wrapped tightly around her son. 'He said there was a body in the suitcase.'

West nodded. It would be in the papers soon enough, there was no point in keeping it a secret at this stage. 'It's the skeleton of a small child.'

'A child,' she said in horror. But her look of horror quickly turned to puzzlement. 'A child?'

West knew what she was thinking. There'd been no reports of a missing child. If there had, they'd all know about it. A missing child stayed in the headlines until found, one way or another.

There wasn't an explanation to offer her, so he addressed himself to the boy. 'You did the right thing, Toby. Thank you.' He looked back at the mother. 'You can leave now, Mrs Ferguson. We'll be in touch.' Turning, he saw a crowd had gathered outside the gate. 'I'll have someone walk you to your car,' he said. 'Where are you parked?'

'On the roadway,' she said, and with an attempt at humour, added, 'I hope I didn't get a ticket.'

West gave a quick smile. Gallows humour. He was used to it.

A raised hand brought Mackin running to his side. 'Walk Mrs Ferguson and Toby to their car, please,' he said, before looking around for Andrews. The garden was empty apart from the technicians working methodically. Already, to one side, a pile of sample containers was building up. Maybe they'd get lucky.

He took a last look around at the sad resting place of the child and walked slowly toward the gate where he pulled the overshoes off and dumped them into the rubbish sack that one of the uniforms had set out.

Andrews was busy instructing the uniformed gardaí. The house-to-house was unlikely to turn up anything useful, but you never could tell and anyway it was standard operational procedure. If they didn't tick every damn box someone would complain. And West was determined not to give anybody cause.

Ken Blundell's face swam into his head as it had done repeatedly during the two months since his death. A death that was a direct result of a foolish decision West had made. He'd been lucky. His career could have ended, but Inspector Morrison had come through for him, telling the powers that be that the decision to send Denise Blundell on an anger management course rather than prosecute her for assault, had been his. Morrison had lied for him, in fact, and as a result, it had quickly blown over. It wasn't something West was going to forget in a hurry. He also couldn't forget, that if he'd followed the rule of the law and prosecuted Denise Blundell, her husband would still be alive.

From now on, he was determined to be a model, law-abiding officer.

He looked up and down the road. Beech Park Road. You couldn't get a quieter suburban street but he wondered bleakly what other horrors were hidden away behind the closed doors. On that maudlin thought, he walked briskly to where Andrews was giving final orders to the enthusiastic gardaí that stood around him with all the eagerness of red setters desperately wanting to get off the leash.

It brought a grin to West's face. Andrews wouldn't let them go until he was happy they all knew exactly what to do. He wasn't a man who believed in improvisation.

'Let's get out of here before the reporters show up,' West said as the last officer headed away.

Andrews took a final look around and nodded. 'Not much more we can do here.'

They were in luck. As they climbed into their car, they saw a van with Raidió Teilifís Éireann blazoned along its side pull up. An eager news reporter climbed out followed by a camera-wielding companion. They'd be looking for someone to question. Without waiting, West put the car into reverse, and took off. 'Phew!' he said. 'A respite, Peter.'

'It'll be brief,' Andrews said. 'Nothing gets the press baying for blood more than the death of a child. We'll have reporters from RTE haunting us until we give them some answers.'

West negotiated the heavy commuter traffic, switching from lane to lane. 'I've been searching my memory,' he said eventually, moving the gearstick into neutral as the traffic stalled. 'We haven't had an unsolved missing child case in Dublin, have we?'

'There was one reported in Cork about a year ago,' Andrews said. 'A mother and a toddler went missing. The mother's body was found in the River Lee a month later, but the child's was never found. It's assumed she drowned. There haven't been any others that I've heard about.'

West shot him a glance. He guessed any police officer with a small child made a point of being aware of what went on. The traffic started moving. He changed into gear and minutes later pulled into his parking space outside Foxrock Garda station.

The desk sergeant, Tom Blunt, looked up as they came through the door. 'A bad one,' he said simply before returning to his computer.

Neither man commented. What was there to say?

2

In his office, West sat behind the desk and picked up the phone. The sooner Inspector Morrison knew, the better prepared he'd be when the phones started ringing, demanding information.

He gave him the little they knew. 'The body was obviously there for several months, Inspector,' he said. 'We've been promised autopsy results later today; until we have more to go on, we're just following standard procedures.'

Inspector Morrison grunted. 'A child. I can already hear the press demanding answers. We've no outstanding missing person reports, I assume?'

'None,' West said. 'It's going to be a difficult one.'

Morrison didn't need to be told. 'Keep me informed,' he said and hung up.

Putting the phone down, West looked up with a half-smile as Andrews came in with a mug of coffee in each hand. He took it without comment. 'Morrison is up to date,' he said, taking a sip.

Andrews sat, pulled a scrap of paper from his jacket pocket and passed it across the desk. 'The date of the report on the squatter. Exactly fourteen months ago.'

'Too far out of the time frame, if Kennedy's rough estimate is anywhere near correct,' West said, picking up the piece of paper and looking at it as if he'd learn something more than the basic date. He tossed it aside and sat back. 'We need to liaise with our friends across the border and in the UK,' he said, 'check if they've any unsolved cases. I don't need to tell you that we'll have to pull out all the stops for this, Peter.'

Andrews shook his head. 'I'll contact Interpol; they'll have a list of missing children. It might save us some time later.'

West saw a look of weariness on his face that hadn't been there earlier. 'Give that to Baxter to do,' he said, correctly interpreting the look on his partner's face. Reading the details of missing children was going to be harrowing. Baxter didn't have any; it would be easier on him.

Andrews smiled but shook his head. 'I'll do it. Baxter is still investigating that suspected arson attack. He's pretty sure it's an insurance scam, he's out with the fire officer having a look around the site.'

West checked his watch. 'What about Allen?'

'He's on leave, back tomorrow, and Jarvis is, once again, helping Foley close one of Sergeant Clark's cases.'

West shut his eyes. Clark was an incompetent, lazy fool but nobody had died because of his incompetence. When he opened his eyes, he saw the glint of sympathy in Andrews' face and said, more sharply than was necessary, 'What about Edwards?'

'Investigating a mugging in Cornelscourt car park.' Andrews shrugged. 'It's the second this week. Edwards thought the first one might have been linked to a series of muggings in Stillorgan Shopping Centre a few weeks ago. He was going to talk to you about it today before we got called out.'

'A series of muggings? Why does that sound like something from a Harry Potter book?'

'You're thinking of Muggles,' Andrews said with a grin.

West held his hands up. 'Muggings, Muggles.'

'Well there was definitely no magic involved here,' Andrews said. 'Three lads arrive in a stolen car, park, and wait patiently until they identify suitable candidates. They strike at the same time, take what they can and scarper. They hit five times in Stillorgan before they stopped. Two weeks later, we had the first in Cornelscourt.'

West frowned. 'Sounds like a high risk for minimal reward.'

Andrews perched on the side of the desk. 'In the five episodes in Stillorgan, there were twelve victims. Altogether, they're estimating their take at over six grand.'

'Six grand?'

'They took their wedding and engagement rings, one of the women had a Rolex, many were carrying designer handbags, and most had over a hundred euro in cash in their purses. They choose their targets carefully.'

'And now they've moved into our neck of the woods.'

'It's certainly starting to look that way. Edwards is definitely convinced they have.' He shrugged. 'But he's been complaining of it being a bit boring around here recently, so it could be a case of wishful thinking.'

'I'd settle for boring for a while,' West said. 'Ask Sergeant Blunt to have the uniforms patrol more regularly for a while. It might make them think twice.'

'Or, if Edwards is right, they'll just move on and hit another shopping centre car park instead.'

West frowned. He knew where Andrews was coming from. This gang should be stopped, not forced to move on. 'Okay,' he said, holding his hands up again in surrender. 'Let's catch these guys.' He picked up a pen and tapped it on the table. 'I'll ask Morrison if we can borrow Garda Foley for a while.' It was a continuing source of annoyance to him that the robbery unit, under Sergeant Clark, didn't handle anything outside of straightforward robberies. Any hint of violence and he declared it West's domain.

'If Morrison agrees, Foley and Jarvis can stake out the car park,' he said, nodding at Andrews, who raised a hand in acknowledgement and left the office.

West picked up the phone to talk to Morrison and minutes later had the permission he needed. Redialling the extension for the robbery unit, he hung up before it was answered. It was easier to deal with Clark face to face.

The detective unit in Foxrock was divided into two sections. Robbery, and everything else. The robbery unit office was on the other side of the station, the office smaller than that of West's unit and generally staffed by Clark and Foley. Assistance was given from West's team as needed – which was often.

Unlike West, Clark didn't have his own office. Instead, he had a desk in a corner of the room; it was set at an angle to give plenty of space behind to accommodate Clark's girth. When West walked in, he was concentrating on the morning paper's crossword puzzle, ignoring the untidy mountain of paperwork in his in-tray. 'What's an eight-letter word for *badge of office*?' he asked without looking up.

West glanced across to where Jarvis and Foley were tapping away on keyboards. He looked back to Clark, noticing the stained tie and worn cuffs. 'Insignia,' he said.

Clark scribbled the word down. 'Perfect. Okay, what's an eleven-letter word for someone unqualified for a task?'

'Incompetent,' West said with more force than was necessary. He knew Clark wouldn't take offence. He, as everyone knew, didn't give a toss.

'Inspector Morrison has given me permission to borrow Garda Foley for a few days,' he said without elaborating further.

Clark normally didn't care what went on, as long as it didn't affect his workday, but losing Foley, even for a few days, definitely would. He lifted his eyes from the crossword and glared at West. 'And what am I supposed to do?'

'Finish your crossword puzzle,' West said and, turning on his heels, walked over to where the two detectives were trying to give the impression they weren't listening. 'Are you nearly finished wrapping up that case,' he asked.

Foley nodded. 'Just need to get this form complete, and we're done.'

'Good, Inspector Morrison has given me permission to borrow you for a couple of days,' he explained. 'When you're finished there come to my office. Both of you,' he added, nodding at Jarvis.

West went back to his office, ignoring glares from Clark as he passed his desk. Back in their main office, Edwards had returned and was helping himself to coffee. 'I hear you have something interesting happening in Cornelscourt,' he said by way of greeting.

Brown was the adjective that best described Mark Edwards. His hair was brown, skin sallow, eyes brown and slightly prominent. He favoured tweed jackets, bought, he told everyone with a complete lack of embarrassment, for a few quid in charity shops. Unfortunately, they too tended to be brown.

'Andrews said he filled you in,' he said, excitement making his eyes sparkle. 'It's definitely the same gang. There were two victims this morning. They attempted a third but were scared off by a dog in the woman's car.'

'Foley and Jarvis will be here in a few minutes,' he said. 'You can fill them in. We're going to stake out the shopping centre and catch these guys.'

Ten minutes later, they crowded into West's office. Edwards took one of the empty chairs, Jarvis the other. Foley dragged a chair through from the main office and squeezed it in beside them.

'Okay,' West said, looking at their eager, intent faces. He gave Edwards a nod. 'Mark, fill them in on what's been happening.'

'It started in Stillorgan shopping centre in October,' he said. 'Every few days, three men arrived, parked, targeted two or three women to attack, and robbed them of anything of value. I have the dates and times on a handout for you.' He flicked through the bundle of papers he held and withdrew a sheet for each of them. He waited until they'd scanned the page before continuing. 'As you'll have noticed, the last one in Stillorgan was two weeks ago. Four days ago, they hit Cornelscourt for the first time. Look at the dates and times, there's no pattern, just a random time on any given day. From the witnesses' statements in Stillorgan, and from our witnesses here, we know there are three of them. But all the victims can tell us is that they're white males of indeterminate age, well camouflaged with hoodies and scarves. They use different cars every time, all of them stolen for the purpose, and all abandoned shortly afterwards. And before anyone asks, they are wiped clean. They're quick, efficient and smart. It doesn't take a genius to see it's the same gang. The security people in both centres have checked CCTV, but they haven't been able to come up with anything useful.'

'So, they hit five times in Stillorgan and, so far, twice here,' Foley said, a finger running over the lines of print on the page he held.

Edwards nodded. 'That's right. In Stillorgan there were twelve victims, and, so far, five in Cornelscourt.'

West tapped the sheet with the back of his hand. 'Seventeen traumatised victims. We've got to stop these guys.'

'Why the same car park?' Foley asked, his brow creasing. 'Wouldn't it have been more sensible to hit a different car park each time?'

Edwards shrugged. 'Maybe it's easier to organise. Hit one place for a few weeks, then move on to the next.'

'Why didn't they organise a stake-out in Stillorgan?' Jarvis asked, frowning as he read the page he held, searching for a pattern that wasn't there.

'It was under consideration,' Edwards explained. 'But the logistics there are more difficult – they have two car parks for example and the gang has hit in both. The main car park also has multiple entrances and exits which would have required extra staff to monitor. We're in the luckier position of knowing from the start what this gang are up to, and we are lucky with a more restricted entrance and exit in Cornelscourt.'

West put his two hands flat on his desk. 'I'm leaving it to you three to organise this. Edwards' – he nodded at him – 'you take the lead. Ask Sergeant Blunt to organise a couple of uniformed gardaí to take with you.' He thought for a moment. 'Ask him to make Garda Mackin one of them, he shows promise.'

When the three stood, he held up his hand. 'Just one last thing,' he said, 'so far these guys have not hurt any of their victims, but stay alert, that may change. We don't want another murder to investigate.'

All three nodded in unison.

'And keep me informed,' West said, and waved them away.

3

When they'd gone, West rang the State Pathologist's Office to get a rough estimate of the time of the post-mortem. Three o'clock. It gave him time to do the necessary paperwork before leaving.

Shortly before one, Andrews appeared in the doorway, a sheaf of paper under one arm, two sandwiches in his hands. 'Chicken, or ham and cheese?'

West smiled. 'Either, thanks.'

The chicken sandwich was passed over. Andrews dropped everything else onto the seat of the empty chair and left, returning, minutes later, with two mugs of coffee. 'I thought I'd fill you in while we had something to eat.'

'Thanks,' West said, biting into the sandwich. 'You didn't get these in our canteen,' he said appreciatively.

'I sent Jarvis out to the new deli, I told them they needed sustenance if they were going to start a stake-out. They're huddled over a desk putting a plan together.' He laughed. 'They don't realise yet how boring a stake-out can be.'

'They work well together,' West said, finishing the first half of the sandwich and reaching for the other. 'What've you found out?'

Andrews wiped his hand on the leg of his trousers and picked up the pile of papers. 'Don't worry,' he said, when he saw West's eyes widen, 'they emailed the details of all the missing persons, not just the one to five age group that I asked for.'

'One to five?'

Andrews sighed. 'It's hard to guess an age from bones. I thought I'd err on the side of caution.' He waved the papers. 'This is what I get for my troubles.'

'Let Baxter have a look when he gets back,' West said, 'he'll be able to narrow it down.'

Andrews shook his head.

'You're stubborn, you know that?'

'I prefer to call it old-fashioned.'

West looked at the clock. 'We'll need to leave soon. The post-mortem starts at three.'

'I could stay here and go through this,' he said, waving the sheaf of papers like a fan. 'You don't really need me, do you?'

West was surprised, and was about to make a smart comment when he saw Andrews' shuttered expression. He was normally more intuitive. Andrews didn't want to see the post-mortem of the little girl. 'Good idea,' he said, picking up his coffee. 'I'll be back in a couple of hours. You might be able to put a name to the child by then.'

Connolly Hospital, where the post-mortem was being held, was formerly known as James Connolly Memorial Hospital, but was generally referred to by most as Blanchardstown Hospital because of its location. West took the M50, made good time to Junction 6 and thirty minutes after leaving Foxrock he was pulling into the car park.

He'd been to post-mortems before so knew that the mortuary, with its dedicated post-mortem room, was to the back of the rambling hospital campus. He skirted around and between the newer structures to the grim, forbidding building, rang the doorbell and was immediately asked to state his business.

'Detective Garda Sergeant West,' he said, feeling foolish, as he always did when speaking to an inanimate object. 'I'm here for a post-mortem.'

He was buzzed through. Inside, they'd done their best to modernise the area, and two reception staff sat in front of large computer screens. One looked up as he entered and held out a hand. 'Identification?'

West took out his card, which was taken and scrutinised with closer intent than he thought was warranted. Did they have a glut of people faking identification in order to see post-mortems?

The receptionist nodded, handed his card back and picked up a phone. The conversation was short. He hung up and gave West an apologetic smile. 'It seems he's a bit behind and is still on another post. You can wait in the canteen, if you want, the coffee is fairly decent.'

He was directed toward a small cluttered room opposite the reception. Aware that he drank far too much coffee, he poured himself one anyway, and sat in a chair near a window overlooking a small courtyard. There were several large pots planted with small trees; acers he guessed, and in the summer, it probably made the view more appealing. Now, however, their bare jagged branches looked as if they would snap easily – like a small child's bones. The thought made him shiver, he put the untouched coffee down and moved away.

By three forty-five, he'd read a four-day old newspaper and every notice on the large, untidy noticeboard. He was checking his watch for the umpteenth time when a smartly-dressed woman put her head round the door. 'He's ready now,' she said and vanished.

'Great,' West muttered when he followed her into a narrow corridor extending in both directions. There was no sign of her and he wasn't sure which way to go. He'd been once before but Andrews had been with him and he'd followed him without thought. A door further up the corridor opened and the same woman popped her head out. It was like some stupid computer game, he thought, beginning to get annoyed.

'Sorry,' she said, 'I assumed you'd know where to go.' She pointed to the door opposite. 'It's just in there.'

She'd disappeared again by the time West reached the door. With a shake of his head, he opened it and found himself in a small anteroom furnished with standard office chairs. On the far side, a door stood ajar. He crossed to it, went through to a viewing platform overlooking the post-mortem room below, and sat.

There was only one person to be seen. Niall Kennedy, barely recognisable in a pale-blue scrub suit and white wellington boots, ones that fit him properly West noticed with a grin. He was sat at a desk tapping on a computer keyboard.

West rubbed tired eyes, wondering how much longer he'd be waiting. Since the Blundell incident, he hadn't slept well. *The Blundell incident.* When had it become that in his head? Sounded like a good name for a movie. He'd have to tell Edel, it would make her smile.

Pushing his hand restlessly through his hair, he wondered if the post-mortem was ever going to start. As if he'd given him a nudge, Niall Kennedy's voice came loud and clear through a speaker set behind him in the wall. Deciding he could do without more voices in his head, he shuffled slightly further up the bench.

'Sorry for the delay, Mike,' the pathologist said, looking up to where he sat and giving a wave of acknowledgement. 'It's been one of those days.'

A gurney was pushed through the double doors into the post-mortem room, the brown suitcase looking lost and abandoned on top of it. He recognised the woman who pushed it as the one who'd half-heartedly shown him where to go. She was dressed now in a scrub suit with her hair caught up in an unflattering disposable mob cap.

As he watched, they lifted the suitcase from the gurney onto the examination table. A man holding a high-spec camera came in and took several photos of it, taking more as they opened the case and reached in to lift the body, slowly and carefully, from the case.

'We'll send the case and what clothes there are to the forensic lab,' Kennedy said for West's benefit before stepping back to examine the small body that lay on the stainless steel. Nobody moved for what seemed like a long time. West was suddenly very glad that Andrews hadn't come. There was something deeply disturbing about the sight of that small child's body, pathetically curved around itself in a desperate final search for comfort.

'The connective tissue has mostly decomposed,' Kennedy said, slowly... almost delicately... stretching the bones out on the table. 'There is some tissue remaining on the right side, where it was in closest contact with the bottom of the suitcase.' He removed some with forceps as he spoke and dropped it into a specimen bottle held out by his assistant. 'We might get something from that,' he said before removing the remnants of cloth from the bones. He shook his head as it disintegrated on contact. 'Most of the fabric has rotted away, I'm afraid.' He peered closer. 'The labels are fairly intact, probably made from different material; they might be able to make out the manufacturer and get an indication as to where she's from.'

The photographer shot the pathologist's every step, the shutter sound loud in the quiet of the room where the only other sound was Kennedy's running commentary on what he saw and did.

How could anyone do this to a child? West pressed his lips together, feeling his gut twist as Kennedy lifted the jawbone between two fingers. It was so very tiny.

'I can give you a close approximate of her age, Mike,' he said, putting the bone down. Her lower molars are just beginning to erupt, but there's no sign yet of upper molars. That puts her age at between twenty-three and thirty-three months.'

Andrews wouldn't be pleased to be right.

Kennedy spoke again. 'I've taken samples for toxicology and DNA. It's impossible, yet, to ascertain a cause of death. There are no bone injuries to suggest she met with violence.' A loud sigh came through the speaker before he continued. 'I'd estimate time of death to be no more than eight months ago.'

West gave him a thumbs up and then, realising that sound was probably two-way, he said, 'Thanks, Niall. Narrowing her age down might help us to identify her. How soon will the suitcase and personal items get to forensics?'

'I know how important this case is,' Kennedy said. 'I took the liberty of asking someone from forensics to come and collect it all. They should be able to start first thing tomorrow, if you can persuade them to skip their usually very long queue.'

With a wave of thanks, West stood and left, making his way back to reception with the images of the small body on his mind.

'Is there someone here from forensics to collect items from the post that Dr Kennedy is doing?' he asked at reception. He'd have a word with them and see if he could persuade them to process the items as soon as possible. If he had to use the *small child* card, he'd do it.

Before either receptionist had time to reply, he was hailed by a friendly voice. 'Detective Sergeant West. Fancy meeting you here.'

For a second, West couldn't place the petite, attractive woman who approached him, his brain quickly flicking through a Rolodex of faces. Clare Island. Of course. He gave the receptionist a wave of thanks and turned to greet the smiling woman. 'Hello, Fiona,' he said, taking the offered hand, 'it's a long way from Mayo.'

She tinkled a laugh. 'Yes, it's city cases only for me these days, thank goodness. No more rushing up and down the country.'

'You're here to pick up the evidence from the Foxrock case?' he asked, unable to believe his luck. Personal connections counted for so much when you needed something done in a hurry.

'Yes,' she said. Her smile vanished. 'I hear it's a child.'

West nodded. 'Dr Kennedy estimates between two and three years old.'

She shook her head. 'How awful. Any idea who it is?'

'Afraid not. We've no outstanding missing persons of that age. So far it's a mystery.' He gave her a slight smile. 'The press will be baying for information...'

'And you'd like the evidence processed sooner rather than later,' she interrupted him, with a knowing slant to her chin.

He gave a quick laugh. 'Just what I was going to ask you.'

'I'll do my best,' she said, 'but I can't make promises.'

'Ms Wilson,' one of the receptionists called, 'they're ready for you.'

'I'll be right there,' she said to him before turning back to West with a hand extended. 'It was good to see you again. Maybe we could have a drink sometime?'

He held her hand in his for a moment. 'I'd like that,' he said, and raised his eyebrows as his phone buzzed. 'I'd better get this.

Whatever you can get us on the child would be much appreciated.' A friendly smile and a nod, and he was outside heading towards his car, answering the call as he walked.

It was Inspector Morrison. 'I expected to have heard from you by now, Sergeant.'

West took a deep breath. 'I've just left the post-mortem, sir, it was delayed. Dr Kennedy was unable to establish a cause of death, but he did give us an approximate age, which should narrow our enquiries. She's between two and three years old. They'll do toxicology and DNA, but we won't have the results for a couple of days.' He waited a moment. When Morrison made no comment, he continued. 'I've asked the forensic department to expedite their processing of the evidence. They may be able to give us more.'

'Right.' The one word was stretched out to convey the inspector's disappointment. 'Well, keep me posted,' he said, and cut the connection.

4

West climbed into his car and tossed the mobile onto the passenger seat in annoyance before retrieving it to ring Andrews. With a few words, he filled him in on the child's age and the meeting with Fiona Wilson. 'She's promised to do her best to have the evidence processed as soon as possible. We'll just have to hope she has sufficient clout there to do so.' He ran a hand over his face. 'I'm heading back now, but I'm hitting rush hour traffic. It's going to take a while.'

It was almost an hour later before he took exit fourteen off the motorway to join the almost static queue of traffic that snaked through suburban roads toward the station, and another twenty minutes of frustration before he pulled into the car park.

When he entered the main office, Andrews was huddled over his desk, a pencil in one hand, ruler in the other. West shook his head but there was no point in saying, yet again, that using the computer would be so much easier. Andrews was stuck in his ways. He was aware his nickname was Detective Plod, choosing to see it as a compliment rather than a criticism of his methods. West agreed with his thinking. Andrews may plod his way through, but he couldn't think of a better detective. If there was something there, he'd find it.

The rumble of his stomach reminded him that one chicken sandwich didn't make up for missing breakfast. Opening a packet of biscuits, he palmed several before pouring two mugs of coffee, adding sugar liberally to one and milk to both. He placed the sugared drink in front of Andrews who automatically dropped the ruler and picked it up.

'Well,' West said, taking a mouthful and following it up with one of the biscuits. He waved one of the others at Andrews who shook his head.

'No, thanks,' he said, putting his mug down to riffle through the pages on the desk. Picking up two, he scanned them before handing them to West. 'It's the underlined two,' he said, 'both from the UK. They're the only children reported missing who haven't been accounted for. One is twenty-six months old, one thirty months.'

He sat back, stretched his arms out, and clasped his hands together behind his head. 'Both are domestic cases, one London-based, the other Cardiff. In each, the mother abducted the child, and neither has been seen since.' He wagged his head side to side. 'I suppose they could have come across on the ferry, hidden the child in the suitcase to prevent being spotted and just blended in. It wouldn't have been difficult, not if they had a bit of money to tide them over.'

'Just the two?' West asked, nodding to the pile of papers.

Andrews dropped his hands and picked up the final sheet. 'I'm just on the last page now. Most of the missing children are older.' He looked up, his eyes bleak. 'So many young teenagers are missing.'

West wasn't in the mood for a protracted conversation about missing children. 'I've got a few things to do,' he said, moving away. Immediately, he felt guilty, and stopped to look back. 'Finish that, Peter, and I'll buy you a pint when you're done.'

He should go home, but he wasn't in the mood for the small talk that seemed to be what passed for conversation at home these days. Picking up the phone he rang Edel. 'I'm tied up here,' he explained, 'don't cook for me, I'll grab something in the canteen.' He hung up with a sense of relief that worried him.

Forty-five minutes later, Andrews appeared at the door. 'Nothing in that last lot,' he said, 'so we've just the two potentials from the UK. Interpol are dragging their feet a bit, but I should have something by tomorrow.'

West shut down the programme he was using and turned the computer off. He stretched and yawned. 'I thought we could go to the Lep Inn,' he said. 'I'm starving.'

'I can't stay long,' Andrews warned him.

West smiled. He knew his partner's domestic routine well. 'I know, I know, Joyce has your dinner waiting, but have a quick pint with me first.'

'Why don't you come home with me?' Andrews said, 'Joyce is always asking you to, and Petey would love to see you.'

West stood and slipped on his jacket. 'Thanks, but no thanks. I'm not really good company these days.' He saw a concerned look flit across his partner's face and looked away. He wanted a pint and some food, not a sermon.

The Lep Inn was busy, as usual, and the noise level was high. West never understood how he managed it but within a few seconds, Andrews had found a quiet, unoccupied table and they sat with combined sighs of relief.

'You going to try a Guinness again?' West said, raising a hand for a passing server.

'No, I'll have a Heineken,' Andrews said.

'A pint of Guinness and a pint of gnat's piss,' West said to the young woman who smiled and raised an eyebrow that told him she'd heard it all before. 'Okay, Heineken,' he clarified.

The two men chatted about the case as they waited. 'Someone must be missing her,' Andrews said, his face grim. 'It's not a newborn, with no history. This child was at least two. Someone would have looked after her, fed her, dressed her.'

West tapped a finger on the table. 'Let's hope forensics turn up something. Dr Kennedy said the clothing labels were intact, they might give us an idea where she was living.'

Andrews shook his head. 'They also might send us on a wild goose chase. Most of Petey's clothes are made in Portugal or Bangladesh or somewhere.'

'Let's wait and see.' Their pints arrived; West took a long drink of Guinness and started to relax. But he should have guessed his partner wouldn't let whatever was on his mind go.

'You need to put it behind you, Mike,' Andrews said, taking a sip of his pint.

West didn't insult him by asking what he meant. Instead, he took another mouthful and sat back. 'I don't mind Morrison watching my every move for a few months, while I prove myself to be a co-operative subordinate. Honestly,' he said, as Andrews raised an eyebrow in disbelief. 'No, Pete, what annoys me, what damn well rankles and makes me want to hit my head on the nearest hard surface, is that I was wrong. *I* made the decision to allow Denise Blundell off that assault charge and allowed her to go off on that, obviously useless, anger management course. Would I have made the same decision if she hadn't been a leading paediatrician? No, I don't think I would have done, and that bloody well rankles too. And there's the gut-rotting guilt, that a decent man is dead because I had the arrogance to play God.'

Andrews frowned. 'If you'd gone to Morrison with it at the time, he'd have agreed,' he said. 'That's why he–'

West, his mouth twisting bitterly, interrupted him. 'Covered it up.' He finished his pint and waved the empty glass at one of the waiting staff who was passing, spotting the worried look Andrews gave him. 'Relax,' he said, 'I'll be fine.'

'I was going to say, that's why Morrison was eager to ensure you weren't held responsible,' Andrews said calmly. 'You made the right choice based on what you knew at the time. Denise Blundell admitted that the stress of her job made her lose her temper. Anger management should have helped. We've seen countless cases where it does.' He put a hand briefly on West's arm. 'You did the right thing. You need to stop beating yourself up about it.'

The new pint of Guinness arrived at the same time as a plate of beer-battered cod and fries with a side order of onion rings, mixed vegetables and garlic potatoes. 'That might put a smile on your face,' Andrews said, shaking his head at the amount of food.

'I forgot how big the helpings are,' West admitted. 'Have a few chips, Pete. I won't tell Joyce.'

Andrews took a few, dipping them one at a time into the tomato ketchup that West poured onto the side of his plate. 'You'll think about what I said?'

West shrugged. 'It's nothing Edel hasn't said to me a hundred times.'

'How are things with Edel? I haven't seen her since Clare Island.'

'Our glorious romantic getaway, you mean?' West said, sprinkling sarcasm on each word.

'Hmmm,' Andrews replied, his mouth full of chips. He swallowed, took a gulp of his beer to wash them down, and tried again. 'You were just unlucky.'

West sniffed. 'Seems to be my middle name these days. I take my girlfriend on a romantic weekend away, and nearly get her killed; then a bad decision I made backfires and a man dies.'

'Poor Mikey.'

West choked on a piece of battered fish. When he recovered, coughing and wheezing, he looked at Andrews with a glint of laughter in his eyes. 'Thank you very much! So, you think I'm acting like a five-year-old, do you?'

'What's that expression about a cap fitting?'

'Can't I feel a bit sorry for myself?' West said, feeling a little aggrieved.

'A little bit, maybe,' Andrews said, taking another drink. 'But that little bit was used up about three weeks ago.'

'Is that the equivalent of a boot up the ass?' he asked, picking up an onion ring with his fingers and popping it whole into his mouth.

'Did it work?' Andrews grinned. Reaching over, he took an onion ring and did the same.

West looked at him for a few seconds before a smile curved one side of his mouth. 'Yes, I think it did.'

The conversation turned to the less contentious issue of work before Andrews checked his watch and jumped to his feet. 'Better go,' he said, 'you can pay for the beer. Payment for the free advice.' He grinned again. 'See you in the morning.'

It wasn't until he was sitting in his car that Andrews realised West had never answered his question about Edel. Perhaps, he thought sadly, it was a relationship that wasn't meant to be. He started the engine and headed home to his family.

5

Edel was beginning to think the same thing herself. Her relationship with West had had a rocky start. 'Rocky,' she muttered, 'admit it, it'd been disastrous.' Maybe it just wasn't meant to be. Before everything went wrong on Clare Island, she'd told him she loved him, but he'd never returned the sentiment. Perhaps, he was having second thoughts.

She'd ignored his advice to stay in her apartment after Ken Blundell's murder, and was waiting outside his Greystones house when he'd arrived home in the early hours of the morning. He'd seemed to take comfort in her presence, but his involvement in the man's death had taken its toll and he'd become distant and withdrawn. By the time his suspension was dropped only a few days later, a coolness had developed between them that still lingered.

It didn't help that she'd become irritable as she waited to hear back from her publisher. She'd written several children's novels, but it had always been her dream to write adult fiction and now she'd done it. However, she was under no illusions. Her children's novels, moderately successful though they were, carried little weight in her ambition to enter the adult market. If what she'd written was no good, FinalEdit Publishing wouldn't offer her a contract.

'Let me read it when it's done,' the director Hugh Todd had said, 'but I'm making no promises.'

She'd finished it a few months before and had worked through several more drafts – changing, deleting, adding, reading and rereading – until she was sick of the sight of it. Finally, she decided she'd nothing to lose and emailed it to him. All she could do then was wait.

'No word from the publisher?' West had asked when he'd arrived home the previous night.

'Please stop asking me that,' she snapped. 'If I'd heard, don't you think I'd have told you?' They ate their meal in an uncomfortable silence that neither made the effort to break; West, because he felt his question was showing an interest in her work and he wasn't sure what he'd said that was so wrong and Edel because she was annoyed that he didn't seem to realise how stressed she was.

'I've some emails to write,' she said when they'd finished. Standing, she took both plates, put them in the dishwasher and left the room without a word. Upstairs, in the spare bedroom she was using as an office, she sat, opened her laptop and stared at the blank screen for several minutes. From downstairs came the distinct sound of doors opening and closing, then the faint sound of the television. He'd watch the news and maybe some documentary about God knows what. Usually, she'd sit and watch with him, they'd hold hands and comment on whatever they were watching.

She hit the *on* button of her laptop with more force than was necessary and brought up the next novel she was working on, reading the last few lines she'd written before starting to type. The buzz of her mobile interrupted her. With a grunt of annoyance, she picked it up, the fingers of her right hand continuing to tap the keyboard.

'It's Hugh Todd,' the voice said, causing her to stop, and grip the phone tighter. 'I'm sorry to ring so late, I've been in meeting after meeting today.'

'That's fine,' she said. She pressed the phone to her ear, afraid she wouldn't be able to hear what he said her heart was thumping so loudly.

'I'm sorry to have taken so long in getting back to you,' he said, 'but you'll be relieved to know I'm ringing with good news. We love your novel. It needs some work,' he added quickly. 'One of my editorial staff, Aidan Power, has it at the moment. He's going to send it back to you with corrections and suggestions.

'As soon as you can, get the changes done. Once we're all happy we can meet up to discuss everything. We'd like to offer you a three-book contract, Edel. We're really excited about this.'

She was shaking when she hung up. Still holding the phone in her hand, she went downstairs. West, as she'd guessed, was sitting on the sofa with Tyler curled up beside him, some news programme flickering across the TV screen.

'Some good news,' she said, coming into the room and perching on the seat beside him. She reached out to rub the little chihuahua who gave her a lick of acknowledgement before dropping back to sleep. 'The publisher loves my book. They've offered me a three-book contract.'

West, who'd been sitting with his eyes closed, going over and over his decision to release Denise Blundell without charge, managed to drag up a smile. He pressed the mute button on the remote control. 'Well done,' he said. She deserved this. He wasn't going to let his misfortune spoil it for her. He pulled her into a hug, annoying Tyler who got up and retired to the armchair. 'Let's celebrate,' he said. 'I'll take you out to dinner at the weekend. We can have champagne.'

Edel kissed him. 'Let's wait until I sign the contract, Mike. I don't want to jinx it.'

He pulled her into the crook of his arm and they sat in silence for a while, each of them lost in vastly different thoughts.

In the morning, he was gone as usual before she was up. He'd rung her during the day to tell her he was busy and wouldn't be home for dinner. It suited her, she got stuck into her writing and didn't move until late evening when she stretched wearily and went down to watch TV. She was enjoying a sitcom that she hadn't seen before when she heard his key in the front door. Muting the sound, she waited for him to join her. 'Rough day?' she asked, when he came in and sat onto the sofa beside her.

She didn't need to ask really; he'd looked preoccupied recently, the Blundell case weighing heavily on him, but now there were lines of strain around his mouth and a sadness in his eyes. 'A tough one, Mike,' she said, resting her hand on his arm.

He nodded and put his hand over hers. 'A body was found in a suitcase, tossed away like garbage. Just a child, about two or three. We've no idea who she is, no child has been reported missing. It's going to be a very tough one.' He picked up the remote and unmuted the sound. Edel took the hint; he didn't want to talk about it.

They watched the end of the sitcom silently. At ten, before the nightly news broadcast, West reached for the remote again and switched it off. 'I don't want to hear their interpretation of what's happening with our case,' he said.

'They'll have dragged in some psychologist to give an in-depth analysis of how a child can go missing without being reported,' she said with a yawn. 'It'll be put down to a break-down in society and family structure. That'll lead to a hundred more discussions that will go nowhere toward identifying the child or who killed her.'

'Such cynicism,' he said, giving her a hug before gently pushing her away and getting to his feet. He reached a hand down to her, she took it and he pulled her up beside him. 'But, yes, that's exactly what will happen. Hopefully, before they have run out of experts, we'll have solved the mystery because their next step will be *why haven't the gardaí solved the case.*'

'Now who's being cynical,' she said with a smile.

Leaving him to settle Tyler for the night she headed to bed. She was asleep before he slid in beside her, and when she woke in the morning, his side of the bed was empty. For a moment, she wondered if he'd come to bed at all, but when she moved her hand over, she found it was warm. He must have just got up. Listening carefully, she could hear him moving around downstairs, and she relaxed.

He came up to say goodbye a few minutes later, peering round the door, his face breaking into a smile when he saw her eyes open. 'Hello, sleepyhead,' he said, coming over to sit on the bed beside her, bending down to press a kiss on her mouth. 'I'll see you tonight.'

She lay unmoving for a few minutes after he left before throwing back the duvet and having a quick shower. Dressed in a T-shirt, jumper and jeans, she headed downstairs for tea and toast, sharing the crusts with Tyler who had a fine line in polite begging.

The secret to working from home, she knew, was a disciplined approach. She made herself start at nine, sitting in the office and switching on the computer. Writing her new novel would keep her occupied until she heard from the editor.

She didn't need to wait long. Late morning, she checked her emails and saw one from Aidan Power.

She opened it. It was short and to the point. He was

delighted to be working with her, excited about her novel and had attached the manuscript with some suggested changes and corrections.

Taking a deep breath, she opened the attachment. At first glance, everything seemed to be highlighted in yellow. She was stunned. Maybe it would be easier to delete the whole thing and start again from the beginning, but after an initial panic, when she looked closely, it wasn't as bad as she'd thought.

She dashed off an email to the editor and told him she'd work through his comments as soon as possible. And then she got down to it.

To her surprise, it was easier than she'd first expected. Some of the corrections were the usual typos that slip through despite checking and rechecking. Others were suggestions she took, nodding her head in satisfaction when a sentence read better for it; some suggestions she ignored. After all, it was *her* novel.

When West rang late afternoon to say he'd be late again and wouldn't need dinner, it suited her perfectly. She'd grab a snack instead of cooking and have extra time for editing. Even with hard work, it was going to take a few days to get it done, maybe longer. But she'd get there.

At least one part of her life was on track.

6

West was pleased to see that the initial flurry of demands for results in the investigation died down within twenty-four hours. There was no grieving family – so no news-worthy sound bites for reporters to latch onto. He'd been right about the plethora of experts who were brought forward to give their opinion, but even they were quickly reduced to sidebars. Within a few days, other news caught the public's attention and, unless something turned up soon, the child would soon be forgotten.

Two days following the post-mortem, West's phone rang.

'It's Fiona Wilson,' the voice said.

'Hello.' West sat back in his chair. 'Good to hear from you. I hope you have some news for me.'

'I managed to get your case expedited,' she said, 'it's surprising how willing people are when they know there is a child involved. I'm heading to your side of the city later this morning, and thought I'd drop the results over myself. There are a couple of things I need to explain, it would be far simpler to do so face to face.'

'Okay,' West said, checking his watch. 'What time do you

expect to get here?'

'Eleven thirty,' she said promptly. 'I'll see you then.'

She hung up before West had a chance to respond. He looked at the phone, slightly bemused, and hung up with a shrug before heading out in search of Andrews.

Baxter was at his desk, fingers flying over the computer keyboard, a lock of ginger hair falling over his eyes. 'Seamus,' he asked, getting the man's attention, 'have you seen Andrews?'

Baxter shook his head, his fingers continuing to pound the keys without the slightest reduction in speed.

'How is the mugging investigation going?' West asked.

Finally, as if giving in, Baxter's fingers slowed and stopped. He ran one hand through his hair, pushing the untidy lock back where it belonged. 'We've spent a total of twelve hours in the car park over the last two days,' he said, 'and there's been no sign of them. We're planning to spend the whole day today. Foley is already there with Mackin, I've just come back to do some paperwork and I'm heading to join them.'

West nodded. It was going to be a long, tiring stake-out. 'Okay, keep me informed, and,' he added, as the other man's eyes flicked back to his computer, 'be careful.'

Baxter grinned and resumed his typing. Minutes later, West, pouring some coffee, saw him stand and leave.

Andrews came through the door at the same time, and West waved him over. 'Fiona Wilson came through for us, Pete. She'll be here at eleven thirty to go through some of the information with us so it looks like we might have something to go on.'

'Good, because we've nothing else,' Andrews said bluntly, sitting at his desk. 'I spoke to a contact at Interpol. There are thousands of misplaced children from conflicts in several countries. She could be one of them, smuggled into the country for any number of reasons.'

West frowned. 'That's taking us in a very different direction,

Pete. I'm not ruling out that she's an Irish citizen who met a violent end, and the family have chosen to cover it up.'

'Or her situation was one that needed to be hidden.'

They continued to discuss the various possibilities until interrupted by a cheerful voice raised in greeting.

'Is this where it all happens?'

The two men turned together. Fiona Wilson stood in the doorway, one hand resting on the doorframe, her head tilted to one side. She waited there a moment before making her way slowly across the room and extending her hand first to Andrews, then to West.

Andrews, who'd thought she was a pretty woman when they'd met on Clare Island, realised the work clothes she'd worn at the time hadn't done her any favours. Now with her hair loose around her shoulders, in a smart dress, and wearing what his wife, Joyce, would call *killer heels*, he thought she was one of the most beautiful women he'd ever seen.

He glanced at West from the corner of his eye. If she was having the same effect on him, he wasn't showing it.

'Come into my office,' West said, gesturing towards the door. 'Would you like some coffee? I have to warn you, it's not very good.'

'I passed a cafe on the way,' she said, shaking her head, 'perhaps when we're done here we could go for a cup?' She took the chair he indicated, sitting and crossing one elegant leg over the other.

West sitting behind his desk, smiled. 'Depending on what you have for us, I might even run to lunch.'

She returned the smile. 'I think with what we've got, you might have to run to dinner.' Opening her briefcase, she took out a sheaf of papers. 'We've sent this to you by email too,' she said, handing the first sheet across to him.

Andrews moved to stand behind him, peering over his shoulder and squinting to read what was written on the page.

'As you can see,' she explained, 'there were no identifying marks on the suitcase. It's a cheap generic type and could have been purchased anywhere.' She handed over the next report. 'The labels on the clothes, unfortunately, had deteriorated too far and we were unable to get any information from them.'

The two men scanned the reports and then, as one, looked over to where she sat, puzzled looks on both their faces.

Fiona smiled reassuringly. 'This is where it gets interesting,' she said, placing the next report on the desk and tapping it with her index finger. 'Whoever this child was, she had sickle-cell disease. Sickle-cell anaemia to be exact.'

Her smile grew broader as she sat back. 'Based on this information, there is a strong possibility that she was of African, Middle Eastern or Asian descent, with a higher likelihood that she was of sub-Saharan African descent. About eighty per cent of all sickle-cell diseases come from there.'

West tried to remember anything he knew about the disease. It was congenital, that was about as much as he could remember. 'Her parents would have had it, wouldn't they?' he asked. 'Aren't congenital diseases registered somewhere?'

She nodded. 'There are a number of registers. There's BINOCAR, for one, that's the British and Irish Network of Congenital Anomaly Researchers, and there's a European register, Eurocat. It only needs one parent to actually have the disease; the other parent may have it or may just be a carrier.'

'It gives us a place to start,' Andrews said.

'There's something else.' Wilson shut her briefcase and sat back in her chair. 'Sickle-cell anaemia may also be what killed her.'

Andrews, who'd moved to sit in the other vacant chair, clenched his hand. This was even better. 'What do you mean?'

She held up her hands. 'It's speculative, I'm afraid. But, given the lack of any other evidence as to cause of death, we consider it a distinct possibility. One of the symptoms of sickle-cell anaemia is breathlessness,' she explained. 'The child's positioning in the suitcase may have restricted expansion of her ribcage and made taking a deep breath more difficult. Theoretically, she may have asphyxiated.'

'She was alive when she was put inside?' West's eyes opened wide.

She held up a cautious hand. 'It's a theory,' she said. 'Unfortunately, there was too much tissue deterioration to allow for a definitive conclusion. But the fact is, this child had sickle-cell anaemia and it *is* one of the side effects.'

'It wasn't something we'd considered,' West said, a frown creasing his forehead. Perhaps they should have done. 'If she was put into the suitcase alive, that changes the direction of our enquiry. When nobody came forward to identify her,' he explained, seeing her puzzled look, 'we considered she may have been smuggled into the country somehow and, as a result, when she died, her relatives were too afraid to come forward. Now it seems she may have died *while* being brought in.'

Andrews frowned. 'She could be the victim of a people trafficking ring.'

'I know someone in the HTICU,' West said, looking at him.

Fiona held one hand up. 'Okay, what does an intensive care unit have to do with it?'

Both men looked puzzled before West gave a short laugh. 'No, sorry, it doesn't stand for an intensive care unit. It's the Human Trafficking Investigation and Co-ordination Unit, a branch of the Garda National Protection Bureau.' He looked back to Andrews. 'Jos Cotter, I'll have a word with him, see if he can offer some advice.' He tapped a finger on the desk. 'Pete, contact someone in the National Immigration Bureau.

Tell them our situation and see if they can offer any assistance.'

Fiona Wilson picked up her briefcase and stood. 'I can see it's not a good time to be dragging you... either of you,' she amended quickly, 'for coffee.' The comment may have been for both, but the smile she gave was directed solely at West.

His smile was perfunctory, his mind focusing on the best use of his limited resources. 'Another time,' he said, standing and holding out his hand, 'you've been a great help, thank you.'

'I'll hold you to that, Sergeant West,' she said and with a nod to Andrews and another smile to West, she left.

'You've got an admirer there,' Andrews said, watching her go with a flicker of admiration.

'She's just being friendly, Peter,' West said, dismissing the woman immediately from his mind to concentrate on the news she'd brought him.

Andrews' eyebrow rose. 'I have a feeling it's not the last we'll see of Fiona Wilson,' he said cryptically. 'I'll go make that call.'

Sergeant Jos Cotter wasn't available when West rang his office. Leaving a message asking him to return his call as soon as possible, he hung up and drummed his fingers on the desk for a few minutes before switching on his computer. It would have been better to speak to Jos first, but there was no point in hanging about. A quick search found contact details for BINOCAR, Eurocat, and the National Congenital Anomaly and Rare Diseases Register. With the phone wedged under one ear, and a pen and pad in front of him, he started into the phone calls and explanations.

Two hours later, he put the phone down and stretched his arms over his head to ease the knots that had built up in his shoulders. He headed out to the main office where he spied Andrews, his phone in one hand, scribbling madly with the other. He stood watching him, mentally considering their next step. At least the reporters had lost interest. It took the pressure off.

'Well, that was interesting,' Andrews said, putting phone and pen down.

'Tell me.' West rested a hip against the desk.

'I spoke to a very helpful woman, by the name of Helga Fischer. It appears there are between 20,000 to 26,000 illegal immigrants living in Ireland at any given time.' He tapped the notes in front of him. 'Oh, and by the way, the politically correct term, as she told me, is undocumented migrants, not illegal immigrants.'

West whistled. 'That's a much higher figure than I'd have thought. Do they know how many of these undocumented migrants are children?'

Andrews shook his head. 'They're understaffed, and over-whelmed.'

West knew the score. It was the same everywhere. 'The three registers I contacted were quite helpful. They wouldn't give me a list of names, but when I told them about our suitcase child they promised to contact the social workers who look after every child with sickle-cell anaemia within a year of our child's age to ensure they are still hale and hearty.'

'That'll take a while.' Andrews sniffed. 'And it's very unlikely to be one of them. A child on a register won't just disappear.'

West nodded. 'True. But someone may have panicked.' When his phone rang, he motioned Andrews to follow him back to his office. 'It might be Jos,' he said, picking up the phone. 'West here.'

He listened for a moment before saying, 'I have my partner, Garda Peter Andrews here with me, I'll put you on speaker.' He pushed the button and immediately Jos Cotter's voice filled the room. West reached for the volume and turned it down slightly. 'Good to talk to you again,' he said, sitting behind the desk. 'I'm hoping you'll be able to help us with a case we have here in Foxrock.' It didn't take long to fill him in. There wasn't much to tell.

'We had some results back today. The child had sickle-cell anaemia so was, more than likely, of sub-Saharan descent. They weren't able to give us a cause of death but have proposed a theory that she might have suffocated.'

'People with sickle-cell anaemia can suffer from breathlessness,' Cotter said, confirming what Fiona Wilson had told them. 'I suppose it's reasonable that someone doubled over in a small suitcase might have had difficulties.'

'Exactly,' West said, pleased to see the theory gaining more credence. 'It's not something we've come across before, Jos. We have more homegrown crimes on our patch. Have you seen children trafficked this way before?'

'I've seen a baby hidden inside a large stuffed toy, Mike,' Cotter said. 'Why not in a suitcase? A two to three-year-old, probably malnourished, she'd be small and light. It would be easy and a case that size wouldn't have drawn attention. They wouldn't have risked flying, of course, not with hand luggage going through scanners, but there are far fewer security checks on ferries.

'Most children we've seen trafficked have been drugged to keep them quiet and compliant,' he said slowly. 'Depending on what they gave her, that also may have had a detrimental effect on her breathing. But, if it is trafficking, it's a bit of a puzzle.'

West caught his partner's eye. Just the kind of thing they liked. A good puzzle. 'What do you mean?' he asked.

Cotter cleared his throat, then noisily took a drink, the sound of his gulps coming clearly over the speaker. 'Human traffickers,' he continued, 'are in it for the money. Bringing in one small child in a suitcase wouldn't be lucrative, not for the risk involved. It sounds more personal. Maybe someone smuggling in a relation.'

'Okay,' West nodded, 'that makes sense, I suppose. Or maybe it was someone willing to pay a lot of money?'

A short laugh was heard down the line. 'I hope they didn't pay upfront then; it sounds like they got a bum deal.'

Andrews closed his eyes at the callous remark, opening them when he heard West ending the call.

'He doesn't mean to sound like a jerk,' West said, seeing his face. 'It's an occupational hazard, I think. I've heard the story of the baby in the stuffed toy before. What he didn't mention was that the baby was dead when he found him.'

7

Over the next few days Edel worked hard on her edits. She had a few friendly emails from Aidan Power asking her how it was coming along, and if she had any questions. By the fourth day, she was finished.

'It's done,' she wrote in an email to both the editor and publisher, attaching the completed edited manuscript. She was delighted to get a reply within a few minutes asking her to come to a meeting the following day.

Next morning, wanting to look the part, she took extra pains with her clothes and make-up. After a final glance in the full-length mirror, she headed downstairs.

West, sipping his morning coffee, stopped to give a soft wolf-whistle when she came into the kitchen. 'You look amazing,' he said, eyeing her appreciatively.

She twirled around. 'You're sure it's okay? I was going for arty and professional.'

West put his mug down and leaned back against the countertop. He let his gaze wander over her, taking in the fitted black skirt, just short enough to show her knees, the pale-pink silk shirt and the tailored black jacket with subtle grey detail.

'Smart, professional and incredibly sexy,' he said with a smile, 'not so sure if you nailed the "arty" look though.'

Edel smiled and brushed back her hair to show multi-coloured chandelier earrings that glinted as they caught the morning light streaming through the kitchen window.

'Ah, now I get it,' he said, moving over to admire them. 'They're lovely.' Stepping away, with a final smile of apprecia-tion, he picked up his mug again. 'I thought you'd met your publisher before.'

'I have,' she said, 'but I've a new editor. It's important to make a good impression.'

He laughed and let his eyes linger on her long legs. 'I think you'll do that.'

She twirled on her high heels. 'I haven't worn these in ages; hopefully I won't make a fool of myself and fall off them. Their office is on Dawson Street; I'm going to drive to the DART station rather than trying to negotiate the roadworks in the city.'

'Good idea,' he said, then his eyes flicked to the clock. 'I'd better get going. Best of luck with your meeting.' He bent and kissed her on the lips. 'Knock 'em dead,' he said.

Edel was still smiling as she slipped on her coat. Maybe they were going to be okay. Handbag and keys in hand, and humming a tune she'd heard on the radio, she locked the house behind her and climbed into her car.

The car park was full when she arrived at Greystones DART station and she swore softly. 'I should have asked Mike to drop me off,' she muttered, driving up and down, eyes peering for a gap in the rows of parked cars. With a yelp, she braked, took the next lane down and pulled into a space. It was just big enough for the car, leaving little room for her to squeeze out and she cursed her tight skirt and high heels.

The train pulled up just as she stepped onto the platform.

The rush hour was over, the carriage half empty. She sat in a seat by the window, hugging her handbag to her chest as the train sped along the coast. It was a blue-sky winter day with sunlight sparkling on the sea, but it was chilly and she was sorry she hadn't worn a scarf.

She smiled. She could buy one, couldn't she? Her publisher's offices were on Dawson Street. After the meeting she could head to Brown Thomas and have a look around. She'd not been shopping in the city for a while.

Tara Street station was the closest stop to her destination. She got off and started down the long platform and, by the end of it, knew she was in trouble. Her shoes were great to look at but they weren't designed for distance and it was a fifteen-minute walk to the Dawson Street office. Maybe if she walked very slowly? Outside on the street, she saw a taxi, and thinking about the arty, professional image she was trying to portray, she grinned and waved it down.

The taxi deposited her directly outside the old Victorian building where the offices of FinalEdit Publishing were spread over the top two floors. She hadn't been back since she'd signed the contract for her children's books three years earlier. A lot had changed in her life since then. Nervously, she rang the door-bell and was immediately greeted and asked to come to the second floor.

The receptionist hadn't changed and recognised her immediately. 'Edel,' she said with a smile, 'how nice to see you again.'

'It's been a few years,' Edel said. 'I've an appointment with Mr Todd.' Glancing at the clock on the wall, she groaned. 'Well I have one, in about forty-five minutes.'

The receptionist gave a polite laugh. 'Better than being late,' she said, 'why don't you take a seat and I'll get you a drink. Tea or coffee?'

Edel, her mouth dry from a nervousness she hadn't expected to feel, smiled. 'Tea would be perfect,' she said.

She crossed the spacious reception area to where comfortable chairs were arranged casually around a low table and sank into one of them with a sigh of relief. Tempted to take off the shoes that now seemed like instruments of torture, she resisted, afraid she wouldn't get her feet back into them.

'There you go,' the receptionist said, putting a cup of tea on the table in front of her. She put some magazines down beside it. 'To stop you getting too bored,' she said with a smile before returning to her desk.

Ignoring the magazines, Edel looked around as she drank the tea. The place had been decorated since she'd last been there. The walls were a muted green, the colour chosen, she guessed, to highlight a collection of very nice paintings. Nice, but a little dull, she thought, reaching for a magazine.

The time passed quickly and suddenly she heard her name called.

'Edel,' the small rotund man said as he approached with hands extended. 'How lovely to see you again.' Hugh Todd took both of her hands in his, then stood back to look her over. 'You look good,' he said, nodding in satisfaction, before waving toward his office. 'Come on in, would you like more tea?'

'No, I'm fine, thanks, Hugh,' she said, stepping into his office. The room was huge and dominated by a large desk littered with books, papers and a small computer screen. But what made Edel stare was the wall behind the desk. She couldn't remember what had hung there the last time she'd been in the office, but it certainly wasn't filled, floor to ceiling, with framed book covers. 'Wow,' she said, moving closer to inspect them. Her eyes sparkled. 'Will mine go there?'

Turning, she blushed when she saw the indulgent look that

Todd gave her. What happened to the arty, professional image she'd hoped to convey?

Her blush deepened when she noticed the tall, elegantly-dressed man standing near the window.

'Edel, I'm Aidan Power, how nice to finally meet you,' the man said, stepping forward to take her hand in a firm shake.

She wasn't vain, but she couldn't ignore the obvious admiration in the man's eyes, then wondered if it was reflected in hers. He was very handsome. Todd indicated a chair and she sank into it, Aidan Power taking the one beside her.

Over the next thirty minutes, Edel asked astute questions about her contract. At the end, she refused to sign until she'd had a chance to look over it again. 'If that's okay?' she said, her tone of voice saying she didn't really care if it were or not. What was that old expression? *Fool me once, shame on you. Fool me twice, shame on me.* She'd learned something from her marriage to Simon.

'Of course,' Hugh Todd said, then steepled his fingers together. 'Perhaps it's time you thought about getting an agent?'

She looked dubious. 'I've never needed one before.'

Aidan twisted in his chair to look at her. 'Children's books are far simpler. Now that you've joined the adult fiction group, you'll need to look at foreign translation, audiobooks etc. Final-Edit Publishing can handle the audio aspect but we don't do foreign translation. A good agent would be able to guide you through that minefield.'

She nodded. It made sense. 'Is there anyone you'd recommend?'

Hugh Todd pursed his lips and met Aidan's eyes. 'Any ideas?'

Power nodded. 'What about Owen Grady? He'd be an excellent choice.' He felt in his inside pocket and pulled out a handful of business cards. 'I think I have one of his,' he muttered, flicking through them and giving a grunt of satisfaction when he found what he was looking for. After a glance at it, he handed it to her. 'It's worth giving him a ring.' Then he smiled. 'Maybe before you sign that contract. Make sure Hugh's not cheating you.'

Edel looked across at the chubby face of her publisher and smiled. She'd dealt with FinalEdit Publishing for years; she'd complete faith in her dealings with them. But Aidan was right, if she was going to hire an agent, she might as well get him to have a look at the contract.

Another meeting was arranged for the following week. 'We're aiming to publish in about nine months,' Hugh said. 'We'd like to launch the second and third in the series pretty quickly,' he warned, 'so you're going to be on a tight deadline.'

'That's no problem,' Edel said, hoping she was right. She'd written her children's books to a deadline, but a fifty-page children's book was easy compared to the 300 or so pages required for an adult one.

'Good,' Hugh said, standing and holding out his hand. 'Unfortunately, I'm tied up for the rest of the day but,' he smiled at the editor, 'I know Aidan is looking forward to getting to know you better over lunch.'

'Absolutely,' Power said, with a glint in his eye that Edel ignored. She'd have been happier if Hugh had come along, but try though she might, she couldn't think of a reason to refuse.

Taking Hugh's hand, she shook it warmly and thanked him again before picking up her bag and coat and turning to leave.

Aidan moved ahead and opened the door. 'I've booked a table at La Maison,' he said, as she passed. 'It's just a short walk away and the food is excellent.'

Edel breathed a sigh of relief at the mention of a short walk, her shoes biting with every step. She tried to relax and enjoy the attention, but the more he talked, the more uncomfortable she felt.

It didn't make her feel any more relaxed when she saw the restaurant. The small, discreet basement restaurant shouted *clandestine meeting*. The steps down to it were steep. Aidan shot an admiring glance at her shoes, his eyes lingering on the curve of her legs, and offered her his hand. 'We don't want our new author tripping and breaking something, do we?'

In the last year Edel had compared her life to an Agatha Christie novel and now... bloody hell, she was drifting into Mills and Boon territory. She laughed aloud and her anxiety vanished. After all she'd been through, she could handle someone as obvious as Aidan Power.

'I think if I hold onto the rail, I'll be just fine,' she said firmly. 'I've managed stairs since I was about two.'

Over lunch she battled to keep the conversation firmly on her work, discussing the edits she'd done, her plans for the next novel and what her hopes were for the future. Power, who'd been so helpful by email, was irritatingly flirtatious the whole time and she decided future arrangements with him would definitely not be done face to face.

She was exhausted by it all, and when they exited the restaurant and she saw a taxi parked at the nearby rank, she pointed towards it and held her hand out to him. 'Thank you for lunch,' she said, 'I'm going to catch a taxi home.'

'If there's anything I can do for you,' he said, holding onto her hand, 'just email me.'

Email – not meet. Definitely, she thought, sinking back against the seat. Shopping was forgotten in the relief of being on her way home. It would cost a fortune taking a taxi all the way to Greystones, but she didn't care.

. . .

'I was shattered,' she told West that night when they sat down for dinner.

He laughed when she told him about the meeting and the subsequent lunch.

'I think he's a good editor,' she said, putting her fork down and pushing the empty plate away. 'But he's utterly convinced that he's irresistible and has such an appalling range of chat-up lines that he's rather amusing.' She watched as West tried to negotiate the last pea onto his fork before giving up and picking it up with his fingers.

'Amusing?' West laughed. 'Does he know that's what you think?'

Edel kept the smile firmly pinned in place. She didn't think it was worth mentioning the hand that seemed to accidentally brush against her breast as Power helped her on with her jacket after lunch, or the suggestion that they meet some evening for dinner. She could deal with it. Far better than she would have done a year ago. 'With his ego, probably not,' she said, with a dismissive wave of her hand. 'Anyway, I'll have little to do with him now that the edits are complete and even less when I get an agent on board.'

'You're going to approach this Owen Grady they mentioned?'

She shrugged. 'They recommended him, it would be silly not to, I suppose.'

Remembering her publisher's warning that they didn't want delays, she rang the agent's number at nine the next morning. She was in luck, not only was Owen Grady happy to represent her; he was available to meet later that morning. So, for the second day in a row, she dressed smartly for an appointment. His office was on Earlsfort Terrace, a twenty-minute walk from the same DART station. The walk would be nice, but definitely not in high heels. Instead, she slipped on a pair of black pumps that weren't quite so elegant but certainly better for walking.

Owen Grady proved to be a much easier man to deal with than Aidan Power. His manner, professional with just the correct amount of distance, put her at ease. He took the contract she'd been given and read through it silently as she shuffled in her seat in his bright top-floor office.

'A fairly standard contract,' he said finally, 'perfectly acceptable.'

'Great,' she said, taking it from him. She could sign it and drop it at the FinalEdit office on her way home.

For another fifteen minutes they discussed what each expected from the other. Translation rights, audio and large-print versions of her work were skimmed over, but in enough detail to leave Edel's head reeling.

At the end, Owen sat back, his rather stern face relaxing into a smile. 'It will be good doing business with you, Edel,' he said.

She nodded. He was definitely a man she could work with. 'You'll email me the details of our contract.'

'Of course,' he said. 'Give me a day or two. It won't be complicated, but it will set out financial details.'

Standing, she held out her hand. 'Thank you for seeing me at such short notice.'

'Actually,' Grady said, standing to shake her hand, 'Hugh gave me a buzz yesterday and told me I might get a call, so it wasn't totally unexpected.'

Edel blinked. Had she been railroaded into this? But no, he'd said Hugh. She trusted him. Had he said Aidan, she might have hesitated. An instinctive distrust of people was also the residual effect of her marriage to Simon. Perhaps it was no harm.

Leaving the office, she headed down Exchequer Street. Yesterday, she'd been too exhausted to shop, but not today.

Luckily for her sense of well-being, she didn't look up at the office she'd just left. If she had, she'd have seen Owen Grady staring down at her, a frown marking his brow.

'Interesting,' he muttered, watching her walk away as if she hadn't a care in the world, 'very interesting indeed.'

8

A week later, West and Andrews sat and went through all the information they'd collated regarding the child in the suitcase. 'It sounds like the title to a bad detective novel,' Andrews muttered.

'Child in a Suitcase.' West considered a moment before shaking his head. 'No, it would be Death in a Suitcase. Much pithier.'

'If it were a novel, there'd be an end to the story,' Andrews said, sitting back with a groan of frustration. 'A happy ending too.'

'Well, we're not giving up just yet.'

But after several minutes reviewing the information they'd collected, even West had to admit defeat. All their leads had come back negative. Frustrated, he clasped his hands behind his head and rubbed briskly, making his hair stand on end. He smoothed a hand over it and picked up the sheaf of papers on the desk, tapping the edges together before putting them down again neatly. 'What about facial reconstruction?'

'What about it?'

'Can we do it?'

'A two-year-old child that nobody has reported missing,' Andrews said, wiping a hand over his face. 'You really think they're going to okay the cost of that?'

West shook his head. They wouldn't because it probably wouldn't help. He pushed the papers away and changed the subject. 'How is the stake-out of Cornelscourt coming along?'

'Pshaw,' Andrews said, 'it's going nowhere. Either the gang has moved outside the city, or they're laying low for a while. The lads are getting fed up hanging around.'

'That's when they'll take their eye off the ball,' West warned. 'I think I'll go and spend some time with them.' He gave the pile of papers on his desk a nudge. 'It beats sitting here thinking about this poor kid.'

Fifteen minutes later, he pulled into a bay in Cornelscourt car park. Getting out, he stood and looked around. It never ceased to amaze him how busy it always was. It was open seven days a week, eight until ten and it never looked any different to now.

It took him several minutes to spot the surveillance team; they were doing a good job of blending in with the casual shoppers. Baxter's thick head of ginger hair made him more obvious. He was standing by the boot of his car with an empty shopping trolley, his eyes sweeping the car park as West approached him.

'Nothing happening, Seamus,' West said, standing on the other side of the car.

'Hi, Sergeant,' Baxter said, 'no, it's been mind-numbingly quiet.'

'Surveillance is ninety-nine per cent boredom and one per cent action. Try to stay focused, boredom can lead to mistakes.'

'We've been moving position every twenty minutes for that reason and breaking for coffee every couple of hours. There are two uniforms in civvies giving us a hand. Mackin is with me.' He nodded across to where the garda stood two cars away.

'Foley has Gemma Ryan. They're covering the car park at the back.'

'What about the multi-storey?' West asked, nodding toward it.

'There are a lot more CCTV cameras inside, plus the exit isn't great, so we decided they were unlikely to strike there. Rather than spreading ourselves too thinly we thought we'd stay out here, but,' he hesitated, 'if you think we should, we could include it in our cycle.'

West shook his head. He'd parked in the multi-storey before and he knew it could be a nightmare to exit. 'No, I agree with your plan.' He looked around the car park. 'Unless we hear they've moved on somewhere else, we'll keep up the surveillance for another week at least.' He rested his arms on the roof of the car. 'I'll go and have a word with Foley and...'

'Ryan.' Baxter supplied the missing name. 'Gemma Ryan. I think Sergeant Blunt borrowed her from Dalkey.'

Sergeant Blunt was renowned for getting staff from other stations when the need arose. 'They owe me,' was all he'd say if questioned as to how he managed it. What he did to curry such favour was never mentioned.

West crossed the car park and had just reached the edge of the building when he heard a shout. He looked around, trying to pinpoint the direction. It came again... a clear, loud *help* coming from the furthest corner. He saw Baxter and Mackin racing to the scene and started to run to join them.

A scream from the other side of the car park stopped him in his tracks. He watched the other two slow before Baxter waved Mackin toward the newer call while he continued on to the first. West ran to join him.

'I've alerted the others,' Baxter said without slowing, 'they'll join Mackin as fast as they can get here.'

They were at the scene minutes after they heard the first

shout. The victim, a middle-aged woman, was sitting on the ground beside her car, the boot open, shopping scattered. She held a hand to her face.

'Gardaí,' West said, bending down to her while Baxter scanned the surroundings to look for her assailant. 'Are you hurt?'

Keeping one hand to her face, the visibly-shaken woman held out her other to show the torn skin on her ring finger. 'He punched me, knocked me to the ground, and pulled my rings off,' she said, 'then he grabbed my bag and ran.'

West moved her hand gently from her face. The skin was broken and it was already beginning to swell and discolour. He was no expert, but he guessed the blow had cracked her cheekbone. 'Okay,' he said, 'stay here. We'll call an ambulance.'

A woman got out of a nearby car. She looked around anxiously and took a step closer, gasping when she saw the injured woman. 'Can I help?' she said.

'If you'd stay with her,' West said gratefully, 'that would be so kind. She's probably in shock.'

The woman nodded and took his place, reaching out instinctively to put a reassuring hand on the injured woman's arm.

Baxter, trying to catch sight of the culprits, found his view hampered by the surrounding cars. Without hesitation, he climbed onto a bonnet. 'There,' he shouted to West, before jumping down and dashing off in pursuit, darting between vehicles, narrowly missing being hit by a van as it pulled out of a parking space.

They converged on the spot where the second assault had taken place at the same time as Foley and Ryan who'd run from the rear car park. Mackin was bent over the victim who'd been treated in much the same fashion as the first, a bruise already colouring the side of her jaw. Blood oozed from a damaged finger onto her pale-blue coat. She was crying pitifully.

'They'd gone by the time I got here,' Mackin said, looking up at them. 'They're bloody fast.'

Gemma Ryan sat on the ground beside the woman and held her uninjured hand, muttering reassurances as the others scanned the car park for a sign of the gang. Baxter, having already discovered the best viewing position, jumped on the nearest car bonnet and scanned the area. 'There they are.' He pointed. 'Two rows down, scurrying between the cars. Two of them,' he called after them as they moved where he'd directed, 'wearing dark hoodies and scarves.'

He stayed on the bonnet, yelling directions to the detectives as the two men tried to evade capture. Mackin dashed to the exit and stopped a car that was leaving, waving his identification at the startled man before directing him to position his Fiesta across the gap. Foley and West split up, trying to hear Baxter's directions over the sound of traffic from the road.

Security men from the shopping centre, alerted to a commotion in the car park, ran to the car Baxter was standing on. They recognised him instantly and offered their assistance.

'Stop people leaving the shopping centre,' Baxter shouted down to them without taking his eyes off the search. 'And stop any more cars from coming in this direction.' Nodding, two security men ran back to the doors to wave people back inside, while a third ran to direct traffic away from the immediate area.

Baxter saw the two men, doubled over and sneaking around the edge of a car. 'Foley,' he yelled, 'to your right.'

Foley swerved to intercept, West chasing down the other lane to join him. Baxter, seeing they almost had them, jumped down from the car and ran to help. The struggle was brief. Baxter, stocky and strong, caught the shorter of the two men in a headlock. Between them, West and Foley brought the other, taller man down. Within seconds, both men were in handcuffs and the three detectives were on their feet, their eyes looking for the getaway car.

As if on cue, they heard the rev of an engine nearby and saw a land cruiser shoot from its parking space. The third member of the gang was making his escape.

The land cruiser increased its speed as it approached the exit and with a look of horror, West saw what Mackin had done, the young garda standing in front of the parked car as if determined to hold his position.

'Get out of the way!' West shouted before starting to run toward him. 'Move!' he yelled again, watching as Mackin realised too late that the car wasn't going to stop. West saw him try to dive to one side just before the cruiser hit the parked car. The rear end of the Fiesta, no match for it, shot into the road, the front jamming into the concrete pillar that housed the barrier that came down at night.

Brakes squealed as cars that were already on the road took evasive manoeuvres to avoid hitting the back of the Fiesta, the land cruiser that kept going, and the cars coming towards them in the other lane. Almost every driver blasted his car horn as if that would help, and for a few seconds it sounded like all hell had broken loose. West and Baxter ran towards where Mackin had stood, leaving Foley dragging the two handcuffed men along behind them.

They expected the worst. There was no way he could have survived the impact. Seeing his body unmoving on the other side of the wrecked Fiesta, West stopped, colour draining from his face. Baxter came up beside him, Foley bringing up the rear. 'No,' he heard one of them say.

9

Gulping, West took a step forward and stopped. In disbelief, he watched as the body moved and Mackin shakily got to his feet. 'Did we get them?' he asked.

There was a collective sigh of relief as they moved toward him. Ryan, who'd given the job of supporting the second victim to yet another helpful member of the public, came up behind them. Seeing he was okay, she headed out to clear the traffic, waving on cars that had stopped to gawk, directing oncoming traffic around what was now a crime scene. With one hand, she stopped the complaints of the Fiesta owner, who gaped in dismay at his car. 'I'll be with you in one moment, sir,' she said, waving another car on with a firm hand.

West insisted that Mackin go to hospital to be checked out. 'You were bloody lucky,' he said. Sometime in the next few days, he'd make time to have a word with him about the wisdom of standing in front of a desperate criminal intent on making his escape.

'I didn't want to let him get away,' he said. 'I failed.'

West shook his head. 'We have his two accomplices. You

think they won't roll over on a mate to escape the charge of attempted murder of a Garda Síochána?'

'So, I did help,' Mackin said with an irrepressible grin.

There wasn't anything to be said to that.

An ambulance's siren was heard in the distance. Baxter and Foley helped the two victims walk over to where they could be picked up when it arrived. West ran an eye over the older of the two women who was still crying and holding a hand to her swollen jaw.

'Your jewellery and bags have been recovered,' he told them. 'They need to be processed as evidence, but as soon as we can we'll get them back to you.'

'Can we have our keys?' the younger of the two asked, looking at him through one eye, the other swollen shut. 'I doubt I'll be driving again,' she said with an attempt at a smile, 'but I need my house keys.'

West nodded to Baxter who held both bags in his hand. The two men had dumped them as they'd made their attempted getaway and they hadn't been difficult to find.

The ambulance crew helped the women inside. Mackin, still insisting he was unhurt, was told he had no choice. 'Standard operational procedure,' Baxter said, pushing him inside, causing West's eyebrow to rise.

'It seemed the easiest way to make him go,' Baxter explained when the crew closed the door. 'He's good, Mike, we could do worse than have him on our team.'

'Well, if ever they allow us more staff, I'll keep him in mind,' West said, knowing that day wasn't likely to occur any time soon. 'Head off to the hospital when you're done here. I doubt they'll keep him long. Make sure he gets home safely.'

A squad car arrived to take the two handcuffed men away. West would make sure they were charged with accessory to attempted murder along with assault, grievous bodily harm and theft. That should put them behind bars for a while.

Order was quickly restored to the area. Gemma Ryan, who had continued to direct traffic, was relieved by two uniformed gardaí whose recognisable uniforms were more effective at ensuring compliance. Shoppers, oblivious to what had gone on, were back to driving around searching for parking spaces. The helpful security guards turned their attention to trying to reduce the chaos and made the entrance to the car park into a combined entrance/exit while the gardaí processed the scene of the crash.

Police photographers were there within twenty minutes. A forensic technical team arrived shortly after and were soon collecting debris from both vehicles.

West guessed the getaway car would be found abandoned later in the day and had a word with Baxter to liaise with the traffic division to be on the alert for it. They might get DNA from it that would identify the driver, and a comparison with glass or paint scrapings collected here would link it to this site.

Every base was covered.

The driver, whose car Mackin had commandeered, was thanked for his contribution in helping to stop the gang and was promised a loan vehicle while a reputable garage repaired his car.

'Have you seen it?' Foley whispered to West when the man had walked away, shaking his head. 'It's totalled.'

West hadn't given it much attention. He did now and grimaced when he saw the damage. Foley was probably right, it looked beyond repair. Morrison would not be happy.

He wasn't going to sacrifice Mackin on that particular altar. It would be reported as being his idea. Thankfully, they'd caught the gang... well most of it, he amended. That would go a long way to appease the inspector.

Foley stayed to monitor the various teams while Baxter headed off to St Columcille's hospital to interview both victims and check up on Mackin.

When he arrived back in the station two hours later, he had the younger man in tow.

'I think they were glad to be rid of him,' he told West and Andrews who were in conversation when he pushed through the door.

Mackin grinned and said nothing.

'Foley is just finishing up,' Baxter said, 'he's hoping you'll wait until he gets here before doing the interviews.'

Andrews raised an eyebrow. 'Wait?'

Baxter blinked and looked from one to the other. He never could be sure when Andrews was taking the piss. 'I just meant...' he started.

West took pity on him. 'He's pulling your leg, Seamus. Of course, we're going to wait.'

Baxter gave Andrews a thump on the arm. 'You are such a bugger,' he said.

'You two can go ahead and start on one of the interviews,' West said, 'I'll wait for Foley.'

Mackin said nothing, but he had big brown eyes that did the talking for him and West wasn't immune to their pleading. 'We'll need you a while longer, Garda Mackin,' he said. 'Write up your account of what happened while we're waiting for Foley.' He turned to walk to his office, stopped and looked back. 'It might be better if you say that having the driver put his car across the exit was my idea. I think the car's a write-off, Inspector Morrison might be a little annoyed.'

'Annoyed,' Andrews said, raising his eyes to heaven, 'he'll be steaming.'

Mackin grinned and nodded. 'Thank you, Sergeant.'

'When Foley gets here, sit in the observation room. You can watch both interviews from there.'

It was a quirk of the station. Because of lack of space, the two interview rooms were joined by one observation room. Sometimes, as now, it had its advantages. When he'd arrived in Foxrock, West had tried to get the team to call the rooms Interview One and Two, but had hit his head against a brick wall, and finally gave in. Within a few weeks he was calling them the Big One and the Other One just as the rest of the staff in the station did.

Foley returned forty-five minutes later with reports that everything in Cornelscourt had returned to normal. He told a groaning West that the mechanics who'd arrived to tow away the Fiesta had laughed when he asked if repairs would be expensive. 'They said it wouldn't even fetch a few quid as scrap.'

'We'd better get some results here, then, hadn't we?' West said.

They headed into the Big One where one of the two men they'd arrested sat at the table, his solicitor sitting beside him, already looking bored.

The formalities were quickly completed, and all four men sat back. West's eyes flicked over the information on the A4 pad in front of him. Ciaran Maguire, twenty-five years old, with a string of convictions that ran into two pages.

'You've excelled yourself this time,' he said quietly. 'Adding an accessory to attempted murder to your list.'

Maguire's upper lip rose in a sneer. 'Don't know what you're talking about. We've never hurt no one.' He shrugged a thin shoulder. 'Well, apart from the odd dig when they weren't co-operating.'

'Both of the women you attacked today are going to require surgery,' West said, his eyes hard. 'That brings your charge up to grievous bodily harm which carries a mandatory minimum prison term. Your getaway driver deliberately drove at a member of the Garda Síochána. That's attempted murder.'

Maguire darted a look at his solicitor and licked his lips. 'I wasn't in the bloody car, was I?'

West shrugged. 'That's why you're being charged with being an accessory.'

The solicitor, who obviously decided he'd better make some effort, asked, 'Did the garda in question identify himself as such?'

Maguire grinned.

There was no point in lying, nor was there a need. 'No,' West admitted, 'he didn't.'

'Ha!' Maguire said, crossing his arms.

'We'll have the charges changed to an accessory to attempted murder of an innocent bystander then, shall we?' West said, picking up his pen and scribbling some notes on the page in front of him.

The solicitor checked his watch. 'Let's cut to the chase,' he said, 'you haven't caught the driver, have you?'

If he expected a response, he was quickly disappointed as West and Foley sat stony-faced.

'I'll take that as a no,' he continued. 'If my client can furnish you with details will that assist in reducing his sentence?'

West stared across the table. It was what he wanted, in fact, what he'd expected. The solicitor knew that, but the game had to be played, and with his memory of Ken Blundell still fresh he wasn't going to make an easy deal.

'If your client furnishes us with information that enables us to catch the driver, we'll be able to discuss terms.'

The solicitor, Enda Careless, sighed. 'I may be careless by name, Sergeant West, but not by nature. I'll want much more than that, before I'll advise my client to assist you.'

'I'm not grassing to the pigs,' Maguire growled.

'Shut up,' Careless said without looking at him. 'If my client can furnish you with what you need, will you drop the accessory to attempted murder charge?'

That was cutting straight to the point. West guessed the solicitor, on a fixed Legal Aid remuneration, wasn't willing to waste more time than he needed. But he'd taken West by surprise. They both knew the charge of accessory to attempted murder was going to be a tough one to make stick. A good defence team could make the argument that Mackin had been partially responsible for putting himself in danger in the first place by blocking the exit.

He opened his mouth to agree to drop this charge but closed it again and frowned. 'I'll have to discuss it with my superiors,' he said.

Careless, raising an eyebrow in surprise, shrugged and looked at his watch again. 'Is this going to take long?'

West shook his head, announced for the recording that he was stopping the interview and left the room. He could have made the decision. Damn it, he would have done a couple of months ago. But now, he was second-guessing his every move. He sighed, and a few minutes later tapped on Morrison's door.

'The solicitor is waiting for our response,' he said, having given a brief but detailed summary of events.

'Mackin wasn't hurt?' Morrison asked.

'No, and anyway, to be honest, I'm not sure if the charge would stick. Mackin did well, but he put himself in a precarious position, and he didn't identify himself as a garda.' West frowned. 'I was surprised Careless went for that. He could have asked for the grievous bodily harm charge to be dropped instead.'

Morrison shook his head. 'Don't be fooled by his bored-looking persona act, Enda Careless is as sharp as a blade. He picked the one you'd be most likely to concede to, and,' he added, 'it's probably the one that young thug is most afraid of.'

West agreed. Despite Mackin's air of bravado, there was a glimpse of fear when the charge had been mentioned. 'So, we'll accept his terms?'

'Play a careful game, Sergeant,' Morrison said, then he smiled briefly. 'It's one you're good at.' The smile was replaced by a sour grimace. 'Can I assume the car is a write-off?'

It was tempting to say he hadn't heard. Easier, too. But honesty forced him to nod. 'The mechanics who towed it away seem to think so. We've given the owner a replacement loan-car until we get something sorted.'

The *something* would be expensive. Morrison's grimace went from sour to curdled and he waved West away with a sharp, 'You'd better get this third gang member, West, get him quickly and put this lot away so that, maybe, I can justify this expenditure to the powers that be.'

'I'll do my best, Inspector,' West said turning to go, then remembering an old adage, *leave on a positive note*, he added, 'Baxter and Foley did well today, and they had excellent assistance from Nick Mackin and Gemma Ryan.'

Morrison nodded in acknowledgement but said nothing. He would, West knew, note the comment down as soon as he left the office. Smiling to himself, he called into the observation room to check on the other interview.

'How's it going in there?' he asked Mackin who was sitting back, legs crossed as if he were at the cinema.

'He's made of tougher stuff than your'un,' he said, nodding towards the man on the other side of the window. Oliver Fearon was a bigger, older man and, whereas Maguire's criminal history was heavy on the robbery side, his was heavier on violence.

West stood listening for a while. They'd made the right choice; this man was never going to give them anything.

Back in the Big One, he sat and the recording was restarted. 'Okay,' he said, looking to the solicitor, 'with your client's history my superior isn't too happy at cutting a deal.' He waited a beat. 'But I persuaded him it was in everyone's best interest.'

Enda Careless gave a knowing smile. 'I thought you might,' he murmured before turning to his client. 'This is the best option for you. Tell them what they want to know. Don't be stupid and fuck it up.'

'You have one minute before I make the same offer to your friend next door,' West said, crossing his arms.

Maguire's lip twisted. 'Ollie's never going to deal with you lot.'

West shrugged. 'It doesn't really matter. We have both of you. We'll just question your friends, your relatives and everyone and anyone you've spoken to in the last year. Uniformed gardaí will swarm your street, looking into every nook and cranny. I bet we'll find plenty to interest us. Your friends will be *so* pleased.'

Maguire paled. He could tell West wasn't joking. Suddenly, taking the deal seemed like a good idea. They were going to find Connor Shields anyway.

Five minutes later, West and Foley left the room together, and Maguire was taken away to a cell. Two hours later, Connor Shields was led in, growling abuse at the two gardaí who held him.

By midnight, they had written confessions from Maguire and Shields, each man trying to offload as much blame as possible on the other. Ollie Fearon, on the other hand, refused to answer any questions, sitting silently sullen in the face of Andrews' and Baxter's best attempts.

'We have him anyway,' Andrews said later as they went over the statements given by the other two men. 'They'll all go down for a considerable amount of time for this. And your boy, Maguire, won't do so well from your deal,' he said with satisfaction, 'both women said it was he, not Fearon, who threw the blows.'

There was a message waiting for West on his desk. The garage had rung to confirm what he already knew. The car was a write-off.

He threw the note toward Andrews who read it and shrugged. 'It's a banjaxed car, not a dead body. We were lucky there, Mike.'

Lucky? West remembered feeling the blood drain from his face when he saw Mackin's body lying on the road. Yes, they'd been damn lucky.

10

Next morning, West left Baxter and Foley to complete the paperwork on the Cornelscourt case while he went over the information he had on the child in the suitcase, looking for something he might have missed. There was nothing. Without identification, it would be impossible to trace her movements. Without a face it was virtually impossible to identify her.

Stymied.

He drummed his fingers on the desk. There must be something they could do. He'd no idea how much a facial reconstruction would cost; he'd no idea if they had the facilities to do it even if funds were available.

He stopped drumming. There was someone who might know. He checked his contacts book and reached for the phone to dial the number. 'May I speak to Dr Kennedy,' he said when the phone was answered, 'it's Detective Sergeant West.'

Put on hold, he held the phone away from his ear. There was only so much terrible music he was willing to listen to. He moved it closer again when the pathologist's cheerful voice hailed him. 'Mike, what can I do for you?'

West smiled. He appreciated someone who didn't waste time

on pleasantries. 'It's about the child in the suitcase, Niall. We're no nearer to finding out who she is. I was wondering about facial reconstruction. Do we have the facility?'

'Not us, I'm afraid, but I know who does. The University of Dundee. They have a computer programme that can extrapolate facial features based on bone structure and nationality. It's in the research phase as yet, but they've had some remarkable results.'

'I wonder if they'd be interested in working on our girl then,' West said, feeling the first stirrings of optimism he'd had with the case. 'I don't suppose you have a contact there, do you?'

'No, I'm afraid not,' the pathologist said regretfully, 'but leave it with me and I'll ask around. I'll get back to you by late morning, if not before.'

Settling for that, West thanked him, and hung up. 'This might work,' he muttered. With little enthusiasm, he switched on the computer and brought up the case audit he'd been trying to complete since the previous month. He was still chipping away at it when the phone rang an hour later. Picking it up in the expectation of hearing Niall Kennedy's voice, he was surprised to hear a female voice instead.

'It's Fiona,' she said, 'Niall asked me to give you a buzz. You asked about the facial reconstruction work they're doing in Dundee. I was at a conference there last year and went to a symposium on it.'

'Do you know if they've done any work with children?' he asked. 'I'm afraid we've run into a brick wall trying to identify that child.'

'They hadn't a year ago, but I've no idea how advanced their research is at this stage.' He heard a sigh, then the rustle of paper. 'I have the contact details of one of the professors who spoke at the symposium. I'm afraid I can't give it to you, but I could contact him, explain the situation and ask him to get in touch with you. Would that work?'

'That would be great,' he said. He wanted to add *can you do it ASAP* but didn't. All he could do was hope she recognised the underlying urgency of his request.

She must have done. 'I'll get right on it,' she said, and before hanging up added, 'you'll owe me, of course.'

He smiled briefly and put the phone down. He should continue the audit and get it finished, but there was only so much time he could spend on bureaucracy without going crazy. Luckily for him, Andrews appeared in the doorway with the offer of coffee. He'd not finished the last one, but it was cold so he nodded.

Coffee in hand, he filled him in on the news. 'Even if Fiona sends an email immediately,' he said, 'it's unlikely we'll hear back for several days.'

But just as West finished his update, the phone rang.

'Is that Garda West?' the voice asked in a distinctive Scottish burr.

'Yes, this is West.' He raised an eyebrow at Andrews.

'This is Professor Alistair McLeod,' he said. 'Fiona Wilson rang us about an interesting case you have there.'

West, who'd expected her to email the man, was gratefully surprised she'd taken the trouble to ring. He definitely owed her.

'Tell me about it,' the professor said.

Another man who didn't bother with unnecessary pleasantries. Keeping to the bare facts, West filled him in. 'We're at a standstill, I'm afraid. Sickle-cell anaemia does indicate she may be of sub-Saharan origin, but that's all we've got to go on.'

'And you say she's between two and three years of age?'

'The pathologist based the estimate on her dentition.'

The silence lasted so long that West wondered if he'd been cut off. 'Hello?'

'Oh, I'm still here. Just giving the situation some thought.

We've not worked on someone so young. We'd have to shift some of the parameters.'

West gave Andrews a thumbs-up. 'But you'll give it a go?'

'Aye, we'll give it a go. It will be interesting to see what we can achieve. But I'll warn you, Garda West, at that age features are very poorly determined. It may not be of much help.'

'But, then again, Professor McLeod, it may give us the break we need. Now,' he said, wanting to get the process started as quickly as possible, 'what do we need to do? And how much is this going to cost us?'

A hearty chuckle came down the line. 'Nay, it won't cost you anything. We're delighted to have this opportunity. All we'll ask in return is for permission to use the results.'

'Absolutely,' West agreed. He'd be sure to tell Morrison; it might go some way toward making up for the car. 'I'll organise to have the child's skull sent over to you in the next few days.'

'No need for that,' the professor said, surprising him, 'all we need are a series of photographs and accurate dimensions of the various bones. I'll liaise directly with Fiona; she knows what I need.'

It was as simple as that.

Then it was just a matter of waiting. The professor had given no indication of time frame apart from his muttering about having to change parameters. West thought it wiser not to ask.

There was enough work to keep him busy. A minor domestic, a few assaults, some dodgy merchandise being sold, and the rumour of yet another new drug on the street, which thankfully, proved to be just that. The routine day-to-day stuff.

It was almost a week before he heard back from Professor McLeod.

'This is a very interesting case, Garda West,' he said, 'we've learned a lot from it. I've sent you the reconstruction by email. As you will see, we went with your sub-Saharan origin. In a child this young, how they wear their hair can make a difference, so we added a variety of different hairstyles.'

West held the phone tightly to his ear. 'Hang on while I pull it up,' he said, tapping the keys.

He opened the email and stared in amazement. 'Wow,' he said, 'this is better than I expected.' He enlarged the image. The child was beautiful; rounded cheeks, luminous eyes, her hair a cloud of curls around her head. There were others with the hair styled differently, but it was this one that generated a frisson of excitement in West. 'How accurate is it?'

'We've had some very good results based on adult skulls, but this is our first child. Bone structure doesn't lie, but as I already mentioned, children's features are poorly defined. We'll only know how close it is, if you manage to identify the child.'

'Well, with this, we might have a shot,' West said.

'Keep in touch, let us know the outcome. The best of luck with it.'

West thanked him and hung up.

He spent several minutes looking at the images before clicking *forward* and sending them to everyone who might be able to identify the child, including the South African Centre for Missing and Exploited Children. He also sent it to the National Centre for Missing and Exploited Children in several countries, to the Salvation Army, and to his colleagues in the National Crime Agency in the UK because, although the child might be of African origin, she could have been born anywhere. All the agencies, he knew, would add the images to their database of missing persons.

He heard Andrews' voice through the open door of his office and yelled out to him to come in.

'Something new?'

West swivelled the computer screen toward him. 'Prof McLeod came through for us,' he said, watching as Andrews' eyes widened. 'There are a few variations,' he added, clicking the key to change the image, 'but this is the one I'm printing out.' He clicked to the one with the curls and saw Andrews smile in agreement.

'If I were her parent,' he said, 'it's the way I'd have left her hair, she's a little beauty.'

'I've forwarded it to every missing person agency I can think of,' West said. 'We might get lucky.'

'Are you going to give it to the press?'

'I'm not sure that's wise. She's a pretty child, but there's nothing distinctive about her. We could be inundated with calls and end up running around like headless chickens.'

'True,' Andrews agreed. 'Probably best to wait and see if we have any feedback from the agencies.'

The very faint hope that someone would have recognised the child died swiftly when there were no replies for a day or two. All of the agencies eventually replied with promises to keep the photograph on their various websites and to circulate it to other groups and charities but, as one wrote bluntly, *I wouldn't get your hopes up.*

West had a long, and very informative, email from the South African Centre. Despite its name, it was involved with missing children over the whole continent of Africa and, more surprisingly, was based in Virginia, USA. It made for a harrowing read. The number of children of all ages missing or displaced due to conflict, famine, and disease was staggering. And, the email emphasised, the numbers they were giving him were conservative estimates. How many of these children ended up being sold was an absolute unknown.

He brought back up the image of their child and shook his head. They might never find out who she was. The phone rang.

'West,' he said, closing the email, wishing he could switch off what he'd read just as easily.

'Hello, it's Fiona. I was wondering if you were free for lunch.'

He stretched and ran a hand through his hair. The company of a charming and attractive woman was just what he needed. 'As it happens,' he said, 'I am.'

'Excellent,' she said. 'Do you know a place called Nutmeg in Monkstown?'

'Yes, I've heard it's very good.'

'It is. I'll meet you there. Say one o'clock?'

'One o'clock it is.'

Hanging up, he checked the time. Eleven. The thought of lunch and pleasant company spurred him on. He finished the audit he'd been struggling with and sent it off to Morrison, hoping it would keep him happy for a while.

At twelve, he switched his computer off, grabbed his jacket and headed out. He met Andrews on the way, his forehead creased, lips a tight line.

'Something wrong?' West asked, hoping the answer wouldn't require him to stay.

'Not really,' Andrews said, shaking his head. 'I bumped into Clark; he was complaining he'd been left high and dry because we took Foley. He had to work for a change so he's not happy.'

'Ignore him, Peter, he's never happy. Anyway,' he said, 'I'm out for a couple of hours. I should be back around four.' He saw Andrews' expectant look as he waited to be told where he was going. Damn it, he wasn't answerable to him. He shuffled off the twinge of guilt and ignored the inner voice that asked the question, *why was he being so defensive?* He was just going to lunch with a colleague, nothing fishy about it.

Nothing fishy at all, but still, he gave Andrews a wave, ignored his surprised look and headed from the station.

11

Edel's determination to get her next novel started gave her little time to think about anything else. Her writing style was disciplined; she outlined the plot, chapter by chapter, and then wrote a biography for each of the characters she intended to introduce. It made for an easier time when she eventually started to write the novel.

Life in the Greystones house had settled into a routine. She wrote from nine until lunchtime when she stopped for something to eat. Afterwards, she went for a short walk to stretch her legs and wrote from two until late.

She became an expert at cooking large meals and freezing portions so she didn't need to cook every day. Their evening meal was never at a set time, West would ring late afternoon and let her know when he'd be home. Occasionally, he'd tell her he was busy and would eat at work. On those nights, she'd write until she was exhausted and have a snack when done.

The worry that their relationship was in trouble never left the back of her mind. West had never said those important words, *I love you* and was still a little distant. She knew Ken Blundell's death preyed on his mind and she tried to be supportive, but every now and then she'd think about her Blackrock apartment with longing. It was peaceful there and the view over the sea would be very conducive to writing. But she just couldn't bring herself to go back. If she did, she knew that would be it.

The bottom line was, she loved him. For the moment, she'd make that be enough.

When she had the plot written out, and her cast of characters ready to go, she started writing the new novel, delighted when it came together easily. Two weeks later she looked down at the word count on the screen and smiled. 'Fifty thousand words. Not bad going.'

It was late morning, the sun was shining. She stretched, reached out to press *save* and switched off the computer. She needed a break.

They were going to a new restaurant in Foxrock village on Saturday. Idly, she considered what to wear. Maybe she should make an extra effort. Clothes shopping, she thought with a grin. Just what she needed.

She'd thrown on her usual slouchy pants and sweatshirt that morning. Her writing clothes, as she called them, definitely weren't suitable for the smart, stylish shops she intended to visit. Pulling them off, she threw them into the laundry basket and opened the wardrobe door. It didn't take long to choose, and minutes later she stood in front of the full-length mirror wearing a baggy grey sweater, thick black leggings and knee-high black boots. The addition of dangling silver and grey earrings and a few silver bracelets brought a satisfied smile to her face. Perfect. Finally, she slipped on a short grey and black jacket and headed down the stairs.

Her purse and keys in hand, she set the alarm and headed off. There were shops in Greystones, of course, but she didn't know them and didn't want to waste time trawling through shops that didn't stock the kind of clothes she wanted to buy.

Instead, she drove down the coastal road to the small village of Monkstown where there were two boutiques she'd shopped in before.

The village was a haven for small artisan shops, boutiques and cafes. Parking was always a nightmare, and today was no different. She tried a few of the side roads before giving up with a grunt of frustration and driving back to Dun Laoghaire where she parked in the public car park. It was a twenty-minute walk back to Monkstown, but it was a lovely day, she wasn't in a hurry, and her boots were definitely made for walking.

In the first shop, she picked out several dresses to try on, discarding them, one after the other, disappointed when none suited.

'We've a new range of tunics in,' the assistant said, 'they'd go lovely with those leggings.' She took two items off the rack and handed them into the changing room. 'Try these on,' she urged.

They did look nice Edel decided a few minutes later, trying on one and then the other. 'I think I'll take both,' she said, unable to decide whether she preferred the blue or sage green.

Carrying the large carrier bag with the shop's name blazoned across it, she headed two doors down the street to the other boutique. Here, she had more luck and found just the dress she'd been searching for.

'This is perfect,' she told the assistant, twisting back and forward to see her reflection in the mirrors. Made of silk chiffon, it fitted perfectly and draped beautifully. It was also ridiculously expensive. She baulked at paying 700 euro for a dress, but just as she decided she couldn't possibly be so extravagant, she imagined West's face when he saw her in it.

'I'll take it,' she told the hovering assistant. Slipping off the dress, careful not to snag it with her bracelets, she dressed and handed over her credit card before she changed her mind.

Out in the street, a carrier bag in each hand, she blew a

guilty breath; 700 euro. For a dress! She'd walked a few steps before she realised, she was heading in the wrong direction, towards Blackrock instead of Dun Laoghaire. Shaking her head at her stupidity, she turned, catching sight of her reflection in the window of the restaurant she was passing and lifting a hand to smooth her hair. She stopped and stared before quickly moving on.

Mike. Mike and a woman. He laughing and looking more animated, more alive than she'd seen him in weeks.

Her heart felt like lead, the weight of it crushing in her chest. Biting her lip to prevent tears falling, she moved as quickly as she could, concentrating on putting one foot in front of the other. She didn't remember the walk, or if she'd passed anyone on the way; she didn't remember the drive back to Greystones or whether or not she'd stopped at traffic lights. Her mind was stuck on that one freeze-frame; the way he'd looked at the woman, his lips parted in laughter, head thrown back, so absolutely relaxed. And the way the attractive, glamorous woman had looked at him, her red lips curved in a smile. They looked so absolutely perfect together.

It didn't take her long to pack; she'd got rid of so much when she left Wilton Road, and quite a lot of her stuff was still in Blackrock. She filled her suitcase and some black bags and piled them into her car. Lastly, she unplugged her laptop and put it on the passenger seat.

She sat in, took a last look at the house, and started the engine.

12

West enjoyed his lunch. Fiona Wilson was a remarkably attractive female and made no effort to hide the fact that she fancied the socks off him. She'd used those exact words, which made him laugh out loud.

When he'd stopped laughing, he looked at her across the table. 'That's very flattering but–'

She held up her hand. 'Don't say it,' she said, with a grin. 'I know you're crazy about that woman I saw you with on Clare Island. Edel, isn't it?'

He nodded. Crazy. It was as good a word as any.

'And much as I find you attractive,' she continued, 'I too am crazy about the new man in my life. But he's an academic. A history professor, would you believe?' She smiled. 'Sometimes, it's nice to be able to talk about work with someone who understands.'

West smiled. 'I'm lucky, then. Edel understands my work only too well.'

Fiona raised a hand to a passing waiter and asked for the bill. 'Now that we know where we stand,' she said, returning her attention to him, 'perhaps we could do this again sometime?'

'I'd like that.'

Outside, West pointed to his car, parked only a few steps away. 'I was lucky,' he said, 'someone was pulling out as I drove up. Where are you parked?'

'I wasn't so lucky.' She shrugged, waving down the street. 'But it gives me a chance to walk off lunch.'

His offer to drive her to where she was parked was turned down. A moment later, he tooted his car horn as he passed her by. He was back at the station by four. In his absence, he saw that Andrews had printed out the image of the child and pinned it to the centre of the main noticeboard outside the interview rooms. Blown up to A4 size, it had a strikingly haunting quality to it. He knew exactly why Andrews had positioned it so centrally; it would serve as a reminder to them all not to forget her.

Paperwork and phone calls filled what was left of the day.

Inspector Morrison rang to voice his opinion on the image they'd received from Dundee. 'They did a remarkable job,' he said.

West guessed he was even more impressed that they hadn't had to pay for the service. 'What about giving the image to the newspapers?' he asked him, holding the phone in place with his shoulder while he finished filling out some forms. There was a lengthy pause before Morrison answered. West pictured him swivelling on his chair, weighing up the pros and cons before coming to the same conclusion that he had.

'It's not worth it. If she hasn't been reported missing, it's unlikely anyone is going to recognise the image, even if it is accurate. We'd be inundated with crank calls, all of which will need to be followed up. We just don't have the resources for that.'

'We've sent it to every agency possible. So far, we've heard nothing.'

'Give it a few more days,' Morrison said, 'then we'll have to move on.'

West hung up and sat back. The inspector was right; they'd move on. He thought of the A4 photo pinned to the noticeboard. But it didn't mean he had to like it, and they certainly wouldn't forget about her.

At five thirty, he called it a day and was putting on his jacket when Andrews walked in.

'The judge threw out the attempted murder charge against Fearon,' he said, leaning against the door frame. 'They're out on bail.'

It wasn't a total surprise. West shrugged a shoulder.

'Ciaran Maguire is kicking up a fuss, claiming he was set-up, that we knew the charge would never have stuck.'

West's eyebrows rose. 'Seriously?'

Andrews smiled and nodded. 'Seriously. I heard that solicitor giving him some words of wisdom.'

'I can imagine,' West said, straightening his shirt cuffs. 'What do you know about him?'

'Maguire?'

A shake of the head. 'Careless. I've not come across him before.'

'No, you wouldn't have,' Andrews said, perching on the side of the desk and crossing his arms. 'I was curious about him myself, so I asked Tom.'

Their desk sergeant, Tom Blunt was a man of few words, but always seemed to know exactly what was going on.

West knew he shouldn't encourage gossip, but he was curious. 'Tell me,' he said, sitting back into his chair.

'Careless worked for a legal team in Cork for several years. When his wife died, a few months ago, he sold his house there and bought an apartment in Mount Merrion.' Andrews hesitated before adding, 'His wife committed suicide.'

'Suicide,' West said, startled.

'He found her,' Andrews said, 'she'd hung herself.'

That explained the bleak look West had noticed in the man's eyes. 'I thought there was something,' he said slowly. Standing, he moved around his desk, put a hand on Andrews' arm and pushed him out the door. 'Let's get home,' he said.

They walked together to the car park, each of them lost in thought.

'See you tomorrow,' West said, reaching his car first.

Andrews gave a wave and walked on.

The traffic to Greystones was slow-moving, giving West time to consider what he'd heard about Enda Careless. Curiosity had made him ask Andrews about him. He'd been a solicitor for several years before he joined the Garda Síochána, and had thought he knew the names of most of those who worked in Dublin but he'd never come across the man before. He smiled at his own arrogance; there were places outside Dublin after all.

He put the man out of his head as he turned the corner onto the tree-lined road where he lived. Perhaps, if Edel weren't too tied up with her work, they could go out for a meal. With that happy thought in his head, he parked his car and got out.

Lost in thought, he was halfway up the path before he realised Edel was sitting on the doorstep. He was brought back to a night, months before, when he'd returned to find her there, a balm for his pain and grief. Now, here she was again, sitting on the doorstep, surrounded by black bags and a suitcase, looking wan.

'Hey,' he said, reaching her in a few long strides. He bent down, saw her tear-streaked face and his heart did a somersault. What could have happened to her? 'What's the matter?' he said, keeping his voice gentle. Whatever it was, they'd get over it. After all, they'd had plenty of experience.

She stood and snuggled into him, taking his arms and

pulling them around her as if to wrap herself in him. 'Hold me tight,' she said.

He did as he was bid. It seemed the only option. 'You're cold,' he said, feeling her nose on his cheek.

'It's the end of January.'

West took a deep breath. 'This may be a silly question, but just why were you sitting on the doorstep?'

It was her turn to take a deep breath. She let it out slowly and pulled away from him a little. 'I was going to leave you,' she said.

'Leave me?' West moved back from her, frowning. He knew he'd been a little preoccupied since the Blundell tragedy, but he thought she'd understood.

She nodded. 'I saw you.'

Okay, now he was... what was that word his mother loved so much... ah, yes, flummoxed. He closed his eyes for a second. What had he done to merit this? Whatever it was, it totally escaped him. Opening his eyes, he met her blue ones full on. 'What are you talking about?'

'Today,' she said, her eyes fixed on his. 'In a restaurant. In Monkstown. With a beautiful woman.' She looked at him accusingly and added the final straw. 'You were laughing with her.'

Fiona Wilson. Of course. What was it she'd said? Ah yes, *I fancy the socks off you*. He remembered he hadn't laughed so hard in a while. There definitely wasn't a reason to laugh now, he thought, looking at the face of this woman he loved. 'That was Fiona,' he said, smiling, 'you've met her. Remember? On Clare Island. The forensic scientist who came to collect the evidence.

'She's been helping us recently with the child we found, it was through her we got that link in Dundee. It came through today, a very clear image of what the child might have looked like. When she rang, neither of us had eaten lunch so...' If it wasn't precisely the truth, it was close enough.

'Oh,' she said. It sounded plausible. 'She made you laugh.'

He shrugged. Laughter wasn't a crime, but perhaps telling her the reason wasn't a good idea. He looked down at the suitcase and bags at her feet. 'You changed your mind?'

'I always seem to be running away, Mike,' she said. 'I thought perhaps it was time I stopped.'

'Why didn't you go back inside?'

She shook her head and gave a rueful smile. 'I was going to go. I'd started the damn car before I realised running away was a stupid thing to do. But,' she said, throwing her hands up, 'I'd put the keys through your letterbox.'

He started to laugh, and within seconds it was a full, deep belly laugh that had her smiling, then laughing along. 'You...' he said, before pulling her back into his arms, 'you're an idiot, but I do love you.'

'What?' She pulled away again and looked at him. There was a moment's silence. 'You do know that's the first time you've said that, don't you?'

He blinked. Surely not? 'I've loved you almost since the first time we met. I told you I did on Clare Island,' he said quietly. Then he frowned. 'Didn't I?'

She shook her head. 'I told you I loved you outside the lighthouse hotel,' she said, putting her hand up to his face. 'When you didn't say it back, I thought I'd crossed a line.'

He thumped his forehead with the palm of his hand, the smacking sound loud in the quiet of the night. 'What an idiot,' he said. 'I wanted to say it but was afraid you'd think I was saying it just because you did. And later, things got in the way.'

'Things!' She smiled. 'We nearly died, Mike.'

He pushed a hand through his hair. 'Bloody hell,' he said, 'what a mess I've made of it.'

She started to laugh again, then they both were laughing.

'We'd better go inside,' he said, 'before the neighbours think we've lost the plot.'

He helped her bring her belongings back in, plugging in her computer, carrying up her case and bags. While she unpacked, he ordered a takeaway from the local Indian restaurant. He opened a beer and drank it slowly while he set and lit the fire in the living room. Tyler was impressed and immediately curled up on the rug in front of the flames. 'Yes, I lit it especially for you,' West said, giving the little dog a gentle rub.

He brought a bottle of red wine, glasses, plates and cutlery through, setting them on the low coffee table ready for the food. Finally, he sat back into the sofa with a sigh and the hint of a smile on his lips. Edel, she fascinated and confused him. He shook his head several times at the complexities of relationships. How much easier it was to understand the workings of a crime case.

Well, apart from the child in the suitcase, he admitted. What other avenue could they explore to identify that child? He hated the idea of giving up, but without any leads he knew they'd at least have to put it on the back burner. They didn't have the time or resources to continue to follow up every case. Andrews wouldn't be happy, but he too would understand. Unfortunately, it was the nature of their job that they just couldn't solve them all.

He put thoughts of work aside when the doorbell rang to announce the arrival of the takeaway.

Edel came down the stairs as he was paying. She'd poured herself a glass of wine and was curled up on the rug beside Tyler when he returned. He unpacked the bags, putting the containers on the table and taking off the lids.

He saw her smile and raised an eyebrow. 'What?'

'You're so neat and tidy,' she said.

He dropped all the lids into one of the bags and tidied everything away before handing her a plate. 'Is that a criticism?'

Shaking her head, she picked up one of the serving spoons. 'You've ordered all my favourites,' she said, looking at the dishes. 'We'll never eat it all.'

But they did, and between mouthfuls they talked, and by the end the food was mostly gone and their relationship was solid.

13

Over the next few weeks, it seemed that Enda Careless was in the station every other day. He nodded at West in passing, but that was as far as their communication went.

Oliver Fearon also paid another visit to the station. This time the charge was assault.

West sat in the Big One and looked across at the men opposite. He knew the solicitor, Alan Mitchell, from his law days. They'd been friends of a sort, attending the same law dinners, going to the same parties, mixing with the same small group of people. A group he was happy to leave behind when he joined the gardaí.

He gave him a friendly nod before turning to the large, dour-faced man at his side. 'Mr Fearon,' he said, 'you were arrested last night following an altercation with Ciaran Maguire. Mr Maguire is in hospital with a broken arm, broken jaw, several broken ribs and concussion.'

Fearon shrugged. 'He fell.'

West stared at him. 'He fell?'

'That's right,' the man said, small beady eyes returning the stare. 'Is he saying otherwise?'

'The garda who made the arrest saw you bending over him, Mr Fearon.'

'I was trying to help him to his feet.' He crossed beefy, tattooed arms. 'Is he saying otherwise?' he repeated.

'My client has a valid question, Sergeant West,' the solicitor said. 'Is the victim saying that my client is responsible?'

Ciaran Maguire wasn't saying much of anything. And when he woke, he probably wouldn't press charges. They could try to force him to testify against Fearon, but odds were it would be thrown out of court. Morrison, he knew, would consider proceeding as a waste of resources.

'No,' he said now, gathering his papers together. 'If you would just make a statement to that effect, we can let you go.'

An hour later, Andrews appeared in his office doorway. 'I hear Ollie Fearon was back in. What happened?'

West threw his pen on the desk, sat back and gave Andrews a rundown of earlier events. 'I could understand Connor Shields beating Maguire up, I suppose. He did give him up to us, after all. But Fearon?' He shook his head. 'Anyway, I had to let him go. There was no point in wasting our time.'

'He'll be back,' Andrews said, 'he always is.'

'He should go down for a while for the car park muggings, that's a given.'

Andrews rubbed a hand over his head. 'He's done time before; he'll do it again. A career criminal, that lad.'

But Andrews, for a change, was wrong.

Two days later, Fearon's career was unexpectedly cut short when he was found with a large knife protruding from his stomach. West and Andrews, called to the scene, parked on the road and entered the laneway where the man's body lay sprawled.

'He's very dead,' Andrews commented, crouching down to peer at the knife.

'As opposed to being a little bit dead,' West said with a smile that faded as he took in the pool of blood. 'It looks like he was killed here, not dumped.'

'A meeting gone bad, maybe?'

'Maybe,' he said, and walked back to the road. From there, the body was barely visible. Frowning, he returned to Andrews' side. 'Fearon was no fool, why would he meet someone down a quiet laneway?'

The pathologist finished his examination and joined them. 'Well there's no difficulty in determining the cause of death,' Niall Kennedy said, pulling off vinyl gloves and rolling them into a ball. 'And the guilty party kindly left the murder weapon behind too.' He patted West on the arm. 'This'll be an easy one for you, Mike.'

'Can you give us an estimated time of death?'

'Taking into account the cold night, I'd say somewhere between midnight and two.' Kennedy yawned. 'I could have done without the early morning call. Betsy is teething; she had us awake all night.'

'Been there, done that,' Andrews said sympathetically. 'We'd a terrible time with Petey, especially with the molars.'

'What about the knife?' West asked, trying to keep the conversation on the murder.

Andrews grinned. 'Sergeant West will know all about it soon enough.'

Kennedy's eyes opened wide. 'Really? I hadn't heard. Congratulations.'

'Please, can we concentrate on the dead man?' West pleaded. Then knowing how gossip travelled, he hurried to set the record straight. 'Don't mind him; I'm not planning on parenthood any time soon.' He pointed towards the body. 'Tell me about the knife, it doesn't look like a run-of-the-mill kitchen knife.'

The pathologist gave Andrews a knowing grin before

turning with emphasised reluctance to talk about death. 'No, you're right there,' he said. 'I'd bet it's a hunting knife of some sort. I'll know more when I remove it.'

With that, he left the two men to their examination of the crime scene. 'Why here?' West said, looking around. The lane was a dead-end; its sole purpose to provide access to the rear entrances of a row of shops. He didn't know what service they provided but guessed Andrews would. 'Do you know what the shops are?'

'A baker, a hairdresser, a newsagent and a butcher's,' Andrews said. 'They do a good trade; this lane would be busy during the day. Only the newsagent stays open late, and it closes at eight.'

'What's on the other side of that?' West asked, nodding to the high wall on the other side of the lane. It was solid, with no gates giving access and too high to be easily climbed, but desperation could make athletes of the weakest.

'A school. It's set back a way, and if I'm right, it's the sports grounds that abut the wall.'

West had no doubt he was right. He'd never met anyone who could store knowledge like Andrews. 'So, we're back to the *why here*?'

'Fearon lives about five minutes' walk away. Maybe he arranged to meet someone and suggested meeting here. It's the only set of shops on the road so it would be easy for someone who didn't know the area to find.'

'Someone who didn't know the area, but who knew him. Fearon wouldn't have wandered down here with someone he didn't know.'

Andrews shrugged. 'Maybe it was someone he didn't know as well as he thought.'

There were several lights positioned near the top of the wall at irregular intervals. Although the morning was dull, and the lane gloomy, they weren't lit. West waved his arms in front of one. 'Not motion activated, find out if they're on a timer,' he said to Andrews.

Andrews nodded, then moved to stand near the body. He took gloves from his pocket and slipped them on before bending down to pick up the dead man's hands, one at a time. Then he stood, peeling off the gloves. 'I've had dealings with this man for several years. You've seen his sheet, he's a thug and invariably his victims end up as Maguire did. But his hands are clean, and I doubt they'll find any tissue under his fingernails to indicate he fought back.'

'Not an argument that got out of hand, then?'

Andrews shook his head. 'I don't think so. It looks to me like he was taken completely by surprise.'

'I agree,' West said, and frowned. Contrary to what the pathologist said, this wasn't going to be an easy case. The problem wasn't lack of suspects, there were hundreds. Ollie Fearon had made a lot of enemies over his lifetime.

They brought Connor Shields in as being a likely candidate. After all, Fearon had beaten up the third member of the team; maybe Connor was next on the list and decided to be proactive.

'Do you know anything about the death of Oliver Fearon?' Andrews asked Shields, wishing he could leave the door of the interview room open. The scent of the great unwashed was already overpowering. Baxter, sitting beside him, was crinkling his nose in disgust.

Shields sat in his *tough man* pose; legs spread wide, bulky arms folded across his chest, eyes in a fixed stare. He didn't answer.

Andrews rephrased the question. 'Did you kill Oliver Fearon?'

It got a reaction, just not the one he expected. Shields reared back, eyes wide. 'You accusing me of patricide? Are you out of your bleedin' mind?'

Andrews and Baxter exchanged startled looks. Connor Shields was Ollie Fearon's son?

'We seem to be missing some relevant information, Mr Shields. We weren't aware that Ollie Fearon was your father–'

'What?' Shields said, and this time he stood and leaned over the table, spade-like hands propping him up. 'What's going on here? Ollie wasn't my father. What're you trying to pull?'

Feeling totally confused, Andrews ran a hand over his face. 'Okay,' he said firmly, 'sit down, Mr Shields. Let's get this knot unravelled.' He waited until the man sat, ignoring the glaring eyes that were focused on him. 'Now,' he said, 'let's start again. What is your relationship to Ollie Fearon?'

'I told you, he's my uncle.'

'Uncle, not father,' Baxter said, holding his hands up when Shields went to stand again, 'okay, just trying to make it clear. You did say we were accusing you of patricide.'

'Yeah, well you did. And that's libel, that is.'

'Slander, actually,' Andrews said. 'Libel is a written defamatory statement, slander is oral. And, just so as you know for future reference, patricide means killing your father, not your uncle.'

Shields wilted a little under the corrections.

'Now, once more, do you know anything about your uncle's murder?'

The response was a shrug of the shoulder and a shake of the head.

Something occurred to Andrews. They'd been puzzled as to

why Fearon had beaten up Maguire. 'You asked him to take care of Ciaran Maguire for grassing you up, didn't you?'

The answer was written on Shields' face, as clearly as if it had been tattooed across his forehead, but he said nothing.

'Would any of Maguire's friends be looking for their own bit of revenge?'

Shields gave the question some thought before shrugging again, then to the detectives' surprise he volunteered information. 'People were scared of Ollie,' he said, 'he had a mean streak and an even meaner temper. There's not anyone I know who'd take him on.'

There was no reason to hold him; they'd never prove he was instrumental in ordering Maguire's beating. Andrews just hoped it wouldn't start a cycle of tit-for-tat assaults.

Back in the office, he turned to Baxter. 'Have a word in Maguire's ear before he's discharged from hospital, Seamus,' he said, 'make him see the wisdom of putting it behind him.' Then leaving him to do the necessary paperwork, he headed to West's office.

'It's pretty clear that it was Shields who asked his uncle to give Maguire that beating,' Andrews said when he'd finished filling him in.

West nodded. 'It makes sense. I'd love to have been there when he came out with the patricide line. I wonder where he picked that up?'

'Probably *EastEnders* or some other soap,' Andrews said, sitting down. 'Then he accused us of libel.'

West laughed in genuine amusement. 'I hope you put him right.'

Andrews grinned. 'Of course, and if I'd known the correct

word for killing an uncle, I'd have added that to the mix and totally confused the lad.' He looked across the desk. 'You know it?'

'As every good solicitor would,' he said, 'it's avunculicide.'

'Avunculicide,' Andrews said, practising the word, . 'I'll remember that.'

West knew he would, and that he'd use it at the first opportunity.

14

Niall Kennedy rang West the following day.

'Hi Mike, I'm doing the post-mortem this afternoon at one o'clock.'

West looked at the clock. It was just after eleven. They'd arranged for some of Fearon's associates to come in for a chat. If he went to the post, he'd be spared listening to one thug after the other. 'I'll be there, Niall, thanks.' Hanging up, he went in search of Andrews.

'I can go if you'd prefer,' Andrews said, putting the clipboard he was holding down on his desk.

West grinned. 'And take you away from those delightful guests you've invited, that just wouldn't be fair, now would it?'

Andrews picked up the clipboard again and read out some of the names. 'Honestly, Fearon knew every damn shady customer on our patch and beyond. We're not going to run out of people to interview for a while.'

West took the list and scanned it. He recognised fewer than half the names. 'Maybe Dr Kennedy can give us something to narrow the field a bit,' he said, handing it back.

'Well, I hope so,' Andrews said, with an exaggerated

sorrowful shake of his head. 'If I have to listen to days of the crap I'm bound to hear today, I'm going to need counselling.'

Smiling, West picked up his jacket and headed out. It was unlikely to take almost two hours to get to the mortuary, but there was a bakery in Blanchardstown that was renowned for its meringues. They were Edel's favourite, he planned to stop and buy some to surprise her.

There was limited parking outside the bakery. He waited; his patience rewarded minutes later when a car pulled out. Inside the small shop, there was a queue of people, giving him time to look around and take in what was on offer. Tempted, he ended up buying a lot more than he'd planned, leaving the shop with the meringues, a loaf of bread, a fruitcake and some Danish pastries.

At the hospital, he parked, took out his mobile and rang the mortuary.

'Can I speak to Dr Kennedy, please?'

He was connected within minutes. 'Kennedy.'

'Niall, it's Mike West, I'm early. I've got Danish pastries if you've time for a break before you start.'

'Perfect, Mike,' the pathologist said, 'tell reception to direct you to the office.'

Several minutes later, West was directed down the narrow corridor to the fifth door on the right. The door was glass-panelled; he could see Kennedy inside pouring coffee. Giving a rap on the door, he opened it and waved the pastry bag.

'Good timing, I usually allow ten minutes from the car park, you made it in eight,' Kennedy said with a grin before reaching a hand out for the bag. 'I have fifty million things to do, you know,' he said, filling a second cup and handing it to him. 'For you, however, or maybe it's for the pastries, I'll take ten minutes.'

Munching, they did the usual chat about weather, holidays and life in general before turning to the specific.

'Thanks for sending me the image of the girl that Dundee did for you, Mike. Any feedback on it yet?'

West brushed flakes of pastry from his hands and sat back. 'We sent it to various agencies; the ones that have replied have done so in the negative. We're still waiting for a couple to get back to us.' Picking up his mug, he took a mouthful. 'Why does everyone have better coffee than we do?' he complained before returning to the subject. 'The image is great, Niall, but even Dundee admit they're not sure how accurate it is. Children of that age, it seems, have ill-defined facial characteristics.'

'You're doing all you can, it might be that this is one you're not going to be able to solve.'

It was what West had been telling himself, hearing it from someone else didn't make it any easier to accept. 'At the moment, I'm busy trying to find who killed our friend Ollie.' Deciding the conversation needed lightening, he told the tale of Connor Shields and his claim that they were accusing him of patricide. 'It descended into farce, from what I gather,' he said, as Kennedy chuckled.

Leaving the pathologist to prepare for the post-mortem, he made his way to the viewing area and sat looking down. To his surprise, Fearon's body was already on the table. His clothes had been removed, but the knife remained, dramatically jutting from his pale, naked body.

Although he listened intently, most of Kennedy's commentary during the autopsy was of little concern to him. He had no interest in how tall the man was, or that he was in rudimentary good health. Only when Kennedy grasped the handle of the knife and removed it, with a sucking sound that was loud in the quiet of the room, did he pay attention.

Putting the knife down on a separate table, the pathologist held a measuring tape along its length. 'The knife is, 300 millimetres in length, with a blade itself measuring' – he moved the tape – '180 millimetres.' He looked up to where West sat. 'That's just over seven inches for those of you still thinking in imperial.'

West waved his thanks. He was trying to mentally convert millimetres to inches and wasn't getting far. Seven inches. That's a big blade.

'The blade is three inches wide and curves inward at the tip. It appears to be composed of steel.' Picking it up, Kennedy examined it closer. 'It has cutting edges on both sides and they appear to be very sharp.' Turning, he looked around for something to try it on, settling for a piece of connecting tubing. The blade sliced through it with ease. 'Correction, based on this small demonstration, the blade *is* very sharp.'

Kennedy placed the handle of the blade under a microscope. 'There's a maker's name. *Wild Ranger.*' He turned to look up at West. 'Generally, the knife injuries we get are caused by kitchen knives, sometimes pocketknives. But this is not something you'd buy in your local department store. I'd say possibly it's a specialist hunting knife. I'll have it sent to forensics; they'll be able to tell you more.'

West waited for the rest of the autopsy, tuning out the irrelevant data about lungs and liver, both of which testified to Fearon's liking for nicotine and alcohol.

'The blade entered the abdomen with lateral force,' Kennedy said. 'It sliced through bowel and almost severed the abdominal aorta. He'd have bled out in minutes. From the direction, the assailant would more than likely have been right-handed.'

West stood, catching Kennedy's eye with the movement. He gave a wave of acknowledgement and left. The rest of the autopsy would be details that wouldn't be of any interest. He'd flick through it all when he received the pathologist's formal report, until then he'd go with what he knew.

Back in the station, he met a bad-tempered Andrews whose mood wasn't improved with what little he had to tell him.

'That's just great,' Andrews said with heavy sarcasm, 'so we can rule out all the left-handed thugs that we drag in, can we? Bloody helpful that.'

'Come and have some coffee,' West said, wishing he'd thought to bring some pastries back. He'd better not mention the ones he'd brought to Kennedy. That would definitely not improve the situation.

Leaving Andrews sitting to cool down in his office, he filled two mugs and headed back.

'Bad?' he asked, when they were both sitting.

Andrews rubbed his face with his free hand and gave a rueful smile. 'I should be used to it, shouldn't I?'

'Did you learn anything?'

'Huh,' he grunted. 'Only that almost everyone we interviewed could have killed him. Not one said he had been sorry to hear the news about his demise; they were just sorry he hadn't departed a bit earlier.'

'What about alibis?'

'Oh yes,' the frustrated garda replied, 'everyone was watching television until the wee hours, then they slept like babies beside their wives, girlfriends, boyfriends, you name it.'

Silence was broken by Andrews slurping his too-hot coffee.

'You think any of them is a likely candidate?' West asked. Andrews could read people better than anyone he knew.

'For every burglary, assault and drug deal that's taken place in the last few weeks, yes.' He put his empty mug down on the desk. 'For murder? No, I don't think so. All of these idiots would punch your lights out for looking at them sideways. But to a man, they were terrified of Fearon; I don't think any of them would have taken him on.'

'We might get lucky with the knife. Dr Kennedy thinks it's

some kind of hunting knife.' He held his hands apart. 'The blade is about this size, Pete. A vicious weapon. It had Wild Ranger stamped onto the handle; it might give us a lead. Get one of the lads to check out specialised knife shops, see if it's a common brand.'

It was a long shot but for the moment it was all they had. 'Are there many more to interview?'

'Just a couple,' Andrews said with a yawn, 'we're speeding through them because nobody has anything to say.' He held up his hand. 'No, that's not quite true. They all said that Ollie Fearon's death was no loss.'

On that note, he picked up the two empty mugs and left the office, leaving West to consider where they should go with the investigation. Despite what Andrews thought, any of the men they'd interviewed could be lying. He picked up the list of the men they'd called in and read a summary of their previous convictions. The only knife crime listed was an assault on a neighbour by a drunken man wielding a dull-bladed kitchen knife.

Very different from the rather expensive-looking knife that was pulled out of Fearon.

He considered previous knife crimes he'd investigated. Simon Johnson and Ken Blundell were both killed with kitchen knives, the first pre-planned, the second spur-of-the-moment. This murder had to have been pre-planned, nobody walked around a suburban street with a hunting knife tucked into their belt.

If that was the best he could come up with, he'd better not ring Morrison just yet. Forensics, he knew, wouldn't get back to him for a day or two. He supposed it would do no harm to give them a buzz, and let them know they'd be expecting the knife in.

He was put through to the forensic lab manager, Stephen Doyle.

'Hi Mike,' Stephen's gravelly voice came down the line. 'What can I do for you, but before you tell me, let me just say the answer is no.'

West laughed. 'I suppose the only reason I ring you is to ask you to hurry something along.'

'Absolutely the only reason,' Doyle said without rancour, 'and the answer is still no. We're inundated at the moment. The only thing I can promise you, is that I'll get to it as soon as possible. Give me a clue as to what to look out for.'

'It's the murder of Oliver Fearon, a hunting knife. There's marking on it, Wild Ranger. It would be a help if you could tell us anything more.'

A deep sigh came down the line. 'I'll keep a look out for it. But I'm not making any promises.'

West had to settle for that and hung up.

In fact, it was two days before he heard back. By then Andrews had followed up the interviews by checking alibis. It was a fool's game; they both knew it and their frustration mounted.

When Doyle rang with information about the knife, West breathed a sigh of relief. 'I hope you have something for me, Stephen.'

'You'll get the official report, of course, but I thought I'd give you a buzz. First of all, the only blood on the knife was from your deceased, Oliver Fearon.'

'Could it have been cleaned really well?'

'I'd go with a no on that,' Doyle answered, 'we took the handle apart, tested the screws and the joins. Nothing. Either it was bought specifically to use here, or your killer has had it a while and never used it. The good news is that there was a clear fingerprint on the handle, the bad news is that we found no match in the database.'

Match or no match, a fingerprint was good news. Now they

just needed to find someone to match it to. 'That's something,' West said, doodling on the notepad in front of him. 'Anything else?'

Doyle's sigh was loud. 'People always want more.' He gave a quick laugh. 'Actually, this time, I do have more. The only place in Ireland that sells this particular brand, Wild Ranger, is a shop just outside Kilkenny city called Outdoor Sport.'

At last, something concrete to go on. 'Thanks, that's a great help,' West said. 'We'd hit a wall here; it was getting us all down.'

Armed with this new piece of information, he headed out to find someone to share it with. Unusually, there was nobody around. He was just about to give up and go back to his office when Andrews, Baxter and Allen walked in together.

'We'd gone for some lunch,' Andrews said, 'were you looking for us?'

'I had some news from forensics,' West said. 'The knife that was used on Fearon is only sold in one place in Ireland, Outdoor Sport, in Kilkenny.'

None of the three looked impressed.

West gave a half-smile. 'Okay, it's not much, but it's something and it might lead somewhere.'

Baxter sat at his desk and frowned up at him. 'What about the internet? He could have bought it online, couldn't he?'

'Could he?' West snapped at him. 'Find out where? See how easy it would be.'

Without another word he headed back to his office.

He was sitting behind his desk when Andrews appeared minutes later and leaned against the door frame. 'Tempers are getting a bit frayed,' he said.

'Is that a criticism of me?' West said sharply, then held his hands up. 'Don't answer that, Peter, and please don't stoop to *if the cap fits, wear it*.'

Andrews, who had opened his mouth to say just that,

grinned.

West saw the grin and relaxed. 'You were, damn you!'

'You took Baxter's head off, and he was probably right. He spends enough time on the internet to know.'

West dropped his face into his hands. The child in the suitcase, and now Oliver Fearon. Neither case looked like it was going to be solved any time soon. Maybe his run of luck had run out. He rubbed his face and straightened. The clock on his wall said four. He'd be damned if he was driving to Kilkenny now.

'Let's go to Outdoor Sport first thing,' he said, 'you and I. We'll get lunch somewhere on the way back, get out of here for a while.'

'Sounds like a plan,' Andrews said, pushing away from the door frame. 'I'll go and put a plaster on Baxter's head.'

The rest of the day went without drama. The post-mortem report told West nothing he didn't already know and the full forensic report just confirmed what he'd been told over the phone.

Maybe they'd get a lead in Kilkenny. Fearon was a minor thug. A bully who was quick with his fists, he didn't have the discipline or intelligence to be more than that. His long and varied crime sheet didn't indicate any involvement with organised crime.

So, who did he get mixed up with?

Someone smart enough to have left no trace. Except for the knife. And a single fingerprint.

Kilkenny, he hoped, would throw some light on the case. He made a quick courtesy call to the local station. As he expected, they offered assistance which he, as was also expected, turned down. Formalities over, he hung up, grateful, not for the first time, that the Garda Síochána was an all-Ireland police force and not divided up into regional areas as in the UK.

At least there was something to be thankful for.

15

West admired the curve of Edel's legs as she stood looking out the window. She was sipping her coffee, lost in thought.

'Are you okay?' he asked, moving behind her and slipping his arms around her waist.

She leaned back against him briefly before turning and smiling. 'Yes,' she said, reaching to give him a peck on the cheek, 'I was just thinking about this meeting.'

'With your publisher?' West asked.

A flicker of annoyance crossed her face. 'With my agent, Owen. Remember, I told you about it last night? He wants to meet with me to discuss overseas rights.'

'Sorry, yes, of course, your agent, not your publisher.'

She moved away from him, refilled her mug from the cafetière and sat at the table with a sigh. 'We haven't spent much time together since we got back, have we?'

Guilt flickered. He'd cancelled their dinner plans at the weekend because he'd been exhausted, wanting to flake out in front of the television and chill. It wasn't fair on her. He sat down and reached across the table for her hand. 'How about we go away for a couple of nights? Not immediately,' he added hurriedly, seeing her expression lighten. 'When this murder investigation is done.'

Edel let her breath out in a puff. 'Okay,' she said, returning the pressure of his fingers. 'And do you know what I'm going to do,' she said, standing and taking her mug to the dishwasher.

'What?'

'I'm going to have A4 pictures of my publisher, editor and agent made up with their names underneath, and pin them to the wall. Maybe if they remind you of criminals you might remember their names.'

West was still laughing as she left the room, his eyes following her, admiring the curve of her bottom in a skirt he was sure he'd not seen before. His eyes narrowed slightly. He hoped she'd follow through with her promise of the photographs. It would be interesting to see what this agent and editor looked like. Smiling as he recognised the green monster lurking in that thought, he brushed it aside. He'd no reason to be jealous. After all, they'd cleared the air; they knew where they stood with each other.

Wishing her a successful meeting, he headed to the station. Andrews was already waiting in the car park, his radio blaring out an old Johnny Cash song that immediately made West decide to drive. His car, his choice of music, and Johnny wasn't on his playlist.

Luckily, Andrews was more tolerant of musical choices and apart from raising his eyebrow slightly when West asked, 'Is Ella Fitzgerald okay?' he said nothing.

Taking the quickest route, the M7 and the M9, they arrived at Outdoor Sport an hour and ten minutes later. The car park to the front of the shop was empty apart from a couple of cars occupying spaces marked, with more emphasis than either thought necessary, *Staff only!!!!'*

'Maybe they're very busy at the weekend,' West said, shaking his head at the four exclamation marks. He was a member of the Garda Síochána, not the punctuation police, but still...

Andrews, opening the car door and getting out, looked around the otherwise empty car park and commented sarcastically, 'Too early for the hunter-gatherer type, is it?' He stretched and looked at the shop. It was an uninspiring set-up. A square, flat-roofed building of no architectural merit.

'They take security seriously,' West commented, noting the see-through security shutters on each of the large front windows.

'And I've counted three CCTV cameras,' Andrews said. 'We might get lucky.'

The solid entrance door didn't encourage the casual shopper. Neither did the signs stating, one above the other, *Restricted Access; Strictly Over Eighteen* and *Entrance at the discretion of the Owner*. At the bottom, in plain font, a smaller sign read, *Welcome*.

'I hope they let us in,' Andrews muttered, pressing the doorbell.

The door was opened almost immediately, leading both men to believe that the CCTV cameras were actively monitored, a fact the middle-aged man who showed them in was happy to confirm.

'We're hot on security,' he said, smiling, before holding out his hand to each of the men in turn. 'I'm Terry Whelan, the manager.' He folded his arms across his chest and eyed the two men. 'So, to what do we owe the pleasure of a visit from the Garda Síochána?'

Neither man was surprised to be identified so quickly, it was something they'd become used to.

West took out his identification and held it out for inspection. 'I'm Detective Garda Sergeant West, and this is Detective Garda Andrews. We're with Foxrock station, in Dublin. We're investigating a homicide where the murder weapon, a hunting knife, has been identified as a Wild Ranger. Our forensic team has informed us that you are the only stockist of this range in Ireland.'

Whelan nodded. 'Come into my office,' he said, 'my brain is sharper with a mug of coffee in hand.' In his surprisingly spacious and luxurious, if windowless, office, he waved them to a seat and offered them a drink. When they were all sitting, he rested his mug neatly in the middle of a coaster and linked his fingers on the desk in front of him. 'Wild Ranger, eh?'

Because it was expected of them, both men said *yes* simultaneously.

'It's a good knife, but not very popular because of its price. The Outdoor Ranger is similar and costs a lot less.'

'So why would someone pay more for the Wild Ranger?' West asked.

'Most hunting knives have one cutting edge,' Whelan explained. 'They're used for skinning and butchering animals. A double blade, like the Wild Ranger, isn't necessary so it was probably just personal choice.'

West and Andrews exchanged glances. They guessed why the man had chosen the double-sided blade. Doubly effective.

'I suppose you want a list of our customers,' the manager continued. 'I should ask for a court order and cite all kinds of confidentiality issues.'

West smiled. 'But you're not going to,' he guessed.

Whelan shook his head. 'Hunting gets enough bad press, Garda West, without some idiot using one of our knives for the wrong reason.'

West blinked at the *wrong reason* but let the man talk on. He was agreeing to be of help, he'd settle for that.

The manager pulled his laptop over and opened it. His forehead creased as he squinted at the screen and tapped the keyboard with one hand. 'Here we are.' He looked at the two men. 'How far back do you want me to go?'

Andrews and West exchanged looks. How far? West, frowning, remembered that Doyle had indicated that the knife was new, probably never used, which would indicate a recent purchase. About to say a month, he shook his head and decided to be more cautious. 'Go back a year.'

It only took a few minutes, Whelan sipping coffee with one hand, tapping his keyboard with the other. 'Okay,' he said, sitting back. 'Six people in the last year purchased a Wild Ranger. Four in person and two on the internet.'

'On the internet?'

'You're surprised? We'd be very foolish not to offer an internet service; many of our customers do all their shopping online.'

'Aren't there restrictions on buying knives online?'

'Same as there are here,' the man shrugged, 'you have to prove you're over eighteen.' He hesitated. 'I'm careful, too careful you might say, but I refuse to provide weapons of any sort to the wrong type, so...' He stopped for a moment, as if weighing up whether to continue or not, then with a shrug said, 'I have a friend who's a garda. I give him the name and he runs it for me. If it checks out, the sale goes ahead, if it doesn't, I tell the person the item he requested is out of stock. Then I blacklist him.'

It was all totally illegal and if it were found out, the garda providing the information would be suspended, and possibly prosecuted. West could have him stopped; it wouldn't be difficult to find out who he was.

Then Whelan would have to supply knives to anyone who wanted to purchase them, as was their right. Personal rights, moral rights, they were an ongoing dilemma. And once again, Ken Blundell came to mind. Perhaps he'd leave things as they were.

'I have the dates and times,' Whelan continued, unaware of the issues he'd raised. 'I've got all the details on the internet customers, of course, and they'll have been cleared by my friend. Of the four who paid in person, three used credit cards, so I'll be able to get those details for you too.' He smiled, nodded and rubbed his hands together. 'I'll have them all printed out, don't you worry.

'The other customer paid in cash. I don't know anything about him, but he'll be on the CCTV. I'll copy the footage of all four customers for you, if you want. It'll take a while, an hour or two; they're spread over several months. You're welcome to wait here.'

'Yes, to the CCTV footage, but no thanks, we won't get in your way,' West said, checking the time. It was only eleven thirty. A very early lunch? 'We'll be back around one thirty.'

'Perfect,' Whelan said. 'I'll have it all ready for you when you get back. I'll make sure of that.'

Thanking the man, the two detectives left. Outside, West moved straight to the car and climbed in, barely waiting for Andrews to close the door before starting the engine and pulling away. 'I don't like the feeling that he's watching us,' he said, when he caught Andrews' look of surprise.'

'Not sure I blame you,' he said. He waited a moment before turning to him. 'Are you going to look into it?'

West didn't insult his intelligence by misunderstanding him. He shook his head. 'I should, I suppose, but do we really want him selling weapons to ne'er-do-wells.'

'Ne'er-do-wells,' Andrews repeated with a chuckle. 'No, I suppose we don't. I wonder if that's the only thing our over-friendly garda does for him though.'

West looked at him sharply. 'You think I should inform on him?'

'I don't think Whelan is to be trusted. In my experience,

when members of the public set themselves up to be holier-than-thou, it is generally for their own benefit.'

'I must admit, his over-helpful manner grated on me.'

Andrews nodded. 'He was so incredibly helpful; we won't need to get a court order to check out anything, will we?'

West's hands gripped the steering wheel. He'd missed it. A quick glance at Andrews' face told him that he hadn't. He never did. 'He's playing us?'

'For some reason,' Andrews agreed. 'I doubt if it's anything to do with our friend Ollie though. Something else entirely.'

The silence lasted until West drew up outside a pub. 'An early lunch?'

'Sounds like a plan,' Andrews said. He looked out the window with a dubious expression. 'Not sure you'll get that here, though.'

He was right. It didn't open until one.

West pulled out his phone and did an internet search. 'There's a hotel about five minutes away,' he said, 'we can get something there.'

The hotel restaurant was closed but the lounge staff were happy to provide them with sandwiches. Andrews, who wasn't driving, had a pint of Heineken that West eyed with disfavour. 'I don't know how you drink that stuff,' he said.

'You say that every time.' Andrews took a large mouthful with obvious pleasure.

West sipped his mineral water. 'I'll talk to Morrison,' he said eventually. 'We can't do anything else. Going to Kilkenny station and asking to speak to someone isn't an option, we could end up speaking to Whelan's pet garda.'

'Don't do anything until we get our CCTV footage anyway,' Andrews said, eyeing the plates that had been put before them. 'Nice,' he decided, picking up a chicken sandwich.

They ate silently, working steadily through the sandwiches, salad and crisps until both plates were empty.

'That was really good,' West said, picking up his water.

'I bet they do a good pudding here, too,' Andrews said, draining his pint.

When one of the staff came to clear the plates, he asked and was brought a menu. Several minutes later, they were both tucking into apple pie and cream. 'Told you they would be good,' Andrews said, more than pleased to be right.

West finished with a coffee, drinking it slowly, his brain ticking over. He could tell Morrison, but what could he do? They'd no proof of any wrongdoing. 'We could get some,' he said, startling Andrews who was busy texting his wife.

'Get some what?'

'Proof,' he said, and as an idea came to him his eyes lit up.

Andrews, seeing his expression, dropped his phone back into his jacket pocket and slapped a hand on his forehead. 'Oh no, what maggot has got into you now?'

West laughed. 'You'll like it, Peter. Listen, Whelan's not giving us the year's CCTV footage, is he? Only the footage that shows the men that came in. What if I speak to a judge, explain that we think our murder weapon was bought there and that we asked for the footage, but when we were given it, we noticed it had been edited. I bet we could get a warrant for the rest and any other helpful information.'

Andrews' eyes narrowed. 'That's very sneaky.'

West grinned. 'Very.'

16

When they returned to the shop, there was one disc and an envelope waiting for them.

'Terry asked me to give this to you when you came back,' a young man with acne-pitted skin said, holding them in limp fingers as if he didn't want to be contaminated by helping the gardaí.

West took them and put them into his jacket pocket without a word. 'Tell Mr Whelan we'll be in touch.'

Resentful eyes followed the two men as they exited into the dull winter sun.

'Pleasant, helpful lad,' Andrews commented.

West didn't reply, his mind thinking ahead to which judge to approach and how to present his argument to achieve the outcome he wanted. Sometimes having a legal qualification acted in his favour. Judge Mahoney always came down hard on knife crimes. He'd try to contact him.

'I'll leave you to go through the disc while I sort out the warrant,' he said.

Andrews, who had his eyes closed, murmured in agreement.

West gave him a glance and smiled. Beer or no beer, his

partner invariably fell asleep. It suited him today; he had things to think about. It wasn't until he pulled into his parking space in Foxrock, that Andrews opened his eyes. 'We here already?'

'You slept all the way,' West said, turning off the engine. 'You'll be refreshed now and be able to watch this.' He handed him the disc. 'I'll join you when I've spoken to Judge Mahoney.'

'Okay, I'll watch it in the Big One, I'll get more peace.' He walked back to the main office with West, grabbed his laptop and headed back to the vacant interview room.

West sat at his desk and considered his options. He needed to speak to the judge. Looking up a number, he dialled, tapping his fingers on the desk as it rang several times. He was just about to give up when it was answered.

'Clerk of court,' a familiar voice said.

'You're still keeping the judges in order, then?'

The hesitation was short. 'As I live and breathe, Detective Garda Sergeant West, to what do I owe this pleasure... no, I don't need to ask, you want something.' A loud sigh was followed by, 'Some things never change.'

'And you were always helpful, Dobby,' West said, remembering how William Dobson had taken him under his wing during those first days attending court.

'So, what's it today?'

'I need to speak to Judge Mahoney. Can you help?'

The sound of voices passing by drowned out his reply.

'Dobby, I missed that.'

'I said you're in luck. If you're quick that is, he has about five minutes before his next case.'

'Five minutes is all I need,' West said, hoping he'd manage to get his proposal out in that time.

The phone went dead for a moment as the call was transferred to the judge's chambers. 'You have two minutes before I'm due in court,' Mahoney said, more than halving the five minutes Dobby had mentioned.

'It's Detective Garda Sergeant West, your honour,' he said, 'we've had a brutal knife crime here in Foxrock resulting in a man's death. We think the knife was supplied from a shop in Kilkenny called Outdoor Sport. They said they'd provide us with CCTV footage of the time in question, but they've carefully edited it and we think they're hiding something. We want to go back with a warrant and get the lot. Gang-related knife crimes,' he added, putting as much conviction into his voice as possible, 'have to be stopped.'

The silence that followed made him wonder if he'd pushed his luck.

'Indeed,' the judge said finally, 'we appear to be on the same wavelength, Sergeant West. Give the details to Dobby and I'll have it drawn up when I finish this sitting.'

Five minutes later, he hung up. Dobby had the information he needed; he'd make sure the warrant was done.

Taking two mugs of coffee with him, he made his way to the Big One, awkwardly holding them in one hand as he negotiated the door handle, finally resorting to kicking the bottom of the door.

Andrews' frown told him he wasn't happy at being interrupted, but his face resumed its usual pleasant look when he saw who it was. 'I thought it was that idiot Clark again,' he said, taking one of the mugs. 'He wanted to interview a suspect. I told him to bugger off to the Other One and leave me alone. He wasn't too happy and went off grumbling about making a complaint.'

The interview rooms, despite their names, were virtually identical. West never cared which one he used, but he knew Clark did. He would complain to Morrison, his complaint would be dismissed, but he would bear a grudge. He always did.

Brushing thoughts of Clark and his moans out of his head, he took a chair beside Andrews and concentrated on the screen.

'I've seen two of the customers,' Andrews said, slurping his coffee and pressing resume to restart the footage. 'Two more to go. Did you manage to get the warrant?'

'Did you doubt me for a moment?'

Andrews grinned. 'Judge Mahoney?'

West nodded and reached to freeze the picture on the screen and peer closer. He shook his head. 'I thought I recognised that guy.' Sitting back, he explained. 'The judge was very happy to give us a full warrant to ensure that Oliver Fearon's death isn't the first in a spate of gang-related knife crimes.'

Andrews looked at him sideways. 'Gang-related knife crimes? That was gilding the lily a bit, wasn't it?'

West shrugged. 'I had a couple of minutes to make my pitch; it had to be a good one. Anyway, he's okayed it, so we're good to go for tomorrow.'

They watched the remainder of the disc in silence. It didn't take long.

The last customer was the one they knew nothing about, the cash buyer. Both men instinctively moved slightly closer to the screen. But they were wasting their time. 'Bloody hell,' Andrews said, sitting back with a frown. 'So much for not selling to dodgy-looking types.'

The cash buyer, with a beanie hat pulled down to cover his hair and dark glasses almost completely obscuring his face, could have been anyone. All they were going to get was an approximate size and body shape.

'But there is one interesting thing,' West said, pressing the backspace key. 'Watch, Pete. See, he must have asked for it by name. The assistant immediately goes and gets the Wild Ranger and hands it to him. He's the only one who doesn't look at any other knives.'

'You're right,' Andrews said, 'the other three looked at one or two others before deciding.'

'I wonder if the original recording has sound. His voice might give us an indication as to where he's from.'

'We'll be able to find out tomorrow. That assistant,' Andrews nodded toward the screen, 'that's the young lad that showed us out. We're not going to get much help from him, I'd say.'

'I doubt if we're going to be popular with anyone when we go back. It will be interesting to see if we can wipe that helpful smile from Whelan's face.'

Andrews removed the disc and switched off the computer. Tucking it under his arm, he picked up his jacket. 'I think we can safely say that we're going to make Outdoor Sport's day,' he said, opening the door with a grin.

17

The first thing that hit West when he opened his front door was the smell of cooking. If his nose was right, and he hoped it was, Edel had made lasagne, one of his favourites. He hung his jacket on the newel of the banisters, threw his tie on top and undid the top button of his shirt. The buttons on his shirt cuffs were next. With his sleeves rolled up, he was definitely in relaxation mode. Smiling, he reached for the kitchen doorknob before stopping with a whispered, 'Damn.'

What was the name of the agent? Hardy? No... Grady. Owen Grady. With a sigh of relief, he opened the door.

'I hope that's lasagne I smell,' he said, crossing the room.

'It certainly is,' Edel said, wrapping tinfoil around garlic bread and putting it in the oven. 'Lasagne, garlic bread and a delicious bottle of Chianti to wash it all down.'

He kissed her on the lips, put his hands on her face and kissed her again. 'Does this mean the meeting with Owen went well?' he asked, stepping back and picking up the corkscrew to open the wine.

'Sit,' she said, 'it'll be ready in ten minutes. I'll tell you about it over dinner.'

He took the wine and two glasses to the table. Taking the far chair allowed him to watch her as she bustled about the kitchen. It was almost a year since he'd first met her; how pale and scrawny she'd been then. Now, she... glowed. It was the only word he could think of that suited.

His mother was nagging him to meet her, as was his sister. He'd been reluctant, afraid to rock the boat or tempt fate. But it was different now. They knew where they stood with each other. He frowned. That was the second time he'd had that thought today. Was he trying to convince himself?

He shook his head and caught her eye.

'Everything okay?' she asked.

'Fine, I was just thinking about work,' he lied.

She placed a plate in front of him, curls of steam rising from the lasagne. 'Well, start thinking about this instead,' she said, putting a basket holding garlic bread in the space between them.

Over dinner, she told him about her meeting. If the name Owen Grady was mentioned more times than he liked, he tried not to let his feelings show. He was just her agent, and he was new, so of course she was going to talk about him. It didn't mean anything.

'That sounds like a good deal,' he said when she mentioned the royalty payments from overseas sales.

'He certainly knows his stuff,' she said, taking another piece of garlic bread and scooping some of the lasagne onto it before popping it into her mouth. 'It's good that we get on so well.'

'Definitely,' West agreed, knowing it was the correct response.

'How did Kilkenny go?'

'We went looking for information on one crime and came back investigating another.'

She raised an eyebrow. 'What? You're kidding me!'

He pushed his plate away and lifted his glass. 'No, seriously,' he said, smiling at her wide eyes.

A few minutes later, she had the full story and was shaking her head. 'Honestly, you and Peter are incredible. Most people would have just been grateful for that Whelan's help, but not you two.'

He held his hands up. 'I have to admit I missed it, at first. It was Peter who pointed out that his helpfulness was just too...' He searched for the correct word.

'Helpful?' she suggested.

Smiling, he nodded and picked up his glass again. 'Once Peter had said it, of course, I knew he was right. There was something a bit odd about it.'

'You've got the unsolved case with the child in the suitcase, and the murder of Ollie Fearon to deal with. And just to make sure you never have a moment; you go looking for more crimes to solve?'

'Like an ambulance chaser, you mean?'

'Something like that.' She swirled the wine around in her glass before lifting it to her mouth and taking a sip. 'It looks like our couple of nights away together won't happen any time soon, doesn't it?'

There was that guilt again, washing through him. He reached across for her hand and rubbed it gently with his thumb. 'I promise, as soon as things calm down a bit, we'll go somewhere.'

'And there'll be no dead bodies.'

'An ambulance chaser and the angel of death,' he said with a smile. 'Are you sure you want to live with me?'

Her hesitation wasn't planned but it was there and they both heard it even as she tried to cover it up with her rushed, 'Of course I do, I love you, Mike.'

But the mood was spoilt.

'There's a programme on that I want to watch,' he said, taking his plate and putting it in the dishwasher. He poured more wine into his glass and took it with him.

'Damn,' Edel said, pushing a hand through her hair. She finished tidying up, switched off the light and went into the hallway where she stood and listened to the rumble of the television. He'd be sitting on the sofa, one hand petting Tyler who would no doubt be curled up beside him.

Suddenly, she felt like an interloper.

18

West didn't know if she was asleep or pretending to be when he went up to bed after midnight. The programme he'd wanted to watch ended hours before, but he didn't want to face into one of those *we have to talk* talks.

He was being unfair. She'd never actually ever said that. But the hesitation, that was real. So, it wasn't all as settled between them as he had been trying to convince himself. He lay quietly beside her, listening to her breathe, and wondered what had gone wrong. It wasn't something he could solve, a bit like his current caseload. He did what he could, he fell asleep.

In the morning, he slipped from the bed without disturbing Edel. Showered and dressed, he headed downstairs, made a pot of coffee and stared glumly through the rain-lashed window as he drank. It wasn't a good morning for a long drive.

He turned when Edel came in. 'Hi, did you sleep okay?'

'Fine,' she said, taking a mug from the cupboard and pouring some coffee.

It was a four-letter word he dreaded. A female weapon guaranteed to bring a man to his knees. He knew, whatever he asked that morning, the response would be the same. He was damned if he was playing into it.

'I'd better get going.' He nodded at the window as he emptied the remains of his coffee into the sink. 'Traffic is bound to be heavier thanks to that deluge.' He bent to kiss her on the cheek. 'I'll see you tonight.'

'Fine,' she said, taking her mug to the table.

He knew when he was beaten. With a last look in her direction, he left, picking up his raincoat on the way. The post was early; he picked it up from the mat, quickly looked through and removed his, and dropped the rest on the hall table.

Traffic wasn't as heavy as he'd expected and he arrived in the car park before Andrews. He thought about going inside but knew, if he did, he'd be waylaid by someone about something. So, he stayed in the car, turned up the radio and opened his post. The first couple were the usual rubbish that he tossed unread onto the back seat. The last, with his name and address handwritten in block capitals, looked to be more interesting 'What's this then?' he muttered, tearing across the top.

He hesitated when he saw the contents. Photographs. Three of them, he guessed, moving the top edges. No letter. Reaching over, he opened the glove compartment and pulled out vinyl gloves. Once they were on, he carefully extracted the photographs.

There were three. And the subject was the same in each. It was Edel as he'd never seen her before, posing naked, legs splayed. They left little to the imagination.

A car pulled up alongside. He put the photographs back into the envelope and shoved them and the gloves into his pocket just as the passenger door opened and Andrews climbed in. He was full of talk about some football match he'd watched the night before so West didn't have to make conversation, the odd *oh* or *really* being enough to show interest and they were well on the road to Kilkenny before Andrews mentioned the upcoming search.

'Edwards picked up the warrant early this morning, your pal Dobby had it waiting for him. He and Baxter will meet us outside the shop. I told them ten.'

West nodded but said nothing. His head was spinning. Who would have sent the photographs? And to what end?

By the time they reached Outdoor Sport, he'd stopped trying to work it out and pushed it to the back of his mind. He needed to concentrate on the job.

Edwards and Baxter were there before them leaning on the bonnet of their car. West pulled up beside them and got out. 'Here you go,' Edwards said, handing over the warrant.

Andrews had already filled the two men in on the previous day's events. 'Just keep your eyes and minds open,' he said to them before he turned to West. 'We might have company from Kilkenny, you know.'

The same thought had crossed West's mind; Whelan's tame copper might indeed show up. 'Let's worry about that, if it happens.'

The door opened as they approached and the nervous, acne-scarred youth of the previous day peered out. 'I thought we'd given you what you wanted yesterday,' he said.

'Perhaps some of it,' West said firmly, reaching the door and pushing it forward to step inside. 'Is Mr Whelan here?'

'In his office.'

West left Edwards to tell the youth that he'd be helping them with their enquiries, while he, Baxter and Andrews went to break the bad news to Whelan.

He was seated behind his desk, the initial look of panic quickly covered by an ingratiating smile. 'Gentlemen, what can I help you with today?'

When West handed him the warrant, he looked at it in

horror. 'I don't understand,' he said, his eyes skimming it, looking for a way out. There wasn't one. Dobby could always be relied on to make sure warrants did exactly what they wanted.

'We just need to look a bit deeper,' West explained, 'you can sit and relax, we shouldn't be too long. It will help speed things up if we had your password for the computer.'

Whelan hesitated, his eyes flicking from one side to the other.

'Your password, please,' West asked again, his voice quiet but firm.

'Outdoorsport,' he said, shoulders slumping in defeat. 'Capital O, all one word, followed by an exclamation mark.'

Baxter nodded, and got to work on the company computer. Whelan hovered nearby, muttering to himself, until he was asked to wait with his staff at the front desk where Edwards had started downloading all the CCTV footage.

Ten minutes later, Baxter looked up from the computer. 'Money laundering,' he said, nodding toward the screen. 'Not a particularly sophisticated operation. They have a set of accounts for the auditor and Inland Revenue, and a second set that shows large amounts of money deposited at irregular intervals, which is then paid out as dividends at *regular* intervals.' He tapped a few keys. 'Not complicated, but it's pretty lucrative. As a rough estimate, I'd say our friendly, ever-so-helpful pal Whelan, is taking home fifty to sixty grand a year.'

Andrews whistled softly. 'Not bad at all.'

'Where's the money coming from?' West asked, peering over Baxter's shoulder.

'Some of the names receiving dividends are known to us,' he said, pointing at the screen. 'Mick Flannery, for instance, he's got a history of drug dealing; and that one, Molly Davis, she used to run a brothel in Camden Street. Looks like she might have moved her business to Kilkenny.'

'Whelan is using this place to launder money for the scum of Kilkenny,' Andrews said. 'And I bet one of the names on that list is our friendly neighbourhood copper.'

'If it proves to be, we'll leave Internal Affairs to deal with him,' West said quickly. There was nothing more demoralising for the gardaí than to have one of their own go over to the other side. Internal Affairs could take that on board. He'd enough on his plate.

Whelan, to their surprise, merely shrugged when they told him they'd uncovered the scam. He asked to make one phone call and returned to his office to make it. They assumed it would be to a solicitor, but it was, in fact, to the owner of the shop who arrived within half an hour, face pale and eyes on stalks.

'I trusted you,' Art Costello repeated, looking down on Whelan who sat, hands hanging between his knees, head bent. 'And I paid you bloody well.' He turned to the gardaí who stood around the desk where Baxter still tapped away on the keyboard unperturbed. 'Will we be closed down?'

West held his hands up. 'Just temporarily, Mr Costello. We'll take your computer away with us; it will allow the team to continue investigating. We'd also like to take all of the CCTV footage for the last year to assist us, both in this, and in the case we originally came here to investigate.'

'Yes, of course,' Costello said, spreading his hands out to encompass the whole office, 'take whatever you want, take everything.' He turned and pointed at Whelan. 'Especially that bastard.'

It didn't take much longer to discover that the remainder of the staff were unaware of Whelan's dealings. The acne-scarred youth who went by the name Buzz, looked at them in disbelief when asked if he knew. 'He's so strict, we couldn't sell a knife to someone who was a day under eighteen. I can't believe he did something illegal.'

Neither could the other two members of staff who were on duty. Whelan had managed to keep his shady doings well hidden.

They packed up the computer and took all the CCTV discs with them when they left an hour later. Costello was relieved to be told he could open the next day as normal and had his staff carry the boxes out to their cars.

West and Andrews, anxious to examine the footage of the cash buyer took the discs, leaving the other two to take, not only the computer, but the grim-faced Whelan as well.

Back on the road, Andrews suggested stopping somewhere for lunch, blinking in surprise when West shook his head.

'Not today, Peter, I've just got too much on.'

They still had to eat, Andrews wanted to say, he had, in fact, opened his mouth to say it when he saw the set look on his partner's face. Something was wrong. Narrowing his eyes, he looked at West for a few minutes, waiting for him to expand on the *too much* that he suddenly had on that prevented them eating. Something had happened since yesterday. That had to mean personal. Edel. He sighed loudly. Since the two of them had met it had been one thing after the other.

'Are you going to tell me what's wrong?' he said, when they'd travelled several miles in silence.

'We're no closer to solving Ollie Fearon's murder or discovering who the child in the suitcase is,' West said. 'Isn't that enough?'

'So that's a no then,' Andrews said calmly. He saw West's quick look in his direction and waited. A few miles further, he was more relieved than surprised when he heard the indicator signal they were pulling into a lay-by.

19

West parked, undid his seat belt and turned to face him. 'I need your help,' he said, smiling when he saw the immediate nod. 'You don't know what it's about yet.'

Andrews shrugged one shoulder. 'Tell me.'

West reached into his pocket and pulled out the envelope. 'Get some gloves,' he said, nodding at the glove compartment.

Andrews pulled a pair from his pocket instead and slipped them on before taking the envelope. Removing the three photographs carefully, he looked at them one after the other.

'It's not her,' West said, hurriedly.

Holding each photo up to the light, Andrews nodded. 'No, but they're good.' He put them back into the envelope and took off the gloves. 'Was there a letter?'

West shook his head.

'If this is blackmail, there will be. And maybe more photos.'

It was what West had thought; it didn't help hearing the confirmation.

'You haven't told her, have you?'

'They only came this morning,' West said, 'but no, I won't be telling her. She's been through enough; the last thing she needs is this.'

'But they're not her, Mike,' Andrews argued.

West ran a hand over his head. 'She has a new agent, a guy called Owen Grady. She's had a few meetings with him recently, and do you know what my first thought was? That she was having an affair with him.'

'But she's not?'

'No, of course she's not. But it worried me that I thought it.'

'You take yourself way too seriously, you know that,' Andrews said. 'Stop wallowing in self-pity. Who sent them to you, and why?'

West felt some of the tension of the day leave him. 'I've no idea.'

'There will be more.'

'Undoubtedly,' West agreed. 'Someone went to a lot of trouble to do them. They have a reason; we just don't know what it is yet.' He started the car and pulled back onto the road.

Back in Foxrock, they sat in the Big One and started on the discs they'd brought back. Each disc was clearly marked with the date and time and it didn't take long to locate their cash buyer. But if they were hoping that having sound would make identifying the man easier, they were doomed to disappointment. He spoke in a barely audible whisper.

The one thing it did confirm was what they'd guessed from the earlier disc. Whisper or not, he asked for the Wild Ranger without hesitation.

'He knew exactly what he wanted,' Andrews said.

'It doesn't get us any closer, though, does it? Get one of the lads to check out the two customers who bought the knives online.'

Andrews nodded. 'I'll chase contact details for the other

three who bought in the shop too. It's best not to leap to any conclusions.'

West agreed, but they both knew this cash buyer was their man. 'What about the CCTV footage from outside?' he said suddenly. 'We haven't seen that.' He reached into the box containing the discs. 'If we're really lucky, we might see his car.'

But they weren't lucky. After a frustrating half hour they managed to find a view of the suspect entering, and shortly afterwards, leaving. If he'd driven to the shop, he'd parked elsewhere.

'It was never going to be that easy,' Andrews commented, taking the disc out and putting it back into its container. 'I'll keep these two and give the rest to Baxter. He can have a fun time looking through them all to see if there's anything else of interest.'

West, leaving him to it, headed back to his office. At his desk, he put on some gloves and took out the photographs again. They'd used an image of her face from Facebook, he guessed. He was no expert, but he knew there were many ways of splicing photos together. There were, doubtless, hundreds of places where they'd got their hands on photos of women in such grotesquely lewd positions.

He put them back into the envelope. The next step would be to take them into the fingerprint office and ask one of the lads there to dust for prints, but he couldn't do it. The station was just too small.

Picking up the phone, he dialled a number from memory. 'Fiona,' he said when it was answered, 'I need a favour.'

The rain had stopped, but surface water had the traffic moving slowly and it took over an hour to get to the forensic office in Phoenix Park. Fiona Wilson came to reception as soon as she heard he was in the building. 'You sounded so mysterious on the phone,' she said with a smile. 'What's so hush-hush?'

'Can we go somewhere?' he said with a glance toward the reception staff.

Her smile dimmed slightly. 'Of course,' she said, placing a reassuring hand on his arm and directing him through the door. 'We can use Steve's office, he's away.'

The office she took him to was small and cluttered. 'Have a seat,' she said, pointing to the only chair in the room while she perched on the desk, one elegant leg crossing the other. 'So, what's the problem?'

It was easier to show rather than try to explain. He took the envelope from his jacket pocket. She didn't need to be told and pulled a pair of gloves from a box that sat precariously on a mound of papers to take it from him.

Her eyes widened as she looked at the photographs. 'I recognise her, of course. She's being blackmailed?'

'It's not her,' he said sharply, and held up his hands. 'Sorry, I should have explained. These were sent to me. It's not Edel; someone has added her face to those...' He waved his hands toward the photographs.

'They were sent to you?' She looked at him, weighing him up. 'Why?'

'No idea,' he said, standing to pace the small room. 'But someone went to a lot of trouble to do this. They must have a reason; I just don't know what it is yet.'

She nodded. 'There'll be more.'

Everyone was an expert. 'That was my thinking,' he said.

She put the photographs back into the envelope and gave him an understanding smile. 'Asking the fingerprint technicians in Foxrock to check for prints would be a bit awkward, I suppose. Give me a few minutes, I'll see what there is to find.' She left, shutting the door behind her.

Relieved he hadn't had to spell it out, he sat again and crossed his arms. There was a clock on the wall, its tick loud and annoying. After five minutes, he stood, took it off the wall, removed the batteries and put it back. He placed the two batteries in the middle of the desk where Stephen Doyle could find them when he got back. Maybe he found the tick soothing.

Restless, he took a book from the small, untidy bookshelf and spent several minutes reading about tissue degradation before closing it and returning it to its place. He'd just sat back into the chair when the door opened and she came in, a frown on her face.

'Not good news, then?'

She shook her head and handed him the envelope. 'Not a single print on any of the photographs. There are several smudged partial prints on the envelope, none good enough for identification. Anyway, whoever took such good care with the photographs was unlikely to be foolish with the envelope.'

'You checked inside?' West asked and shook his head in apology when he saw her eyebrow rise. 'I'm sorry, of course you did.'

Relenting, she put a hand on his arm again. 'It doesn't mean he won't make a mistake next time, Mike. Come back to me if you get anything else.'

Thanking her, he made his farewells and headed back to Foxrock. He couldn't spend any more time on it. Not until something else turned up.

Back in the station, he'd sat behind his desk when Baxter appeared in the doorway. 'I got contact details for the two online purchasers,' he said, brushing ginger hair out of his eyes as he spoke. 'One lives in Kerry, the other in Westmeath, and both were able to offer alibis for the night in question without hesitation.' He dropped the pages he was holding and shrugged. 'Both checked out.'

'Thanks, Seamus,' West said. 'Did you check that the knives are still in their possession?' He saw by the suddenly arrested look on Baxter's face that he hadn't. 'Just in case they were stolen, have gone missing, were loaned to a friend stroke ex-wife stroke lover.' West grinned to lessen the implied criticism.

'I'll get back onto them,' Baxter said, turning away.

By the end of the day, the team had managed to contact everyone who'd bought a Wild Ranger from Outdoor Sport. West stood in the main office and listened to their report. Almost all of the purchasers had concrete alibis for the night of Fearon's murder.

'Barry Shelton, in Kilkenny, wants to know how he's supposed to supply an alibi when he lives on his own and didn't see anyone from leaving work the day before to going to work the next morning?' Allen said, leaning back in his chair.

Andrews, perched on the side of his desk, asked, 'Does he have a criminal history?'

Allen shook his head. 'Not even a parking violation.'

'Talk to his place of work, see if he was there until the end of the day, and if he was there as usual the next morning, that's the best we can do,' West said. 'Okay. We've eliminated the possible so we're left with the one probable. Our cash buyer. We don't have much to go on. Estimating his height from the CCTV, he's about five-ten, is of medium build, and Caucasian. That's not going to get us far. I've sent the disc over to the IT department to see if they can do anything to sharpen up either the image or his voice, or hopefully, both.'

He saw the doubt in the four sets of eyes that stared back at him and smiled. 'Yes, I know, it's a long shot...'

'A very long shot,' Andrews interrupted.

'Very, very,' Edwards added.

West held both hands up in surrender. 'Okay. A nigh impossibility but it's all we've got.'

20

'What are you going to do about those photographs?' Andrews said before he left for home.

'There's nothing I can do at the moment,' West said, throwing down the pen he was using and sitting back. 'I took them to be tested for fingerprints. They're clean.' He saw Andrews frown. 'Don't worry, I didn't take them to the fingerprint office; I went across to the Park. Fiona Wilson had a look at them for me.'

The frown cleared. 'That was a good idea. You two have become pretty pally, haven't you?'

'I like her,' West said simply and left it at that.

Andrews, seeing he wasn't going to get more, nodded and left.

West watched him go with narrowed eyes. A friendship between him and the attractive forensic scientist was always going to raise eyebrows, no matter how innocent it was. There were still men, Andrews being one of them, who didn't believe in friendship between a man and a woman. He shook his head.

He'd planned to stay late and do paperwork but being honest with himself, he was just putting off the inevitable. With a sigh, he took the photographs from his pocket and put them in his desk drawer. There was no point in worrying until the next step was taken.

One thing he was sure of, he was going to protect Edel from any fallout.

It was dark when he got home, and he was surprised there were no lights on in the house. Edel's car was still parked where it had been this morning, so if she'd gone out, she hadn't gone far. Maybe to the local shops, he thought, putting his key in the lock and pushing the door open.

It was dark in the hallway, but he didn't switch on the light. Sometimes, he found the darkness soothing after a day under the glare of the neon lights in the office. He hung his raincoat on the newel, dropped his keys into the hall table drawer and headed to the kitchen. Tyler didn't come rushing over, so she must have fed him before she went out. Relaxing, he opened the fridge, flooding the room with light, and took out a beer. He was momentarily blinded when he closed the door, finally giving in and switching on a light.

He was disappointed to see no evidence of anything cooking. His belly rumbled in sympathy and he had a sudden regret that he hadn't agreed to stop for lunch with Andrews. He'd had no breakfast either. So apart from numerous mugs of coffee, he'd had nothing to eat all day. He shook his head. No wonder he didn't feel too great.

The beer wasn't the best idea, but he poured it into a glass anyway and opened the cupboard to search for something to eat. A jar of olives and a packet of crackers. Things were looking up. Opening the fridge again, he found some cheese that had gone a little hard around the edges. Humming, he took out a plate, opened the crackers and olives and minutes later was balancing the plate on top of the glass to open the door into the lounge. He'd watch the news. When Edel came home, they could go out for something to eat or get a takeaway.

'Hi.'

The plate, awkwardly balanced, fell to the floor with a clatter, cheese and crackers landing on his feet, olives skittering across the floor in every direction. The noise startled Tyler who'd been curled up asleep on the sofa. He barked at West and growled at the olives before being picked up and put out into the hallway.

West shut the door on him, put his pint down and stepped over the mess on the floor to sit beside Edel who was curled up on the end of the sofa. The room was only lit by the streetlights outside, but even in their shadowy light, he could see her face was tear-stained, her eyes swollen and red.

'What the hell?' he said, shocked. He pulled her into his arms. She was unresisting, almost limp. He held her for several minutes without saying a word.

It was Edel who pulled away, wiping her face with her sleeve. 'It's just one thing after another, Mike,' she said, her voice breaking.

'What is it?'

She rubbed her eyes and gulped before pointing to the table. 'Have a look.'

An envelope. He knew what was inside. Picking it up, he took the photographs out and looked at them. Similar, but different poses. 'Where did you get them?'

She sat bolt upright. 'You aren't surprised?' Slapping her hand to her forehead, she groaned. 'You got them too?' She dropped her hand. 'Oh God, please don't tell me they were sent to the station.'

'No,' he said, 'here, this morning.'

'Here?' She looked at him suspiciously before taking a deep

breath and letting it out in a shuddering gasp. 'You weren't going to tell me, were you?'

'No, I wasn't. You've been through so much I wanted to–'

'Protect me? There you go again, treating me like a child... or worse,' she said, standing and moving away to the window, 'treating me like a victim.'

He dropped the photographs on the table. 'Tell me what happened.'

She stayed facing the window, her voice catching as she told him. 'I had a call from Hugh Todd this morning. My publisher,' she reminded him. 'He asked me to call in to see him; he was very mysterious and wouldn't tell me anything over the phone.'

'When I got there, I knew immediately something was wrong. He wouldn't look me in the eye and there was no offer of a drink, none of the usual courtesies I'd come to take for granted.'

There was silence for a few minutes. West could hear her cry and wanted to go to her, but there was a chasm between them. Once more, whether she liked it or not, she was a victim.

'He told me they were ending my contract, not just for the current book, but also for the children's books I've written, and they wouldn't be looking to do business with me again.' She turned then and looked at him. 'I've known him for almost five years.' She moved to the armchair and sat. 'I was so shocked and stunned I couldn't speak. When I finally managed to ask him why, he just handed me those.'

'But he must have known they weren't photos of you,' West said.

She smiled sadly. 'I don't think he really cared if they were, or not. He'd had a phone call first thing from Books Ireland Inc; they're the biggest wholesale supplier of books in Ireland. They'd also received some photographs, and on the back of each was a list of the children's books I've written. They weren't too happy, as you can guess, and will be withdrawing all of them from sale.'

West tried to think of something positive to say. But he wasn't a fool; in today's world image was everything.

'If I wrote erotica,' she said, with a smile, 'they'd use it to promote my books. But a children's author must be above all that sleazy stuff. My new novel is a family saga, it wouldn't do much for that either.'

West's stomach growled. He needed food. 'I missed lunch,' he said apologetically, deciding that saying he'd also missed breakfast might be a bit of an overkill. 'I'll order a takeaway and we can sit down with a bottle of wine and see what we're going to do about this.'

He didn't wait for a reply. The takeaway menus were in a drawer in the kitchen; he pulled the local Indian one out, rang them and ordered an assortment of food. It was probably too much, but his growling stomach egged him on.

An open bottle of red wine in one hand and two glasses in the other, he headed back to the lounge, pleased to see she had switched on some lights and looked a little calmer.

He opened the wine, poured a glass and handed it to her, waiting until she'd taken a sip before moving away to pick up the food he'd dropped on the floor earlier. He piled it on the plate and brought it into the kitchen where he dumped the lot into the bin. Tyler lifted his head expectantly, but one look from West made him reconsider moving from the comfort of his bed.

Returning to the lounge, he picked up his pint of beer and sat beside her. The silence was awkward, filled with things they both wanted and didn't want to say.

'I–' Edel started, turning to him, shaking her head and smiling when the doorbell interrupted her. 'It doesn't matter,' she said, nodding toward the door.

West put his beer down and left the room, returning minutes

later with a bag of food hanging from each hand. He placed them carefully on the table and left again to fetch plates and cutlery.

Edel unpacked the bags, spreading the containers out on the coffee table and taking off the lids. 'There's way too much,' she murmured, taking the plate he handed her and spooning a little of each dish onto her plate.

'It's always a bad idea to order a takeaway when you're starving,' he said, opening a bag holding two naan breads and handing her one. He broke a piece from his and dipped it into the sauce on his plate, watching her from the corner of his eye. She was playing with her food, trying to appear brave; his heart twisted.

He wasn't sure how to say what needed to be said. Before his hunger was satisfied, he'd had enough and pushed his plate away. 'You need to report this, Edel,' he said firmly, 'make it official.'

She looked at him with wide eyes. 'You have to be joking.' Her laugh verged on hysteria. 'Report it, and have people, maybe some of your colleagues, drooling over photographs they think are of me? Maybe copying them, putting them online. Are you out of your bloody mind?'

'It won't be like that,' he said, but there was no conviction in his voice. Secrets had a tendency to escape, no matter how hard you tried. 'I'll keep it between Andrews and me.'

'I should have guessed you'd show him.' She dropped her plate on the table with a clatter. 'Who else has been gawping at them? Who else?' she demanded when he didn't answer.

'I needed to get them checked for fingerprints. I took them to one of my colleagues at the forensic office in the Park.'

'And did he drool over them?' she said, sneering.

'She,' he said, trying to stay calm. 'Fiona Wilson, you've met her.'

She took a deep breath and let it out slowly. When she spoke, her voice was less ragged. 'Did she find anything?'

He shook his head. 'They were clean. Whoever's doing this, they're not completely stupid. We might have more luck with the ones that were sent to the bookshop. If he took the time to write on them, he might have left some trace. I'll get someone to pick them up tomorrow.'

She shook her head. 'No, I don't want that. I'll take care of this myself.'

'Don't be ridiculous,' he snapped, frustrated. 'This is a police matter. You, more than anyone, should know how dangerous it is to get involved with criminals.'

Standing, she wrapped her arms around herself and moved across the room to stare out the window. 'This is personal,' she said softly, 'and I think I might know who it is.'

He had to strain to hear what she said. 'You think you know who it is?' he repeated, unsure if he'd heard her correctly.

'Aidan,' she said, turning around. 'Aidan Power, the editor. He was so helpful when we communicated online, but when I met him... there was something not right. He made my skin crawl.'

She pushed her hands through her hair and stood there a moment, eyes wide, looking wild. 'It's not something I can explain. He just gave me a bad feeling.' Dropping her hands, she smiled slightly. 'Female intuition, or as you and Peter might say, *a gut feeling*. However you describe it, he just made me feel uneasy.'

He held up his hands. 'I'm not going to knock that feeling, Edel. But what motivation could he have for trying to destroy you, personally and professionally.'

She shrugged. 'There isn't always a motive, is there?'

West frowned. She was right. There wasn't always a motive. Sometimes it was a case of being in the wrong place at the wrong time. But this didn't fit here. Someone had gone to a considerable amount of trouble to make those composite photographs. And the recipients were carefully chosen to cause the most harm.

The photographs were addressed to him. 'Does Aidan know about me?'

A shrug. 'I don't know. What difference would that make?'

West told her.

'I suppose I might have mentioned you,' she said. 'But if I had, it would have been your first name. I wouldn't have used your full name, there was no reason to.'

'But he knew you were living here in Greystones, not in Blackrock?'

Edel frowned. Did he? She'd filled in forms, what address had she used? Embarrassingly, she couldn't remember. 'I don't know,' she finally admitted. 'They may have my address here, but they definitely wouldn't have had your surname.'

West smiled reassuringly. He knew she believed what she said. After all, he'd heard it so many times. People would swear blind they hadn't told someone something, and get embarrassed when faced with proof that they had but had forgotten. All it needed was the wrong person to get the right piece of information for it to cause untold damage.

Edel picked up her wine glass, drained and refilled it. She stood, swirling the wine around, and looked at him. 'I mean it, I'll handle this myself.'

Putting his empty beer glass down, he poured a glass of wine and sat back. 'How about a compromise,' he suggested. 'You have a word with your pal, Aidan, and I'll do a bit of a background search on him. Strictly under the radar.' He watched as her eyes narrowed, wondering if there was a catch.

'Strictly under the radar and no official garda investigation?' she said.

'Nothing official,' he agreed, nodding. There was no point in enlightening her. Many of their investigations were unofficial. Neither was there any point in telling her that he was going to look into the others too: the publisher Hugh Todd, and her agent Owen Grady.

He hid a smile at how easy their names came to him once he was viewing them as possible criminals. Under the circumstances, she was unlikely to find it amusing.

21

Edel contacted Aidan Power by email the next morning. She decided on a simple, short *Can we meet today?* and hoped he'd be intrigued enough to agree.

He was, and immediately responded. *Two o'clock, The Coffee Pot on Harcourt Street.*

Perfect. And that was her one-word reply. *Perfect.*

She took out the photographs and looked at them again, her nose crinkling in disgust at seeing her face attached to a body in such a lewd, compromising position. They were well done, if she hadn't known better, she'd have been fooled. For a second, she wondered if West had been, and shook the thought away.

She sat back in her chair and sighed. She should be writing, but couldn't drag up any enthusiasm for it. Anyway, finding another publisher might be hard. A thought crossed her mind. Owen Grady. Had he received a set of the photos? It wasn't something she wanted to ask over the phone. How can you gently drop into a conversation, *have you recently received compromising photos of me?* She gave a dry laugh and ran her hands through her hair, holding it away from her neck before dropping it. The best thing to do was to go and see him before her meeting with Aidan.

She'd have to dress carefully. More than ever, she needed to portray an efficient professional image. It would take a while to get those photographs out of her mind. For a moment, she felt ill at the thought. She'd waited such a long time for the success that had been within touching distance, and now it had been destroyed. Someone was going to be held accountable. Straightening her shoulders, she took a deep breath.

In her room, she opened the wardrobe and searched for an appropriate outfit. She discounted anything frivolous, colourful or anyway revealing. Eventually, she pulled on navy trousers and a navy polo-neck jumper. When she pulled on a navy coat, she checked herself in the full-length mirror. It was a little severe, and a stark contrast to the wanton woman in those photos. Would they see it as a case of the lady protesting too much?

She'd pinned her hair up in a tight knot. Undoing it, she shook her head, ran her fingers through her hair and checked again. Much better. Grabbing her bag and her keys, she headed out.

The car park in Greystones was, as usual, full. Giving up after a few useless circuits, she decided to drive to the city. Maybe she'd do a bit of shopping.

She found parking easily in the Stephen's Green centre but the idea that Owen Grady had seen the photographs was preying on her mind and she couldn't relax until she knew one way or the other. The walk to Harcourt Street took her through the Green. Even this early in the year, with a cold breeze biting, it was full of people either sitting, hanging over the bridge taking photographs, or people like herself taking the most scenic route from one place to the next. A vacant seat overlooking the pond beckoned her to sit for a while; she ignored it and walked briskly to the agent's office.

The receptionist was surprised to see her but was as cordial as she had been the previous visit leading Edel to believe the photographs hadn't been sent. Tension eased a little and she took the seat indicated while she waited to see if Owen was available.

'He'll be free to see you in ten minutes,' the receptionist said when she returned, adding with a smile, 'Help yourself to coffee.'

The vending machine was hidden behind a large, leafy and very artificial plant, and it served surprisingly good coffee. Ten minutes later, Edel's cup was empty, there was still no sign of the agent so she helped herself to a second one. She'd taken her first sip when he appeared through a door to her right, a slight frown between his eyes when he saw her.

It was hard to know if the frown indicated a state of disapproval or not. She didn't know him well enough to tell and predicted she'd be second-guessing many things from then on.

'Come on through to my office,' he said, standing back to allow her to pass into the narrow corridor.

His office was as she'd remembered or maybe a little untidier. She sat without invitation and waited for him to take his seat behind the desk.

'You were lucky,' he said, his voice giving nothing away. 'I'd planned to be out this morning, but a meeting was cancelled. Now, what can I do for you?'

Edel had been so sure he'd have seen the photographs, that she hadn't planned what to say if he hadn't. She laughed nervously. It was only a matter of time before he heard the news from Hugh Todd. It was better if he heard it from her. Damage limitation, wasn't that the term they used?

'There's a problem,' she said, and watched as his frown deepened.

'You've signed a contract,' he said, tapping his pen on the desk.

It was her turn to frown. She shook her head. 'No, it's not that,' she said, 'I don't want to get out of my contract, I'm very happy for you to continue as my agent.' She gave another nervous laugh. 'Unfortunately, you may not feel the same.'

He leaned forward. 'Perhaps you'd better tell me what this problem is.'

There was no easy way to tell him. Reluctant as Edel was for anyone else to see the photographs, showing them to him was easier than putting it into words.

Grady took the envelope she handed him and looked at the contents with a raised eyebrow. 'Well,' he said, putting them back. 'I can see how this could be a problem. I'm just not sure why you've come to me. If someone is blackmailing you, you should go to the gardaí.'

'They're not photographs of me,' Edel said, horrified. Reaching out, she snatched the envelope from his hand.

He shrugged. 'It looks like you.'

'It was made to look like me, but I can assure you,' she said, lifting her chin, 'that it is most definitely not.'

There was a moment's silence, broken only by Grady's pen tapping on his desk. 'I'm still not sure why you've come to me with this.'

Edel sighed loudly. 'To be honest, I thought you'd have already seen them.' She looked him in the eye. 'Similar photographs were sent to Hugh Todd, Books Ireland Inc and my partner.'

'Ah,' Grady said, dropping the pen and sitting back. 'Hugh is as strait-laced as they come, and Books Ireland Inc definitely wouldn't have been too pleased to see one of their children's authors in such compromising photographs. I'm sure Mike wasn't too happy either.'

'Books Ireland Inc rang FinalEdit Publishing and said they were pulling all my books.' She felt tears well and fought them back. 'Hugh rang me. He's cancelled my contract for both the children's books and the new saga. It seems there's something in the small print that states I must refrain from engaging in activities that could bring me or the publisher into disrepute.'

Grady nodded. 'Exclusion contracts are common. It's a shame you don't write erotic fiction,' he said, 'they could use it to promote you.'

'Well, I don't,' she snapped. Then, feeling tears welling again, she said quietly, 'What am I going to do?'

Grady scratched his head, ran a hand over his face and looked at her intently. 'What do the gardaí say?'

She shook her head angrily and waved the envelope. 'I'm not involving the gardaí. You think I want these spread about? It's bad enough that you and Hugh have seen them, never mind how many people at Books Ireland Inc. But it stops there. Anyway,' she said, putting the envelope back into her handbag, 'I think I know who might be responsible.'

Grady's eyes widened. 'You do?'

She ignored his question. 'If I can sort it out, prove it isn't me in those photos, can I recover?'

'I might be able to get you a publishing contract for your new book,' he said, and stressed, 'only might.' He picked up his pen and drummed it on the desk. 'If you can prove you're innocent, we can definitely reduce the damage, but it better be soon.' He tossed the pen down and crossed his arms. 'I think it will be a difficult proposition with your children's books. Books Ireland Inc aren't going to take the risk. It might be wise to withdraw them for a few years, and then republish them under a pseudonym.'

Much as she disliked the idea, it made sense.

Seeing her accept the necessity, the agent pushed a little

more. 'It might be as well to approach a different publisher with your new novel under a pseudonym too,' he continued. 'They'll have heard the gossip, of course, it's too small a business not to, but under a different name they could brush it aside.'

For a moment, Edel agreed, and then Simon came into her head. He'd used a false name to trick so many people. Pretence. It was a trap for the foolish. 'No,' she said firmly, 'on second thoughts I won't use a pseudonym, not for my children's books, not for my saga. I'll clear myself, and I will fight for the right to be published under my own name.' The corner of her mouth lifted in an attempt at a smile. 'After all, what is it they say about there being no such thing as bad publicity?'

Grady tried to persuade her, but she wouldn't budge. 'Okay,' he said, holding up his hands in defeat. 'If you clear your name, I'll see what I can do but there are no guarantees.'

She picked up her bag and stood. 'There rarely are, Owen. But I can give you one. I will clear my name.'

Her head held high, she left the office and went back down Earlsfort Terrace. She'd only gone a few steps when something struck her, and her pace slowed until she stopped completely. Turning, she glanced up at the office she'd just left and saw Owen Grady looking down at her. She held his gaze for a moment before raising her hand in farewell, as if it were the most normal thing in the world to do. Then she walked on.

She didn't stop until she was back inside Stephen's Green. Then she sat on the first bench she came to and drew a ragged breath. *I'm sure Mike wasn't too happy.* Her relationship with Owen had been strictly professional, there had never been any reason to mention Mike so how did he know his name?

Hadn't she felt railroaded into taking Grady on as an agent? Maybe he was the one who sent the photographs?

Aidan had recommended him. Were they in it together? But

for pity's sake, what reason would they have? Mike was right; she should report it to the police. She went as far as taking out her phone before changing her mind and putting it away again. It would be better to wait until after she'd seen Aidan Power.

Then she'd decide what to do.

22

There were hours to kill before Edel's meeting with her editor. She thought about going to Brown Thomas and headed in that direction only to change her mind when she got to the door. Beautiful clothes, the fragrance of perfumes, and the smell and feel of good leather handbags and shoes weren't going to work today. Instead, she kept walking and turned onto Wicklow Street. When clothes and perfume didn't help there was always chocolate.

A few minutes later, she was sitting in Butlers Café with a cappuccino and a selection of chocolate sweets going over and over her conversation with Owen. She tried to remember the tone of voice he'd used, or whether he'd looked uncomfortable at any time. With a sigh, she was forced to admit he'd looked relaxed the whole way through. He'd shown little expression even when faced with those hideous photos. Was it because he was responsible? She dropped her head into her hand. This was proving more of a conundrum than she'd anticipated. She finished the chocolates and sat back. How would Mike handle it? Wouldn't he gather all the information first, and not jump to conclusions? It was what she needed to do.

At ten minutes to two, she headed back down Grafton Street and skirted around Steven's Green onto Harcourt Street. As she walked, she tried to keep her focus on three things: Aidan Power made her feel uncomfortable; he'd suggested Owen Grady as an agent; and Owen knew something about her that he shouldn't.

The Coffee Pot was busy. According to her phone it was exactly two o'clock but there was no sign of the editor. Having already had more than her fair share of caffeine she ordered herbal tea and looked around for a seat. There wasn't a table free but she quickly and surreptitiously weighed up the various customers and approached a table where a lone woman sat in front of a nearly empty cup.

'Would you mind if I sat here?' she said with a smile, indicating the empty chair.

The woman shook her head. 'I was just leaving anyway,' she said, lifting her cup and draining it. With a friendly nod, she stood and left.

Edel took off her jacket, dropped it on the vacant chair and sat back with her eyes fixed on the door. She checked the time. He was late. It was another fifteen minutes before he arrived. Not hurrying, she noticed, instantly annoyed to see him saunter through the door.

He crossed the café to her table. 'A meeting ran later than expected,' he said, without offering an apology. 'Can I get you something to drink?'

Perhaps, after all, caffeine might be necessary. 'I'll have a double espresso,' she said. The queue at the counter was slow, giving her time to observe him as he stood waiting to be served, hands plunged deep into his expensive-looking leather jacket. Everything about him was overdone. His clothes, the impeccably shiny shoes, and hair that she guessed wouldn't move in a hurricane.

She quickly pasted a smile in place when he glanced over

and caught her staring. He didn't return the smile, giving her a *what-can-I-do* shrug at the slowness of the queue, and looking away.

'I think the barista is new,' he said, when he finally returned bearing her espresso and a macchiato.

'Thanks,' she said, adding a sachet of sugar to her cup and stirring briskly. She took a sip, put the cup down and looked him straight in the eye. 'I'm sure Hugh told you about the photographs,' she said. 'I'm determined to find out who is responsible.'

He looked away. Crossing one perfectly-creased trouser leg over the other, he picked up his cup and took a sip, pausing as if to savour the taste, before taking another and never looking her way.

If he was trying to provoke her, he was doing a good job. Her hands clenched into fists; sharp words poised on her lips. Taking a deep breath, she looked around the small coffee shop. Couples, singles, workers, shoppers, tourists. They were all here, dealing with whatever life threw at them. Letting her breath out slowly, she relaxed and released her hands; to lose control wouldn't help, she could wait him out.

'Hugh was really shocked,' Power said finally, drawing her attention back to him.

She met his gaze. 'He really thought the photos were of me?'

'Weren't they?' he said, his voice cold.

Her audible gasp wasn't in response to his remark, but to a sudden revelation. The admiring looks he'd sent her way, the flirtatious remarks he'd made, they were a lie. It was there in the sneer; in the derisive look he gave her. He didn't like her. She closed her eyes for a second. When she opened them, he was staring at her, much as she had been staring at him a few minutes before.

'Why do you dislike me?' she asked, deciding she had nothing to lose.

'What's to like?' he said, looking at her as if she were something he'd scrape off his shoe. 'You're not nearly as good a writer as you think you are, and now it seems your morals leave a lot to be desired.' He gave a harsh laugh. 'Thank goodness, I don't have to pretend anymore.'

Shock left her incapable of words. It was tempting to get up and run from the café but she refused to give him that satisfaction. The veneer of friendliness had gone. All she could see was contempt and dislike... no, more than that... disgust.

'I don't understand,' she said, hating the plaintive quality in her voice. She cleared her throat. 'Why did you agree to meet me?'

He shrugged. 'I thought it might be fun.'

Fun? She put a hand over her mouth as her lower lip started to tremble. She wasn't going to cry. Dropping her hand, she lifted her chin. 'You sent those photographs, didn't you.'

His laugh was unexpected. 'You see, I was right. This is fun.'

'But you did send them.' Edel pushed. 'I don't want to go to the gardaí, but I will if you don't admit it and tell me why you would do such a thing.'

He finished his coffee and pushed the cup away. 'It's getting boring now. Women are like that, they never know when to shut up.' When she sat silently looking at him, he sighed loudly. 'No, you stupid bitch, I didn't send the damn photos. Why would I? If you want to spread your legs for every cock in Dublin, why should I care?'

She was taken aback. She'd been so sure. But despite the crudeness of what he'd said, she believed him.

Hurriedly, she gathered her thoughts. If it weren't him, who was it? 'How well do you know Owen Grady?' she asked.

'Hardly at all,' he said, checking his watch. 'Anyway, much as

I'm enjoying our little chat, I have a meeting to get to.' He stood, and without another word or look in her direction, left.

Edel watched him go, her eyes narrowed. It was obvious he'd lied about how well he knew Owen. Why?

She smiled. It was time to put the real detectives on the case. Taking out her phone, she pressed the speed-dial button for West.

23

West had other things to worry about that day. Morrison was demanding results. Where he was expected to get them, he wasn't sure.

'IT couldn't do anything with the disc,' Andrews told him over the rim of his mug.

'At least you had the good sense not to say I told you so,' he growled.

Andrews smiled. 'There is some good news,' he said, shaking his head when West's frown vanished. 'Don't get too excited, it may not go anywhere,' he added hurriedly. 'Jarvis spoke to one of Ollie Fearon's mates who told him he should speak to a guy Fearon had done some work with recently, name of Richie, no surname, but he told Jarvis where he'd find him. He and Allen have gone to talk to him.'

'Good,' West said, 'let's hope this gives us something. Morrison is nagging me for results.'

'You're spoiling his solve-rate averages,' Andrews said with a grin.

'Is Baxter here?' West said, ignoring his comment.

'Sure, he's in the office. You want me to get him?'

West sat for a moment. Unofficial or not, once he started a search it was garda business. 'I want to do some digging on some new men in Edel's circle,' he said slowly.

'Unofficially,' Andrews guessed.

West's lips set in a grim line. 'She doesn't want to make an official complaint in case the photographs fall into the wrong hands.'

'Sounds like they already did,' Andrews said reasonably.

'I think she was afraid of a bunch of lecherous gardaí drooling over them.'

'Well, if you give me the names you want checked out, I'll give them to Baxter and tell him to be discreet.'

'Discreet but thorough,' West said, taking a piece of scrap paper and scribbling the names down before handing it over.

'I'll get him on it straight away,' Andrews said and left the office.

West spent the next hour answering emails from the various agencies he'd asked for help in identifying the suitcase child. None offered any assistance or told him anything he didn't already know. It was a cold case and getting colder. They'd nowhere to go with it. Regretfully, he knew they'd have to put it on the back burner unless something turned up within the next couple of days.

Emails dealt with, it was tempting to go and ask Baxter if he'd made any headway with the names, but it was also a waste of time. If anything interesting turned up, Seamus would let him know. Instead, he rang the head office of Books Inc and asked to speak to the managing director, Elliot Mannion.

'This is Detective Garda Sergeant West, from Foxrock,' he introduced himself when he was put through. 'I believe you received some pornographic photographs in the post yesterday.'

There was a moment's silence before a quiet voice said, 'I didn't contact the gardaí.'

'No, I'm aware of that,' West said, and wondered for the first time why the man hadn't. 'I'll explain if I may, but not over the phone. In your office perhaps, or maybe,' he said when there was a further protracted silence, 'you'd prefer to come here?'

It always worked. Mannion quickly agreed to see him. 'I'm assuming discretion will be offered,' he said.

Discretion? It was a book wholesaler, not a bank. But what did he know; maybe the corporate world of bookselling was cut-throat? Anyway, there was no point in antagonising the man. 'I can assure you of our full discretion, Mr Mannion. I'll see you in about an hour.'

He slipped on his jacket and headed out to the office. Baxter was tapping away on the keyboard with his left hand and scribbling furiously with his right. If there was something to be found, he was the man to find it.

Andrews, he could see, was busy doing the rota, a job he proclaimed to hate, but which he did with incredible diligence. Nobody complained about their shift patterns in Foxrock.

'I'm heading out for a while,' he said to him, watching as he put his finger on the line he was checking before looking up.

'You want me to come with you?'

'And take you away from that,' he said, nodding toward the sheaves of paper on the desk before him. 'No, it's okay. I'm heading out to Books Ireland Inc.,' he explained. 'The photographs that were sent there were written on. I'm going to pick them up and take them out to Fiona. We might get lucky this time.'

'We're due some luck, we haven't had much recently.'

Luck, so much of their job depended on it. They could work all hours, question everyone under the sun, and it still came down to one four-letter word. Shaking his head at the thought, West left.

The head office of Books Ireland Inc. was in the seaside town of Bray, in a huge Victorian building overlooking the sea. There were four parking spaces in front, and here luck was on his side. One of the spaces was empty.

Granite steps led up to a heavy wooden door. A neat sign, positioned dead centre, asked customers to use the doorbell to gain access. West fingered the brass door knocker beneath the sign with a hint of regret before pressing the indicated bell.

Immediately, a light, friendly voice answered. 'Books Ireland Inc., can I help you?'

West bent his six-foot frame slightly to speak into the intercom. 'It's Mike West, here to see Elliot Mannion.'

A buzzer sounded and he automatically pushed the door open and stepped into a small, poorly-lit hallway. Light came from the open door on the right. He headed towards it and stepped into a modern office where a plump young man sat behind a desk crammed with three computer screens.

'Mr West,' the same light, friendly voice greeted him, 'come in and take a seat. I'll let Mr Mannion know you're here.'

The chairs were comfortable. West sat and crossed his legs. In his experience, people liked to do one of two things. Play the power game and keep him waiting or betray an inherent nervousness in being questioned by the gardaí by seeing him immediately. It amused him to try to anticipate which it would be. Guessing from his brief conversation with the man that he'd go for the power play, he was surprised when, less than a minute later, the receptionist came over to him. 'Mr Mannion will see you now,' he said, and pointed back into the hallway. 'If you go up two flights of stairs, it's the first door on the right.'

The stairway had an elegant curve that West admired as he took the two flights with ease. He stopped outside Mannion's office, shaking his head a little when he noted the imposing sign stating, *Managing Director*. Mannion was obviously a man who knew his own importance. West knocked smartly.

The *come in* came immediately, and he pushed the door open into a large office. It had a corner aspect with windows on two sides making it very airy and bright. Winter sun flooded through, causing him to squint slightly as he looked over to where Mannion remained seated behind a modern steel and wood desk.

'Thank you for agreeing to see me,' West said.

'It didn't appear as if I were being given a choice. Have a seat.'

The chair he indicated matched the desk and was surprisingly comfortable. 'Very nice,' West said, sitting back and resting his hands on the broad armrest, his fingers automatically moving to feel the smoothness of the wood.

'Timothy Higgins. Cork. I like to support young designers when I can,' Mannion replied, sliding a hand over the top of his desk. 'But you haven't come here to talk about modern design, have you?' He slid open a drawer and took out an envelope, holding it firmly in his hand. 'I'd be interested in knowing how you found out about these.'

West smiled. 'And if I don't tell you?'

'Well, I suppose I could just drop them back in the drawer, but,' he said with a sigh, 'it's not really the kind of *artwork* I like to have around me.'

West's smile faded. 'They're photographs of my partner, or at least that's what they're purporting to be. They're not, but they are good composites.'

'Edel Johnson is your girlfriend?' Mannion's voice was part shock, part surprise.

'Yes. I was sent similar photographs, as was Hugh Todd. Someone is trying to destroy Edel, personally and professionally. They've already done a fairly good job on the professional end of things.'

'But not the personal,' Mannion said, raising an eyebrow.

'Trust is an important part in any relationship.'

'Image is an important part of an author's relationship with her reader,' Mannion countered. 'Probably the most important part, after the book itself.' He dropped the envelope on the desk and sat back. 'We had no choice but to pull her books from sale.'

'Guilty until proven innocent, eh?'

Mannion shook his head and tapped the envelope with one finger. 'With these? I'm afraid not, it's more a case of guilt by association and, unfortunately, even if she's as innocent as a newborn, the association will last.' He looked at the detective with a grim expression. 'We're talking about children's books.'

'Are you saying her career is finished?'

Mannion sighed. 'The general public has the concentration span of a gnat, Sergeant West. One could be infamous one day and a nonentity the next.' He tapped his nail on the wooden surface of his desk, the sound loud in the quiet office. 'If I may make a suggestion?'

West nodded.

'Withdraw her novels from sale wherever she has them. Wait several months, or even a year, then release them under a pseudonym.'

'You'd stock them again?'

'Under a different name, yes.' He nodded. 'But she'll need to find a new publisher. I know Hugh Todd. He's a very unforgiving man and is also paranoid about protecting the reputation of his publishing company.' He shrugged. 'There's no way he'll take her back.'

'There are other publishers,' West said.

'There are, but you're fooling yourself if you think they won't know about all this.' He nodded toward the envelope. 'This is a very tight-knit business.'

West frowned, then remembered the sign on the door. Self-importance and image, they went together. 'You're the biggest book wholesale company in Ireland, aren't you?' He waited until the managing director nodded before continuing. 'In that case, publishers will listen to what you say?'

'Of course,' Mannion said, before nodding with a wry smile. 'Yes, I see where you're going.' He held his hands up. 'Yes, okay, when... and only when... she's waited a few months and rein-vented herself with a pseudonym, she can tell any publisher she goes to that I said we'd be happy to stock her books again.' He shoved the envelope across the desk. 'Tell me, Sergeant, do you know who is responsible?'

West shook his head. 'Not yet. But,' he said, his eyes narrow-ing, 'I'll find out.'

Mannion smiled. 'I have no doubt. Please, give Edel my regards and apologies. And now' – he stood and stretched a hand across his desk – 'it was good to meet you, but I really must get on.'

24

Minutes later, West was back in his car. Taking out his phone, he rang Fiona Wilson's number. 'I've got some more photographs,' he explained after exchanging greetings. 'He's written on these and I'm hoping we'll get lucky.'

'Am I your go-to girl for private fingerprint analysis?' she said.

He could hear the smile in her voice and laughed. 'Absolutely,' he said. 'How about I bring them over now, and afterwards we go for lunch. There must be somewhere nearby?'

'I know just the place,' she said. 'I'll see you when you get here.'

The M50 was busy and it was just over an hour later that West pulled into the car park outside the Forensic Science building.

The receptionist had been told to send him straight through when he arrived. Fiona was sitting behind a desk in a large cluttered office that was obviously used by several people. Luckily, at the moment, she was alone, a pair of glasses perched on the end of her nose. She looked up at him when he tapped gently on the open door. 'Mike,' she said, taking off the glasses and tossing them onto the pile of papers that covered one side of the desk.

'Fiona,' he replied, smiling across at her.

She held out her hand. 'Gimme,' she said. 'I'm starving so will be motivated to get these done as soon as I can.'

The envelope handed over, she told him to take a seat and headed off.

West answered some emails on his phone. Then, from curiosity, he did an internet search on Elliot Mannion, and was still reading about him when Fiona came back. He put the phone away and stood. 'Anything?'

She shook her head. 'Afraid not, he's very careful. The writing is light and unsteady and I'd guess, although I'm no handwriting expert, that it was someone writing with their non-dominant hand.'

'An easy disguise,' West agreed. 'We can take it to an expert if we find a suspect. Some things are harder to change.'

As he spoke, Fiona took a raincoat from a coat hook behind the door. 'Let's go before I die of starvation,' she said. 'I missed breakfast this morning.'

The day was cold and grey. 'We can walk if you're not in a hurry,' she said, when they'd left the building. 'It'll take about twenty minutes, but driving can often take as long.'

Nodding in easy agreement, he fell into step beside her and they chatted about trivialities until they crossed Conyngham Road. He looked at her, perplexed. 'Where are we going?'

'I thought I'd take you home,' she said with a quick smile. 'I made a quiche yesterday and planned to have the rest for lunch. There's enough for two.' When he said nothing, she turned to look at him. 'There's a pub we can go to, if you prefer, but they do tend to be very busy around here and it's hard to have a private conversation.'

He glanced at her. 'Quiche sounds fine.'

'So real men do eat quiche,' she muttered with a chuckle.

'This man eats anything as long as it's not still moving on the plate,' he returned and launched into a story of being on holidays in Indonesia as a student and being faced with a plateful of seafood, one item of which started moving across the plate as he ate. Soon they were swapping horror stories of meals eaten in strange places and any discomfort West felt at eating in her apartment was dismissed.

They were only a few minutes from it when the rain started and, as it often did that time of the year, it came down in a deluge. She pulled up the hood of her raincoat and quickened her step. 'We're almost there,' she said, pointing to the apartment block in front of them.

It was only a few minutes, but the rain was heavy. Inside the front door of the apartment block, she turned and looked at him. 'Oh, my goodness,' she said, 'you're soaked.'

West shook his head, sending droplets flying, and wiped his face with his hand. 'I have a raincoat,' he muttered, 'shame I wasn't wearing it.'

She pressed the call bell for the lift. 'I'll get you a towel once we're inside,' she said.

The apartment was a penthouse, spacious and bright with views over the River Liffey and the Phoenix Park from its wrap-around balcony.

'This is very nice,' West admired, as he dried his face and hair with the towel she'd given him.

'I bought it a few years ago,' she said. 'I was living in Terenure at the time and wanted something closer, where I could walk to work if I felt like it. When plans were submitted for this development, I jumped at it.'

'A wise buy,' he said, combing fingers through his damp hair. 'I lived in an apartment in the city for a while, but it wasn't as nice as this.'

'Greystones is nice though, isn't it?' she said. She put her hand on his jacket and screwed up her nose. 'You can't sit in those wet clothes. Hang your jacket on the back of the chair in front of the radiator and give me your shirt. I'll throw it in the tumble dryer. It will be dry in a few minutes.'

He shook his head, feeling slightly embarrassed. 'I'll be fine.'

'Don't worry; you won't have to sit around in a state of undress,' she said with a laugh. 'I've lots of scrub tops here. They come in handy. I'll fetch one; you can slip it on and give me your shirt.' She left the room as she spoke and came back with a scrub top in her hand, holding it out until he had no choice but to take it.

With a raised eyebrow, she left the room as he took off his jacket and hung it on the back of the chair. He loosened his tie, took it off and tossed it on the seat. His shirt was wet, especially around the shoulders. Peeling it off, he slipped the scrub top on. It was tight, but it covered him. It would do. Short-term, anyway. He could imagine the raised eyebrows if he wore it back to the station.

Fiona returned, took the shirt and threw it into the dryer. 'Sit down,' she said, indicating the dining area, and busied herself in the kitchen

He sat, looking out the window. Even in the rain, the view over the park was stunning. On a summer's day, it would be a delightful place to sit. He said so as she came over, a plate in each hand.

'Yes, you'll have to come back then, it really is lovely. Okay, there you are,' she said, putting the plate before him. 'The afore-mentioned quiche, with some trimmings.'

'Very nice,' he said, waiting until she sat before picking up his knife and fork and tucking in. 'This is very good,' he said.

She nodded her acceptance of the compliment. 'I like to cook.'

'Your history professor is a lucky man. Which university is he with?' he asked.

'He's a *very* lucky man,' she said, correcting him. 'He's in UCD.'

West grimaced. 'Not an easy commute from here.'

'Oh, he doesn't live here,' she said, spearing a piece of tomato with her fork, 'he has a house in Clonskeagh, just a short walk from the university. We're both used to our own space so it works perfectly for us. He stays over at weekends, or I stay over at his.'

'Mutually beneficial,' West said, forcing a smile. It wasn't something he understood. His space was better with Edel in it. With a sigh, he pushed away his plate.

Fiona, hearing the sigh, assumed it was one of satisfaction and smiled. 'There's apple pie,' she said, 'and cream.'

'No, I really should get going, but thank you, this was very nice.'

'I'm sorry I hadn't better news for you about the photographs. I hope you catch whoever did this. Edel must be devastated.'

'It's not easy for her,' he agreed.

'Or for you, I suppose,' she said, and reached across to lay her hand briefly on his. 'If you ever need to chat, you know where I am.' She laughed and stood. 'Now I'd better get your shirt, you can't go like that.' Taking it from the dryer, she shook it out and handed it to him. 'See, it's good as new,' she said.

As before, she left him to change, disappearing into one of the other rooms. It took him a few seconds to get the scrub top off, easing it over his head and having a moment's panic when it became stuck. It would have been embarrassing to have to call for her help. It would also be embarrassing, if she came back and found him standing there, hands up in the air and the top stuck tight. With a grunt, he managed to get it off without doing damage, pulled his shirt on and did up the buttons. He slipped his tie over his head and tightened it before checking himself in a wall mirror. Normal service resumed.

Despite the heat from the radiator, his jacket was still damp. It would have to dry in the car. Checking his watch, he grimaced; it was time to get going. He looked towards the door to the hallway, wondering whether he should give her a call, when she appeared, buttoning her coat. 'Ready,' she said with a tilt of her head. 'It's stopped raining, but I'll bring an umbrella, just in case.'

But they were in luck and the rain stayed at bay as they walked briskly back to the Forensic Science building.

'Thank you again for lunch,' he said, as they reached the car park. 'Next time, it will be my treat.'

'Next time,' she said with a smile and tilt of her head, before leaving him with a casual wave.

Sitting into his car, West checked his phone. There was a missed call from Edel, but when he rang her it went straight to voicemail. He wondered how her meeting with Power had gone. It would be so much better if she left the detective work to him. He drove back along the M50, mulling over who could be responsible for the photographs.

Baxter greeted him as soon as he entered the station. 'I think I have something,' he said.

'Great, come into my office,' West said, taking off his jacket as he walked.

'Edel is waiting in there; she arrived about an hour ago. I didn't think you'd mind.' He dropped his voice. 'She looked a bit upset.'

West looked toward his office door, a slight frown on his face. 'Thanks, Seamus,' he said, 'I'll give you a shout in a few minutes.'

Opening the door, he prepared himself for tears, surprised to find a very sombre Edel sitting there, legs crossed.

'I tried to phone you,' he said, hanging his jacket on the back of an empty chair before sitting down. 'You're looking very navy,' he said, glancing at her. 'Very business-like.' Personally, he didn't like the outfit. It made her look paler than usual. He looked at her more closely. She *was* paler than usual. 'Are you okay? How did the meeting with Power go?'

'I think they're both in on it,' she said, her voice brittle. 'Aidan Power and Owen Grady. It's some kind of conspiracy against me.'

West felt his heart drop. He sat in his chair and looked across the desk at her.

A conspiracy theory.

Just what he needed.

25

'Tell me what happened?' West said quietly.

'You don't believe me?' Edel accused him, running her hands through her hair.

'Just tell me what happened,' he repeated.

She took a deep breath and started her story. He didn't interrupt, although a number of times she went off on a tangent that left him confused.

'Okay,' he said, when her voice trailed away. 'Let me get this straight. You went to see Owen Grady, and you showed him the photographs–'

'Only to make him understand,' she interrupted. 'I was so sure he'd have already seen them that I was taken unawares, and it was the easiest way...' She stopped and sighed loudly. 'It seemed like a good idea.'

'And he mentioned me by name. You're sure you've never used my name in conversation?'

She shook her head, loose hair swinging. 'There was never any reason to. We've never met socially. Your name would never have come up. I don't think even Hugh knows your name, why would he?'

'Indeed,' West said and looked down at his desk to hide his expression. When he continued his voice was cooler. 'And afterwards, you went to meet Aidan Power.'

'Yes, and don't forget it was Aidan who recommended Owen as an agent.'

West nodded. 'Yes, so you said. You mentioned to me before that you found Power pleasant and helpful as an editor.'

'He is a good editor. On a personal level, I'd found him a little too flirtatious, too touchy-feely, but today he was obnoxious and rude and he made it quite clear that he doesn't like me at all.' She frowned at the memory. 'He doesn't rate me highly as a writer either.'

'And you think he lied about his relationship with Owen Grady?'

She met his eyes. 'He definitely lied, then he couldn't leave the café fast enough.'

'Would he have recommended Grady as an agent if he hardly knew him?' West said. He'd no idea how things worked in the publishing industry. 'I suppose he might have known him by reputation.'

Edel sighed loudly. 'I suppose.'

'Elliot Mannion said the publishing business is a small one. Maybe everyone knows everyone else.'

'Elliot Mannion,' she said, her eyes opening wide. 'The MD of Books Ireland Inc.?'

'I went to see him to pick up those photographs. There was always a chance that whoever wrote on them might have got careless and left some trace. Unfortunately, we weren't so lucky.' He could feel her eyes boring a hole in him.

'You had no right. I haven't made an official complaint.'

'I told you I'd look into it unofficially,' he said with a shrug. He saw her mulish look grow and as quickly fade.

'It doesn't matter,' she said wearily, 'I was going to ask you to make it official, Mike. They're in it together; you'll be able to find out why they're doing it.'

He saw her wan look, the air of defeat that settled over her like a cloud. 'If they're responsible, we'll get them. As it happens, I asked Baxter to do some digging into all three men; Todd, Grady and Power. He just mentioned that he found something, so let's get him in here and hear what he's got to say.'

He opened his office door. Baxter was perched on the side of a desk chatting to Andrews. Both men looked up as the door opened. 'Come on in,' he called, returning to his desk.

Andrews nodded a friendly greeting at Edel and took the vacant chair while Baxter pushed paperwork from one corner of the desk and perched on the spot.

'Make yourselves at home,' West said, rescuing the papers that had been in an orderly pile. He shuffled them back together and placed them in a drawer. 'Right,' he said, looking up at the younger man's freckled face, 'tell us what you found.'

'There's a lot available on Hugh Todd,' Baxter said, 'and having read most of it, my conclusion is that what you see is what you get. A straight-up, well-respected, conservative family man. In business, he's regarded as tough, but fair.

'Aidan Power has worked for FinalEdit Publishing for three years, before that he worked with Oisin Dubh Publishing for almost ten. He left following a falling out with the owner, with whom he'd had a seven-year relationship. From all accounts,' he looked around the room, 'and there are multiple, it wasn't an amicable split. Power arrived home to find his partner in bed with a woman.'

'Finding out your partner of seven years is a lesbian, might make him a little bitter,' Andrews said.

Baxter grinned. 'No, you have it wrong. Power's partner was Oisin O'Leary. Power is homosexual. The insult was that O'Leary strayed with a woman, not another man.'

'Ah,' West and Andrews said in unison.

'So, it isn't me he doesn't like,' Edel said, drawing three pairs of eyes toward her. 'He blames women in general for his partner's cheating. Although,' she frowned, 'he made it seem personal.'

'Maybe you look like her,' Andrews suggested, 'or maybe you've the same colouring. It might have brought it back to him.'

'It might be worthwhile checking to see if he ever enacted any form of revenge on the woman O'Leary was with.'

Andrews nodded. 'I'll look into it.'

Baxter shuffled on the desk. 'I'm not finished,' he said with a grin. 'In fact, I've left the best to last.'

'Well?' West said.

'Guess who Owen Grady is related to?' Baxter said. Getting a warning glance from Andrews to stop playing games, he hurried on. 'He's Amanda Pratt's brother.' He glanced over to Edel. He didn't have to spell it out; they all knew who she was. The widow of Cyril Pratt aka Simon Johnson, the man Edel still thought of as her late husband. Andrews gave a low whistle. He'd interviewed Amanda Pratt; she was a piece of work.

Edel looked shocked, her face even paler than it had been. She turned wide eyes to West but said nothing.

West was checking the time. Five o'clock. If they were in luck, they might catch both men in their offices. Giving Andrews a nod, he said, 'Ring Power and Grady, ask them to come in. If they refuse, tell them we'll send uniformed gardaí to their offices in the morning with a warrant.'

Andrews didn't need to be told twice. He left and seconds later they heard his deep voice in conversation.

Baxter, with a quick look at Edel, shuffled to his feet, murmured something inaudible and left the room, pulling the door closed behind him.

West knew there was no point in asking her to go home; she

wouldn't go and they'd end up having a row. He was about to suggest that she stay in his office until after they'd interviewed the men when she turned sad eyes on him.

'Amanda Pratt's brother,' she said, and shook her head. 'It seems I'm never going to be able to put that whole terrible ordeal behind me.' Standing, she walked a few steps, turned and walked back. 'The whole situation was explained to her, wasn't it? She knows it wasn't my fault.'

He nodded. 'A family liaison officer went and explained the details. Peter said that there was little love lost between her and her husband, and a very healthy life insurance policy has left her and her two children well cared for.'

'You don't think she bears a grudge?' Edel said, sitting back in her chair.

'I don't see why she should,' he said, trying to reassure her. But the one thing he'd learned from working with the public was that there was no accounting for what they did. Perceived grievances could be held for a long time by some people. Maybe Grady held a grudge on his sister's behalf.

Andrews knocked, and stuck his head around the door. 'It took a bit of persuading,' he said, 'and a heavy emphasis on uniformed gardaí in squad cars arriving with sirens blazing to escort them in tomorrow morning. But finally, our two law-abiding, upstanding gentlemen saw sense and agreed to come of their own accord.'

'Good. Show them into separate interview rooms.'

Once Andrews had gone, he turned to Edel. 'Before they get here, I'd like you to make an official statement. It will just make our lives a little easier and ensure that there'll be no room for them to wriggle out of any charges.'

'Yes,' she said, 'of course.'

'Good.' He slipped a few sheets of paper across the desk. 'Just write exactly what happened, starting with the phone call you had from Hugh Todd and finishing when you came into us today. Take your time.' He stood up. 'I'll get you some coffee; we're going to be here for a while.'

He left her to write her statement and sat in the office with Andrews and Baxter. 'Any word from Jarvis regarding that friend of Ollie Fearon's?' he asked.

Andrews shook his head. 'They've had no luck chasing him down as yet. They're still looking.'

It was the way the job went. 'Slowly, slowly catchy monkey.'

'Never understood that expression myself,' Andrews said. 'Why would anyone want to catch a monkey anyway?'

'To chop off the top of their heads and eat their brains,' Baxter suggested. He grinned when they both looked at him. 'It was in that Indiana Jones movie.'

The phone rang. Andrews, answering it, gave the other two a thumbs-up. 'Show him into the Big One.' He hung up. 'Aidan Power has just arrived. Sergeant Blunt says he doesn't appear too happy.'

'Let's give him a few minutes to settle into his new accommodation,' West said, picking up his mug. 'Some day,' he said conversationally, 'we're going to invest in some decent coffee.'

They waited five minutes. Baxter sat in the observation room while the other two went to speak to an obviously annoyed Aidan Power. They took the two seats opposite him; West introduced himself and Andrews and warned Power that the interview was being recorded.

'Just a formality, you understand,' West said, looking at the face of the man who sat opposite, lips and eyes narrowed, a frown on his forehead. 'Thank you for coming in to help with our enquiries.'

Power's lips curved into an unattractive sneer. 'It didn't look as if I had much choice. Come in now or be dragged here in a blaze of publicity tomorrow. Now,' he snapped, 'tell me why I'm here.'

'You know about the photographs purporting to be Edel Johnson that were delivered to Mr Todd and Mr Mannion.'

'Is that what this is all about?' Power said, sitting back with wide eyes. 'Has that stupid cow said it was my doing?' He slammed his hands on the table. 'I told her it was nothing to do with me.' Crossing his arms, he sneered. 'She said they weren't photographs of her. Well, it looked bloody like her to me.'

West took a deep breath. 'No, Mr Power, they're not of her. The photographs have been forensically examined and have been proven to be composites. Now,' he said, looking him in the eye, 'if you are, as you claim, innocent of any wrongdoing in this regard, can you explain your obvious antagonism towards Ms Johnson.'

Power looked down his nose at him. 'Antagonism? I just don't like the woman. So, sue me.'

West and Andrews stayed silent. It was obvious there was something more to it than that. They could wait.

'Oh, for goodness sake,' Power said, uncrossing his arms and resting his hands on the table. 'If you must know, although why it's any of your business I don't know, but if you must, I'll tell you.' He ran a hand over his face. 'Once upon a time,' he started, 'there was an enthusiastic young man who fell in love with an older man and was happy for many years. One day, this inno-cent young man came home and found him in bed with a woman. A woman,' he repeated with disgust. 'He was devastated.

'Many years later, this somewhat cynical and world-weary man fell in love again. When he started to hear his new love talk about a woman they both knew, he began to suspect the same thing might happen again. And he was angry.' He stopped and looked from West to Andrews. 'The end.'

'The first older man, that was Oisin O'Leary, I assume,' West said, letting the man know they'd already done some digging.

Power gave a sad smile. All anger was gone. Gripping one of his hands in the other, he said, 'It took me a couple of years to come to terms with what happened. When I met Owen, I thought, maybe, I was getting a second chance.'

West and Andrews resisted the temptation to look at one another. Power and Grady were a couple?

'That's Owen Grady, isn't it?' West said, going for it.

Power nodded. 'Stupidly, I'm the one who suggested him to her. Owen's trying to build his client base. She looked to be going places, and I thought I'd be doing him a favour.'

'What happened?' West nudged when he didn't speak for a while.

'He met her, and it was all Edel this, and Edel that, until I could hardly bear it. When I accused him of having feelings for her, he laughed and told me I was getting paranoid.'

'So, you sent the photographs to destroy her professionally?'

Power, who'd drifted off into his own little world, looked up sharply. 'What? No, I tell you, I didn't send the damn photographs. I wouldn't destroy anyone professionally, and certainly not personally. I've been there; I wouldn't inflict that kind of pain on anyone.'

The two detectives exchanged glances. They believed him.

'One last question,' West asked. 'Why did you lie to Ms Johnson when she asked you if you knew Owen Grady?'

'I wasn't getting into a discussion about Owen with her,' he said simply.

West saw the truth in his eyes. He hadn't wanted to get into a discussion with her about the man he loved because he was afraid she'd admit to having an affair with him.

He pushed back from the table and stood. 'This interview is terminated,' he said for the benefit of the recording, stating the time and date. He looked down at the seated man. 'We've no further questions for you, Mr Power. Thank you for coming to assist with our enquiries.'

Power stood. All the fight had left him during the recounting of his story. Without a glance at either of the detectives, he left the room.

26

West and Andrews joined Baxter in the observation room.

'Power and Grady,' Baxter said when they sat down. 'That was a bit of a surprise, wasn't it? They've kept that quiet, nothing on social media about their being an item.'

'What did you make of his story?' West asked him.

Baxter ran a hand through his ginger hair, making it stand on end. 'He went from confrontational to pathetic very quickly. I think his bravado is all front, and the innocent boy who was so hurt by O'Leary is never very far away.'

West hadn't expected such a thoughtful reply. 'Yes, I think you're probably right,' he said. 'Has Grady arrived?'

'About ten minutes ago. He's waiting in the Other One,' Baxter said. He moved to the water cooler in the corner, filled two paper cups and handed one to West.

'Thanks.' West drained the cup, scrunched it and threw it into the wire rubbish bin as Andrews walked in. 'Right,' he said to him, 'let's go and see what Grady has to say for himself. If Power didn't send the photographs, maybe he did.'

Owen Grady looked up and smiled when they came into the

room. West introduced himself and Andrews and they sat in the chairs opposite.

'This interview is being recorded, Mr Grady,' he said before stating the date and time and the names of those present.

When he'd finished, to the surprise of both detectives, Grady laughed and said, 'This is great, really great.'

West and Andrews exchanged glances. Was he on something?

'You seem to be unusually happy about being here, Mr Grady.'

'I am,' Grady said, 'and I'll tell you why, shall I?'

'Well, if it saves us having to go and get the police doctor to certify that you haven't taken any mood-altering drugs, that would be of benefit,' West said caustically.

'No, I'm on a natural high. You see, after years of watching authors have their novels published, I decided to write one myself. A crime novel, Sergeant, set in Dublin. This,' he waved his hands around the room, 'will allow me to give it veracity.'

'We're happy to be of use,' West said, wondering if the day would come when people stopped surprising him. He certainly hoped not. 'Perhaps you can return the favour and answer some questions for us.'

'Fire away,' Grady said, 'I've nothing to hide.'

'Not even your relationship with Aidan Power?'

Grady's smile faded a little. 'Keeping it quiet was his idea, not mine.' He shrugged. 'He has trust issues.' He looked from one detective to the other. 'You've hardly brought me here to ask about my relationship with Aide, have you?'

'No,' West said, 'you're here to assist in our investigation into the photographs that were sent to FinalEdit Publishing and Books Ireland Inc. purporting to be of–'

'Edel Johnson,' Grady interrupted him. 'Is that what this is all about? She was in with me earlier today. You can't think I've anything to do with sending them?'

'During your conversation you mentioned her partner's name. She maintains she never told you about him.'

'I know her partner's name, and therefore I'm the guilty party. Seriously?' He shrugged dismissively. 'I must have heard the name somewhere.'

'From your sister, Amanda, maybe?'

All trace of good humour left Grady's face. 'I should have guessed she'd come into this somewhere. Yes, okay, I probably heard his name from her. She told me all about what happened to that piece of shit she married. For a while, she became obsessed with the other life he'd led and tried to find out everything she could about it, especially about Edel Johnson, where she moved to, what she worked at et cetera. She knew about her relationship with some garda who was involved in her husband's case.' He stopped and closed his eyes briefly. 'Of course,' he said, staring at West. 'Mike West. I'd forgotten your surname until now. I've heard a lot about you.'

'Would that obsession have led Amanda to send those photographs? Trying to destroy Edel personally and professionally to get revenge?'

Grady shook his head firmly. 'She's over that. Cyril was an idiot, but at least he had the wit to have good life insurance. Money is a good balm, you know.' He smiled. 'As is the new man in her life, he must be good for her, she looks happier than I've seen her in years. The past is behind her, she's moved on.'

They'd have to follow it up, but if he were right it looked like Amanda Pratt was out of the picture.

But he wasn't giving up on Grady yet. 'Why did you take Edel on as a client?'

He held up his hands. 'I swear, I didn't know who she was until I met her. I recognised her from photographs Amanda had shown me during her obsessive phase.' He frowned. 'I would have assumed she'd go back to using her maiden name. Why did she hang onto the surname Johnson? It wasn't as if she was ever legally married to the lying toerag.'

West looked as if he were going to ignore the question, then with a sigh, said, 'Cyril stole the real Simon Johnson's identity, and as a result, he was killed. Edel made a promise to his sister that she'd keep the surname in his memory.'

'Edel's a pretty decent sort, isn't she? I watched her walk away from the office both times she came to see me, wondering what she ever saw in the likes of Cyril. He was a waster. A total dick. I never knew what Amanda saw in him, but, much as I love my sister, I'd be the first to acknowledge, she's a bit rough. Edel is in a different league; good-looking, very classy and intelligent. I'll never understand why she fell for him.'

'He was a good liar,' West said, 'and the truth is, people generally see what they want to.'

Grady nodded and looked West straight in the eye. 'I can see why you might have thought we had something to do with those photographs, but I swear we didn't.' He shook his head slowly. 'Amanda has the capability, don't get me wrong, but if she'd been going to do something, she'd have done it a long time ago.'

West, catching Andrews' quick look, nodded. There was nothing here. 'We had Mr Power in earlier,' he said, watching Grady's eyes widen in surprise.

'Aide? You can't think he had anything to do with this?' His voice became high-pitched, and he blinked rapidly. 'Seriously, Aide isn't capable of inflicting that kind of harm.'

'No, maybe not,' West conceded. 'He has, however, shown a level of animosity toward Ms Johnson that warranted looking into.'

'Animosity?' Grady's forehead creased. 'I thought they got on okay.'

'Perhaps you should stop talking about her in such an admiring fashion. I gather Mr Power had an unfortunate experience with Oisin O'Leary.'

Both detectives watched as the penny dropped with a resounding clunk. Grady slapped his forehead with his hand. 'He's jealous of her?' He crinkled his nose. 'No disrespect, Edel's lovely, but she's a *woman*.' He stood up. 'I assume I can go. It looks as if I have some explaining to do.'

At West's nod, he smiled. 'Thank you,' he said, reaching out his hand. 'If you ever get tired of being a garda, a role as relationship counsellor might suit you.'

On that note, he left with a cheery wave.

'Well,' Andrews said, crossing his arms. 'We went pretty rapidly from three potential suspects to none.'

'Get someone in Cork to check out Amanda Pratt, will you? I think Grady is telling us the truth but we'd better be sure.' He ran both hands through his hair. 'Edel is not going to be happy.'

It was an understatement. Edel was furious. 'It had to have been one of them,' she said when he told her what had happened. She paced his small office, her arms wrapped around her waist as if trying to hold herself together.

'They had reasonable explanations for everything,' he said, keeping his voice calm.

She dropped down into the chair and rubbed her face. Everything he'd said sounded reasonable. 'Aidan was jealous of me?'

'It looks like it. Power has trust issues because of a previous bad experience. When Grady sang your praises, he must have thought history was repeating itself.'

'That's just great,' she said bitterly. 'So, if they're all squeaky clean where does that leave me?'

West checked the time. 'Let's go and get something to eat,' he said, 'we can talk about where we go next.'

'I'm not hungry,' she said, and shook her head. 'Sorry, I'm being childish. That's a good idea. Let's go somewhere nice.'

The general office was empty apart from Baxter sitting in front of his computer, fingers tapping. 'We're going for something to eat, Seamus,' West said, 'would you like to join us?'

He shook his head. 'I want to get this written up, and then I'm heading home. Tanya is still unpacking; she'll kill me if I don't get home to help.'

'Who's Tanya?' Edel asked, as they made their way to the car park.

West pressed the key fob to unlock his car. 'His girlfriend,' he said, as they sat and fastened seat belts. 'They've been together a couple of years, I gather, and just recently bought a house in Gorey.'

'Nice,' she said, but her mind was on other things and the conversation ground to a halt.

West drove to Greystones and parked outside a small Italian restaurant near the marina. 'This okay?' he asked, turning to look at her.

She smiled. 'Perfect. There's nothing in this world that can't be solved by pizza and a glass of wine.'

27

The restaurant was busy. The owner, a Sicilian with a charming smile and expansive manner, showed West and Edel to a table near the back window with a view over the marina. He handed them menus with an elaborate flourish and left them alone.

'Mushroom and artichoke,' Edel said, 'my perfect pizza topping.' She closed the menu with a snap.

West closed his. 'Seafood pizza for me.' He handed her the wine menu. 'You decide, I don't mind what we have.'

The Sicilian returned to take their order. 'It's a lovely wine list,' she said, 'is there a white wine you'd recommend?'

'Certo,' he said pointing to the menu, 'this is very good.' He grinned. 'Sicilian, like me.'

Pizzas and wine ordered, they sat back to admire the view.

'It's beautiful,' she said, looking out at the lights of the marina.

'Beautiful,' he echoed, looking at her.

She laughed. 'Stop being Mills and Boonish, Mike.' But she looked pleased all the same. 'I'm not dressed for a romantic night out,' she said, looking down at her navy clothes. 'I still haven't worn that dress I bought.'

He reached for her hand and held it tightly. 'I promise, we'll get a weekend away soon. In fact, I know just the place.'

She tilted her head. 'Not a lighthouse in Clare?'

'No, not this time,' he said with a smile. 'It's a hotel, near Aughrim. It has a spa and an award-winning restaurant. I'll send you the details and you can see what you think.'

The wine arrived, the manager chatting about its provenance while he uncorked the bottle. He poured with great ceremony and waited with a look of anticipation on his face as they tasted.

'Oh, that is very nice,' Edel said.

'Excellent,' West agreed, raising his glass to the man.

The manager made a little bow of acknowledgement and left them once more.

A burst of laughter came from a table on the other side of the restaurant. It drew Edel's eyes and she stared for a moment, a wry smile on her face. 'I was so happy when I got that damn publishing contract. I felt like all my troubles were over and now look at me.'

'We will find out who did this,' he said, taking her hand again.

'Did?' she said. 'You think it's over?'

West hadn't even realised he'd used the past tense. Did he think it was over? No, he sighed, it probably wasn't. Nobody was going to go to that much trouble without achieving what they'd set out to do. Which was? His eyes narrowed. Professional and personal destruction? The photographs had certainly achieved their aim at destroying her professionally. Pulling out of it would be a tough struggle. Personally?

She was waiting for an answer. 'No,' he said, squeezing her

hand. 'I'm sorry, I don't think so. Someone wants to cause you trouble, Edel.'

'They're doing a pretty good job,' she said, draining her glass and refilling it. She held the bottle towards him. 'Another glass?'

'I'm okay,' he said, 'maybe when I've had something to eat.'

As if they'd heard him, a waiter weaved his way through tables with a plate in each hand. He deftly placed one in front of each of them, leaving them with a *buon appetito* and a smile.

Ignoring the cutlery, Edel picked up a slice of her pizza and took a bite. 'Delicious,' she said, finishing the slice in a few mouthfuls and immediately reaching for the next.

West was more of a knife and fork man when it came to pizza. He cut into his and nodded his approval as he ate the first bite. 'We'll follow up on Amanda Pratt, just to be on the safe side,' he said, pouring himself a second, smaller glass of wine.

'But you don't think she's involved?'

He swirled the wine around. 'No, I don't. Grady says she's moved on. Whoever did this, it took time and effort. The photographs are good.' He smiled at her pantomime-outraged look. 'You know what I mean.'

Laughing, Edel nodded. 'Yes, if I didn't know better, I'd swear they were me.' Lifting her glass, she looked at him. 'Tell me truthfully, when you opened them, did you think, even for a second, that they were of me?'

He smiled. His moment's suspicion that she might be having an affair with Grady seemed unworthy of a mention. 'Not even for a millisecond,' he said.

Curiosity lit her eyes. 'Why? They *are* well done. You really need to look carefully to see that they're composites, so why were you so sure?'

'Well, firstly because I know enough about you to know you'd never pose for something like that, and secondly because unlike Aidan Power I don't have trust issues.'

'Is there a *thirdly*?' she asked, smiling at him across the table.

'I love you, and would never believe anything bad of you,' he said, 'will that do?'

She nodded before standing to reach over and kiss him on the lips. 'I think so,' she said. Sitting again, she refilled her glass and held the bottle toward him. 'You won't have more?'

He shook his head and picked up a glass of water instead. 'I'd better not.'

'I've been thinking,' Edel said. 'Self-publishing is perfectly acceptable these days; I don't know why I didn't think of it before. I can self-publish my family saga and concentrate on my next novel.' She cited all the writers who'd successfully self-published and who swore they'd never go the traditional route.

'Is it the same as vanity publishing?' he asked, knowing very little about it apart from a vague memory of reading about people who paid thousands to have books published and never made a penny. 'Don't they charge a fortune?'

'It's not the same,' she said with a shake of her head. 'There's no financial outlay with self-publishing. I just decide which platform I want to use, download my novel, choose a cover and that's it. It's published.'

West put his wine glass down. 'That's it?'

She smiled. 'I could do it straight away, but I need to make sure it's as good as if FinalEdit were publishing it. That means finding and hiring an editor. It also means employing a cover designer; I don't want it to look amateurish. I will also have to learn about marketing which will be something completely new for me.'

'Ah,' he said, picking up his wine again. 'I see; you'd have to do all the advertising and promoting yourself.'

'Yes, it'll be a challenge, but I think I can do it.' She lifted her chin. 'I'm a good writer, Hugh wouldn't have taken me on if he hadn't believed in me. I'm not letting whoever is sending those photographs destroy my career. Self-publishing isn't easy; I have a lot to learn but I will succeed. Meanwhile, I'll write the next novel and keep going.'

He smiled at her determination. 'I predict a bestseller,' he said and raised his glass in a toast. 'Here's to your success.'

Finally, the wine was finished and the restaurant almost empty. 'I think we'd better leave,' West said with a smile and a slight nod toward the hovering waiter.

Outside, the mild night and clear, starry sky prompted him to suggest a stroll along the marina. They walked hand in hand in silence for a while and stopped to look out to sea.

West put an arm around her shoulder and pulled her to him. 'We're good together,' he said simply. And then, because the mood had become a little serious, he told her about his lunch in Fiona's apartment.

She was slightly taken aback at first. This was, after all, the woman he'd been laughing so uproariously with in Monkstown.

'She has a penthouse in one of those lovely apartment blocks between the Park and the Liffey, with fabulous views over both.' He told her about the sudden downpour they'd been caught in on the way there, and Fiona's kindness in providing an alternative while she put his wet shirt into the dryer. 'Unfortunately,' he said, 'getting into it was easier than getting out, so there was I, hands in the air, trying to wriggle my way out of a scrub top that was several sizes too small, expecting her to come back any moment. It could have been so embarrassing.' He held his arms up to demonstrate and wriggled his body frantically.

Edel smiled. Seriously, what had she been worrying about? As West continued his contortions, she started to giggle.

'It wasn't funny,' he said, grabbing her in a bear hug.

She giggled louder and kissed him soundly on the mouth. 'What an idiot,' she said fondly.

Back home, by mutual agreement, they went straight to bed and made love until after midnight.

Then, relaxed, sated and sure of their world, they slept.

28

Waking early, West resisted the temptation to stay just where he was. Instead, he kissed the sleeping woman beside him and got up and had a shower. Instead of hanging around drinking too much coffee, he decided to go into the station and get some work done.

He arrived early enough to chat with the night shift, swapping stories with officers he hadn't seen for a while before heading to his office to switch on his computer and check emails. There were a number from various children's groups he'd reached out to. But, like the others that had replied, they had nothing positive to offer.

The child in the suitcase. It looked like she was going to be left with that name and that didn't sit easily with him. The team, especially Andrews, wouldn't be happy having to put it to the back of the pile, but they'd understand. Despite their best efforts, they just couldn't solve them all. They'd leave that reconstructed image of her on the noticeboard, and they wouldn't forget.

The Ollie Fearon case was also stagnant. He had half a mind

to head out with Jarvis and Allen to interview that friend, if they could find him. He sighed, they wouldn't appreciate him tagging along and, if he were honest, he'd just be in the way. Opening his diary, he groaned. More damn audits due. This one an audit of their response time.

He wished he could do an audit of the time wasted doing them instead of proper police work but he was afraid if he suggested it, even with heavy sarcasm, Morrison would think it was a good idea. The man did love his audits. He might rarely interfere with what went on in the detective division yet forget to do the damn audits and he'd pester him for days.

He pulled up the relevant forms and figures and started on the tedious job of transferring one to the other. He'd made little headway when he heard voices outside and Andrews' cheerful face peered around the door.

'You're in early. Coffee?'

He nodded, saved what he'd done and sat back with his hands locked behind his head.

Andrews returned moments later, a mug in each hand. Handing one to West, he sat down. 'Jarvis and Allen are heading into the city first thing,' he said. 'They're hoping to catch Fearon's pal before he heads off to do whatever it is he gets up to.'

'Let's hope when they find him that he has something to tell us,' West said, picking up his mug. 'Before I forget, will you contact someone in Cork to have a look at Amanda Pratt?'

Andrews nodded. 'I thought I'd ask Tom to do that. He has a lot of contacts down there.'

'Good idea,' West said and put the woman out of his head. 'You know, I half expected to find more photographs in the post this morning. It seems to me, whoever is responsible, they've left the job half-done.' He saw Andrews' puzzled frown. 'The photographs were sent to professional contacts, and they did a bloody good job there. But they were also sent to me. That's personal, Pete.'

'You think they'll try again?'

'I just can't think that they'll leave it at that, or what motive someone would have for trying to destroy her.'

Andrews sipped his coffee thoughtfully. 'She has been involved in a number of high-profile cases. Maybe she's picked up a follower?'

West nodded and smiled grimly. 'A stalker? That's what woke me so early this morning. If it isn't someone she knows, it's someone who has his sights on her for some reason, and what you say makes sense.'

'I wouldn't put it past that young Finbarr,' Andrews said with a shake of his head. 'I'm sure we haven't heard the last of that young gurrier.'

West laughed. 'I agree but for the moment Finbarr is safely ensconced on Clare Island. Edel has kept in touch with Sylvia. She says Finbarr has been very supportive.'

'Hmmm,' Andrews said, 'I can't imagine that will last.'

'No. Probably not.' West put his half-empty mug down. 'I think we'll just have to wait until whoever it is takes the next step. Meanwhile, Mother Morrison will be shouting for this damn audit, so I'd better get back to it. Let me know as soon as Jarvis and Allen get in contact.'

Dismissed, Andrews took his mug and headed out to have a word with Tom Blunt about Amanda Pratt.

Sergeant Blunt, a big man who listened intently, remembered everything and said little, was a popular garda, liked by both the uniforms and detectives. Andrews found him in his office directly behind the front desk.

'You busy?'

A shake of his head gave Andrews the answer he wanted. He closed the door, sat in the only other chair in the office and told Blunt exactly what he needed from him.

'It's really just to make sure she is as settled down there as her brother is making out,' he finished. 'Have you someone who you can trust to check her out discreetly?'

Blunt gave the question some thought before saying, 'Garda Libby Forster.'

Andrews didn't know the name, but if Blunt thought she was up to the job, that was good enough for him. 'Perfect. Thanks, Tom. I'll leave it to you then.'

And that was that job done. Andrews often thought that if they could just get on with their job without excess chat and paperwork, they'd get a lot more done.

His phone was ringing when he returned to his desk. He reached it just in time. 'Andrews,' he said.

'It's Jarvis. We've found the guy; he has some interesting things to tell us. We're bringing him in; we think the sergeant needs to hear what he has to say.'

'Okay,' Andrews said, 'I'll let him know. What time do you expect to make it back?' He listened, asked a couple more questions, hung up and went to West's door.

'Jarvis and Allen are heading back. They're bringing Fearon's friend with them. Jarvis says you'll want to hear what he says.'

West looked up from his computer screen. 'Did he give you any indication what it's about?'

Andrews shook his head, a frown of annoyance on his brow. 'I've noticed that to be a trend with the lads recently. They're all becoming divas, wanting to ramp up the excitement before communicating anything.'

'Let them have their fun. Did they say what time they'd be back?'

'About eleven. I'll go and book the Big One before Clark lays claim to it. I spotted him lurking around a while ago.' With that, he vanished from sight.

West returned his attention to his computer screen. With a bit of luck, he might get the audit finished before they got back. He probably would have done, only his mind started to wander. They'd obviously found something interesting. He hoped it would be enough to put someone in the frame for Fearon's murder. They could do with getting one of their outstanding cases solved.

Forcing his attention back to the numbers and columns on the screen, he kept it there until Andrews once more appeared in the doorway. Perhaps he should have shut the door. With a deep breath, he looked up. 'What?'

'Just wondered if you wanted some more coffee,' Andrews said, arms crossed, shoulders resting against the door frame.

West saved what he'd done and shut down the programme. There was always tomorrow. 'Yes,' he said, 'and a biscuit if Clark hasn't pinched them all.'

Andrews returned with two mugs and a packet of biscuits. 'I hid them when I saw him around this morning,' he admitted, dropping the packet on the desk. 'He's a pig; he'd just eat the bloody lot and look around for more.'

Fig rolls. West's favourite. He opened the packet and took out a couple before pushing the remainder across the table. Andrews shook his head and patted his belly. 'Joyce has had to sew trouser buttons on a few times recently. She says I've put on weight and blames my inability to say no to a biscuit.'

West smiled. Joyce Andrews was a tiny woman with a huge personality. She was also a wonderful cook. He'd eaten in their house often enough and had seen the meals she put in front of her husband with the same instructions every time, *get on the outside of that.* He didn't think the odd biscuit Andrews ate in the station made a huge difference, and he said so.

'I told her I ate a packet a day here,' Andrews said, grinning from ear to ear. 'I'm not stupid, if I told her I only ate the odd one, she might think about cutting down my meals. I told her I wouldn't eat any more biscuits and this way, we're both happy.'

'You're mixing with the wrong sort too often,' West said with a shake of his head.

They switched to talking about their caseload until they heard voices approach, Sam Jarvis and Mick Allen jostling one another as they tried to be first into the office with the news.

'This is going to make your eyes widen,' Allen said.

'Widen? More like pop from your head.'

Andrews gave West an *I told you so* look that was ignored.

'How about you grab a couple of chairs and tell us,' West said. 'Where have you put...'

'Richie Gallagher,' Allen said, supplying the name. 'He's sitting in the Big One.'

'Right,' Andrews said, 'will one of you tell us what's going on?'

Jarvis, with a look at Allen, nodded. 'We'd called round to Gallagher's flat a few times yesterday. He was never there so we went to a few places where he was supposed to hang out, without any luck. It was beginning to look like he'd done a runner. This morning, early, we decided to give his place another try and there he was, cool as you please. He swore he didn't know we were looking for him, said he was busy all day yesterday and didn't get home until very late.'

'Busy doing what?' Andrews asked.

Allen met Jarvis' eyes and they both shook their heads. 'We wanted him to talk to us about what Fearon was into, so we didn't ask him,' Allen said with a shrug. 'In fact, when he looked a bit nervous, we told him we hadn't the slightest interest in what he was doing, that we just wanted to know about Ollie Fearon. He was very forthcoming then.'

Jarvis nodded. 'He said Fearon had contacted him last year and asked if he were interested in doing a bit of smuggling.'

'Drugs,' Andrews said, shaking his head.

'No, not drugs. People.'

29

'People?' West and Andrews exchanged looks.

Jarvis nodded again. 'Fearon told him they'd go over in a camper van or something similar and bring people back hidden in a false bottom. Gallagher was paid five k upfront and another five when they arrived back in Ireland. He did it twice, then he didn't hear from Fearon for a few months. About seven months ago, he bumped into him and asked if there were any more trips planned. Fearon laughed and said he was going solo. He told Gallagher that it was more lucrative for him, he got to keep all the money for himself.'

Jarvis stopped and ran a hand over his face. 'He was bringing children over. Gallagher said some were for families who wanted a relative rescued from migrant camps, but not all of them. Fearon didn't care as long as they coughed up the money. He said it was less risky than trafficking adults. He went over with a suitcase, spent some time in a hotel, organised someone to bring the child in question to a designated space, then the child was squeezed into the case and carried back on the ferry.'

'You see now why we wanted you to hear his story,' Allen

said, his face grim. 'It puts a different spin on our child in the suitcase.'

West sat stunned, his mouth hanging slightly open. Not in his wildest imagination would he have linked the child in the suitcase to Ollie Fearon's murder. He closed his mouth and gulped. 'So, Ollie Fearon may have been paid to bring our child to Ireland?'

'That's our guess,' Jarvis said, jerking his head to include Allen. 'But then, probably because of the sickle-cell disease, she dies before he can deliver her.'

'Leaving one very unhappy customer,' Allen said.

'Who got his revenge by killing Fearon,' Jarvis added.

West nodded; mostly, it made sense. 'Why wait till now though? The child died around six months ago. Why wait until now to get revenge?'

'What's that expression about revenge being a dish best served cold?' Andrews asked.

West shook his head. 'She was a child, hardly more than a baby. If it were family, I think they'd have acted immediately.'

'Maybe it wasn't family,' Jarvis said. 'According to Gallagher, Fearon was happy to supply children to whoever paid him. We all know what that means.'

Unfortunately, they did. Was Fearon supplying paedophiles? 'Let's go talk to Gallagher,' West said, standing, 'maybe we can persuade him to remember more of the details.'

But Richie Gallagher, intimidated by the grim-looking men who sat opposite, had no more to contribute. In fact, he was desperately trying to recant all he'd told them. 'Made it up, didn't I?' he said, looking wild-eyed at the detectives.

Allen and Jarvis had made the right call to get as much information out of the man while he was in an expansive mood. Despite reassurance that he wasn't being charged with any crime, he insisted he knew nothing, getting more and more panicked as the minutes passed.

Finally, almost an hour later, West shook his head. 'Get him out of here,' he said to Jarvis. He didn't have to tell Gallagher twice, the man leapt up and was out the door before anyone could change their mind.

'It's a shame we can't arrest him for people trafficking,' Andrews said, as the door closed behind him.

'With him spouting that he made it up to impress the lads,' West said with a regretful shake of his head. 'We've no proof. I think we should just be grateful he was initially so forthcoming.'

They headed out of the room together and stopped in the corridor outside where the main noticeboard covered most of the wall. The photo of the reconstructed child's face was there, its central positioning unchallenged. 'So maybe someone wanted the poor child,' West said. 'I just hope it was for the right reason.'

Back in his office, he picked up the phone and rang Morrison.

'Inspector,' he said, when the phone was picked up. 'I have some news for you regarding two of our cases.'

'Well, I hope it's good news,' Morrison said bluntly.

'Of a kind,' West said. 'It appears that our child in the suitcase might be linked to the murder of Ollie Fearon.'

'What?'

West smiled, remembering his own reaction to the news. He decided to take the man literally. 'It appears that our...'

'Yes, yes, I heard you the first time,' Morrison said testily. 'Are you sure?'

'Jarvis and Allen have just interviewed someone who knew Fearon. He told us about his involvement in trafficking.' West decided it was in his best interest to leave out the details of

Gallagher's involvement. He wasn't too sure the inspector would agree with letting him leave. When Ken Blundell's face popped into his head, he batted it aside. 'It was adults initially,' he continued, 'and then, it appears, he found smuggling small children to be more lucrative.' He waited a moment before he added the clincher, smiling to himself as he thought of what Andrews would say. Maybe it was diva behaviour, but sometimes it was allowed. 'He carried them across in suitcases, Inspector.'

'Well, well,' the inspector said, obviously as stunned as they had been with this turn of events. 'A very interesting twist, Sergeant. Is this going to assist in solving both cases?'

West had no idea, but he wasn't going to say that. 'It's opened up a range of possibilities, sir.'

Morrison, who had to play politics every day, said, 'Indeed,' and hung up.

The smile on West's lips faded as he sat back in his chair. A range of possibilities. He couldn't think of one. Clasping his hands across his stomach, he twirled his thumbs, and thought hard. It was worth reinterviewing all Fearon's associates. It would also be worthwhile showing Fearon's photograph around. He was getting his customers somewhere. He picked up a pen and started writing.

When Andrews appeared in his office doorway a few minutes later, he waved him in and tapped the list he'd made. 'Have Fearon's photograph emailed to any sub-Saharan embassy we have in Dublin, Pete. He may have been sourcing his customers there. Same with any immigration assistance groups. In fact, anywhere you can think of. We need to narrow this down somehow.'

Andrews took the list and nodded. 'Gallagher said he'd been given five k upfront and another five on completion. Fearon was more than likely receiving a lot more, but even at a conservative estimate we're talking about twenty grand. I think embassies may well be a good place to start.'

Unsure where sub-Saharan Africa started or ended, Andrews emailed the photograph to every embassy on the African continent that had an office in Dublin. To his surprise, less than an hour later, he had a reply from one of them.

30

'The embassy of South Africa,' he said, standing in the doorway and grinning at West who had returned to working on the audit.

'You're kidding me,' West said, taking the email and skimming over it quickly before rereading it slowly. 'So Fearon has been seen at the embassy several times?'

Propping his shoulder against the door frame, Andrews nodded. 'I rang them and spoke to a Jason Betterman. He said Fearon called several times with spurious questions about applying to work in Cape Town, and vague queries about health and welfare. Initially, he was viewed as harmless. They began to be suspicious when he just started hanging around, and he was told to take a hike.' He waved a hand. 'They put it more politely but it amounted to the same thing. The time frame gels with what Gallagher said.'

'It might be worthwhile going to speak to them,' West said.

'How about at three?'

'You've already organised it?' West said with a shake of his head. 'Where is the embassy anyway?'

'Earlsfort Terrace. We'll need to leave pretty sharpish.'

West closed the audit with a sigh of relief. He'd get it done, eventually. Morrison, he knew, would be far happier with a result in the case than a result in the audit. Actually, he reconsidered; he'd want a result in both. But he would just have to settle for one.

Less than an hour later, they were searching for a parking space on Earlsfort Terrace, West unwilling to park illegally and stick up a Garda business card, and Andrews arguing they should. It was an old argument that thanks to his seniority, West always won.

'There,' he said, spying a car pulling out several yards ahead.

They walked the short distance to the Earlsfort Centre, following directional signs for Alexandra House where the South African embassy was located.

'It's on the second floor,' Andrews said, pushing open the door into a wide ground-floor reception area. A security guard stood to one side, and two reception staff sat behind a long, curved desk.

There was no stairway visible; signs directed the two men toward a lift, which took them past the watching security man. West could feel the man's eyes boring into them. Not much would escape him, he guessed. It might be a good idea to have a word with him before they left.

The reception area on the second floor was smaller. Again, it was manned by one security guard and two reception staff, both of whom were dealing with customers.

Rather than wait, they approached the security guard and explained who they were looking for.

He gave them a quick once-over before nodding and walking to a wall-mounted phone. Moments later, he returned and indicated that they follow him.

'A man of few words,' Andrews muttered as they followed him down a short corridor.

The guard stopped abruptly at the third door. He knocked on it, pushed it open and waved them inside without a word.

Jason Betterman stood with a smile. Tall and gangly, he reached a hand across the desk to shake their hands. 'Cal is a great security guard, but social niceties aren't his forte, I'm afraid. Please, have a seat. May I offer you a drink?'

Both men declined. 'Thank you for replying so promptly to our email this morning, Mr Betterman,' West said, following introductions. 'We're investigating the possibility that this man, Ollie Fearon, was responsible for the death of a young child. She was found in a suitcase. We've recently learnt that Fearon used this means to smuggle children into the country.'

'In a suitcase? You're kidding me.' Betterman grimaced. 'Mind you, I shouldn't be surprised. We stop one means of people trafficking and they come up with another.'

'The child in question was around two years old. Malnourished, she would have been small for her age. And children,' Andrews said with a sad smile, 'are remarkably limber.'

'She had sickle-cell anaemia,' West told him. 'We're running with the theory that she died from lack of oxygen. Fearon was paid, probably very well, to bring her into the country. When he opened the case and found the child had died, we think he panicked and dumped her. He has subsequently been murdered. We've only recently discovered the connection.'

'You think whoever paid him to bring over the child, killed him when he didn't deliver?'

'He was murdered recently; she died around six months ago. But yes, we're running with the theory that whoever paid him, also killed him. We just need to find who his contact was.'

'You think that's why he was hanging around the embassy?'

West shrugged. 'People at refuge centres probably wouldn't have had the wherewithal to pay him. Embassies were the other option.'

'I'm not sure why,' Betterman said, his forehead creasing as he tried to see where the detectives were going with this. 'South Africans would have no problem bringing their children here legally.'

'But Fearon was here in the embassy,' West said, frowning. 'And he wasn't here for travel advice.' He was close, he knew it. 'What about illegal immigrants to South Africa? Isn't it true to say that your townships can have upward of several thousand illegals at any one time?'

Betterman smiled grimly. 'Unfortunately, that is true of some of them. However, there would be no point in coming to me for help finding someone there. If they were undocumented, there would be no way I could trace them, and even if I could, I couldn't help. Illegal immigrants to South Africa are sent back to their country of origin, wherever that may be.'

West's frustration was clear. 'We have it on fairly good authority that Fearon was smuggling children into Ireland. He was hanging around your embassy several months ago, and six months ago a child from the sub-Saharan continent was found suffocated in a suitcase.'

Betterman held his hands out. 'I'm not disputing your argument, Sergeant West; I'm just not sure how I can help you.'

West rubbed a hand over his face. 'You might not have been able to help bring the child out, but did you have any requests of that nature?'

'Have you any idea how many queries we deal with on a daily basis?' he said. 'Hundreds. The desk staff deal with most, pointing people in the right direction, giving them answers to simple questions. Many of the requests and queries wouldn't even have been logged.'

'Can we speak to them?'

'Sure,' he said, picking up the phone. 'It will have to be one at a time.'

Betterman sat back with his long arms crossed while West questioned each of the two desk staff. When the second left the office, he shook his head. 'I'm sorry we couldn't be of more help. I do hope you find who you're looking for. Although' – his face turned harsh – 'to be honest, it sounds like your Fearon got what he deserved.'

People always said that when a bad guy got killed as if it was poetic justice of a sort. There was nothing poetic about murder, no matter who the victim was. Thanking Betterman, they left the office.

In reception, they stopped to speak with the security man before they left the second floor. He looked at the photograph they handed him, shook his head, handed it back and said nothing.

'Do you reckon he can speak?' Andrews said before the lift door had even closed.

Suddenly, the guard put one muscular arm between the two doors, causing them to bounce open. 'Goodbye, and have a nice day,' he said, and stood back.

West and Andrews exchanged looks when the door closed. 'Jesus,' Andrews said, 'that'll teach me to keep my big mouth shut.'

Since West had been thinking much the same thing, he didn't comment.

The security man they'd seen in the main reception wasn't around when they exited the lift. They lingered, Andrews reading information leaflets on the noticeboard, West checking messages on his phone.

They didn't have to wait long before he reappeared. He came through a door on the far side, his eyes sweeping the room to check it was as he left it. When his eyes landed on the two detectives, they stayed there.

'Maybe he'll be chattier,' Andrews said as they crossed the

reception to speak to him.

They were in luck. As soon as they introduced themselves, the man's face relaxed into a smile. 'I guessed; you might as well wear a uniform it's so obvious.'

'We're looking for information,' West said, ignoring his comment. 'You might be able to help.' He took out the photograph of Ollie Fearon. 'We know this man was seen around here several months ago. We're wondering if you remember him.'

'Sure,' the man said, handing the photo back. 'He called up to the South African embassy a few times, and he hung around here until I told him to sling his hook.' He shrugged. 'Never saw him again after that.' His expression turned mean. 'When I tell someone to go, they generally stay gone.'

'How do you know he went to the South African Embassy?' Andrews asked. 'There are other businesses in the building, other floors he could have got out at.'

The guard jerked his head toward the lift. 'I watch the floor number,' he said. 'I know where everyone goes.'

'Do you remember seeing him with anyone?'

A group of people came through the door, chatting loudly. The security guard's attention was immediately diverted to them and he watched as they got into the lift and until it stopped at a floor. He nodded as if he'd guessed rightly and returned his attention to the detectives.

'The third or maybe fourth time he came in, he didn't go upstairs at all. Instead, he hung around the noticeboard, taking his time reading the posters, writing stuff down. He'd look up when the lift door opened and watch as people came out. Drugs was my first thought; I thought he'd approach some of what I considered the more likely candidates but' – he shook his head for emphasis – 'he didn't. It wasn't until a young woman came out, her eyes red from crying, that he moved. I don't know what he said, or what she said. Seconds later, he walked off, leaving her alone.

'Next time he came in was a few days later. Again, he didn't go upstairs, just hung around the noticeboard writing stuff down. Just when I thought he was going to head off, the lift opened and a woman came out. She was stunning.' He waved his hand in front of his face like a fan. 'I'm talking smoking hot here. He followed her, stopped her outside and spoke to her for a long time. I watched her open her bag, take out something and hand it to him, then she put her hand on his arm and they went off together.'

West frowned. 'Any idea who she was?'

The guard shook his head.

'Did she come from the embassy floor?'

'I've no idea,' he said, 'I didn't see her come in. I'm the only security guard on this floor; they're supposed to relieve me from the other floors if I need to take a leak. They never do, so I have to leave the place unattended for a few minutes now and then. They don't complain because each floor has its own security guard anyway. Since I didn't see her coming in, I've no way of telling where she went, and I don't watch the lift when it's coming down. She could have been visiting any of the floors.'

'Okay,' West said, 'thank you. You've been a great help.' He started to walk away, Andrews at his side. They'd gone a few steps when something struck him and he stopped. He smiled at Andrews. 'The lift has CCTV,' he said.

They both took a deep breath. This was it; they were going to find the woman. And when they found her, maybe they'd find out the name of the child in the suitcase. Finding out who killed Ollie Fearon would be a bonus.

31

It took two days to get permission to view the CCTV footage from the lift; the building's management company cited privacy despite West's assuring them that they'd no interest in anyone apart from one particular woman. Finally, a court order persuaded them to co-operate.

The security man, Bob Singer, was easily persuaded to come out to Foxrock to look at it when he was promised he'd be paid for his time. 'A consultant's fee, I assume,' he said, and mentioned a sum that caused their eyes to widen in disbelief. He wouldn't budge, guessing they'd never find one woman among all the females that visited the building in the course of several days. He was right, and despite Andrews' protestations, it was agreed to pay him what he asked.

Since Singer was only able to provide a rough idea of the month, they allowed several weeks either side to allow for error. They sat in the Big One and watched the discs one after the other. Copious amounts of coffee were consumed and several packets of biscuits munched before they heard what they'd been waiting for.

'That's her,' Singer said, spraying biscuit crumbs over the table in his excitement.

West and Andrews leaned in and watched the woman as she stood impassively in the lift until it opened on the second floor.

'The South African Embassy,' West said.

She stepped out and vanished from sight. They checked the time on the screen and watched until she appeared again only six minutes later, her face now hard and grim in contrast to the expectant look of earlier.

'It looks like she was quickly dismissed,' West said. He pressed the repeat button and watched again as she arrived and as she left. The guard was right. She was stunningly beautiful. 'Get some hard copies,' he said, 'let's see if we can find out who she is.'

Back in his office, hard copy in hand, he admired the woman's bone structure. She really was lovely. Did that mean she would be easier to identify? He hoped so. Folding it in four, he put it in his jacket pocket and sat thinking about their next step.

Andrews came in moments later. 'I've sent an email with her photograph to all the embassies as before. I also sent it to an immigrant woman's support group, and a few other places I thought might be relevant.

'You're assuming she's not Irish then?' West said. He laughed when he saw Andrews lost for words; it was a rare occurrence.

'Relax, I'm kidding you, it's a fair assumption based on what we know, but we could be wrong and need to look at the alternative. Perhaps she's an Irish woman looking for assistance from the embassy, maybe to trace a young relative? When they tell her they can't help, she comes outside and meets Fearon. He offers enough sympathy to have her spill her sad story, then he offers to help her.'

Andrews pulled up a chair and sat. He thought for a moment. 'Lots of refugees have made it out of their countries and gained refugee status wherever they land. But often they've left loved ones behind. That's where people like Fearon excel. They find these vulnerable people and exploit them because they have no choice. Oh, and by the way, I had replies from all the embassies. Fearon was recognised by two others. All he had to do was wait; someone would eventually arrive, desperate and willing to pay whatever he asked.'

'Whoever this woman is,' West said, 'we'll find her. Her face is not the kind you forget in a hurry.'

While Andrews busied himself sending the woman's photograph to every conceivable group, West made a few phone calls. If the woman was trying to get a child into the country, she may have tried the legal route first. He had a contact in the family court, a solicitor he'd been friendly with in a different life, and he didn't mind asking for a favour.

'I'll send you her photo, Dominic,' he said after several minutes on the phone, the first five of which were spent in catching up.

'Great, I'll have a look, and send it to a few people I know who may be able to help. We must meet for a drink sometime, Mike,' he said.'

'I'd like that, Dom,' West said, knowing they never would. The other man knew the same, the social intercourse of life. It had been much more prevalent in the law circle he'd worked in; he breathed a sigh of relief, not for the first time, at having left it all behind him. But he knew Dominic would do as he asked. It was a long shot but one worth trying.

Morrison would be happy with some movement in both cases. He just hoped the information led to a conclusion. At least, they were doing something.

He gave a thought to Edel's case, smiling as he realised it had become that in his head. The Blundell Incident, Edel's Case, why did he feel the need to label things?

He tapped a finger on the desk as he thought about it. He'd expected something more by now. The arrival of the post in the morning made them both stop whatever they were doing and stare toward the hallway with a sense of trepidation. He'd pick it up and sort through it, relieved when it turned out to be the usual glut of circulars and bills.

The sense of waiting was taking its toll. Edel's face had become drawn, her mood irritable. She'd stopped writing too, shaking her head when he mentioned it. Instead, she passed the time watching daytime television, and cooking more and more elaborate meals that they sat over in virtual silence.

Still mulling over her, he was startled when his phone rang, picking it up with a more than usually curt, 'West.'

'Mike, hi,' a female voice said. 'You sound busy, sorry for interrupting you. I'm in the area and wondered if you were free for a coffee.'

'Fiona,' he said, recognising her voice immediately. 'Sorry, I was miles away.' He checked the time. An hour out of the station would be just the thing to clear his head and give him room to think. 'Yes, I could do with a break right now. Are you in Foxrock?'

'I'm in Cornelscourt,' she said. 'I'd just pulled into the shopping centre, when I realised it was not too far to Foxrock and thought of you. Join me here; I'll buy you a coffee.'

'Perfect, see you in about fifteen minutes.'

He made a vague reference to meeting someone when he passed Andrews in the office and walked on before questions were asked. Andrews wouldn't believe there was nothing in it apart from a pleasant friendship so what was the point explaining?

. . .

West saw her immediately when he pushed through the doors of the café. She was sitting, one crossed leg gently swinging, as she watched the world go by. Her face was turned in the other direction so she didn't see him as he approached. He took the opportunity given and let his eyes drift over her. A gauzy black shirt was matched with a fitted black skirt. A chilly outfit for a very cold day. He guessed the dark cream leather jacket that had been thrown casually onto a vacant chair was also hers.

'Hello,' he said, bringing her eyes lazily back to him.

'Hello yourself,' she said, and nodded toward the coffee on the other side of the small table. 'It should be okay; I've only been sitting a couple of minutes and I did ask for it extra hot.'

Smiling, he sat and sipped it. 'Perfect,' he said, sitting back with a sigh. 'This was a good idea.'

'You look like you could do with a break. You're paler than I remember, and your eyes look tired.' She tilted her head to one side. 'Personal or work?' she said, her voice soft. 'Remember, I told you I was a good listener.'

Personal or work? It was a good question. The line between both was constantly being blurred. Time and time again, he and Edel were put into situations where she was occupying the role of victim and he the policeman. After Clare Island, it was their turn to have a long period of calm, yet here they were again, thrown back into those well-dug holes.

'No, that's okay,' he said, picking up his cup again. 'To be honest, it's just nice to be away from all the mayhem for a while and pretend I'm just a guy having coffee with an attractive woman.'

She smiled. 'Happy to oblige,' she said and proceeded to chat about her upcoming holiday to Miami, telling him about the hotel, the friends she was going to meet there. She drifted from there to places she'd been in the past, her favourite cities, favourite restaurants.

As she chatted, he could feel himself relaxing. 'I've enjoyed this,' he said, checking the time. 'Unfortunately, I need to get back. Maybe we can meet up again soon; you're as good as a tonic.'

She walked out with him, her hands buried deep in the pockets of her leather jacket. 'Thanks for coming, Mike,' she said when they got to her car. 'I always enjoy chatting with you.' With a smile, she leaned into him and pressed a kiss on his cheek. 'See you soon.'

He watched as her car pulled out and gave a wave before heading to his. He felt better; his head was clearer, now maybe things would make more sense.

The look on Andrews' face when he returned told him that his partner knew exactly where he'd been and he wasn't happy about it. He ignored him and returned to his office. Resisting the temptation to shut the door, he sat behind his desk and reached to switch on his computer, stopping when the desk phone rang. He picked it up. 'West.'

'It's Dominic, I need to see you.'

There was no disguising the urgency in the man's voice. West gripped the phone tightly. 'You've news about the woman?'

'I can't talk here,' he said, his voice a barely audible whisper. 'Meet me somewhere, preferably today.'

'How about the lobby of Randolph's,' West said. The boutique hotel near the courts was one he'd often used for meetings in the past.

'Perfect. I'll see you there in an hour.' Dominic Farrell hung up before West could argue that an hour was cutting it fine to get from Foxrock to the city centre and find parking to boot. It might just be one of those days, when he did what Andrews always wanted him to do, and park illegally.

Thinking of Andrews, he looked up and saw the man hunched over his computer. It was probably a good idea to take him along. He knew he was giving him the perfect opportunity to complain about his meeting with Fiona, but that would come regardless of how long it took. Andrews was never one to forget when he felt he was in the right.

It was essential to have someone with him if Dominic had something important to tell him. He wasn't going to be pulled into any old boys' network. He was a member of the Garda Síochána; anything the man had to tell him was going to be official.

Andrews nodded when he filled him in. 'So, you want me to come with you to *this* meeting?'

To West's surprise, that was as much as he said about his meeting with Fiona. Maybe he'd decided it was as innocent as he'd said. More likely, he thought, Andrews had discussed it with his wife, Joyce, and she told him he was being stupid.

Whatever the reason, he was happier to have a peaceful drive through the usual mayhem of Dublin city traffic.

As he'd guessed, despite checking numerous side streets and nearby car parks, there was no parking available. Seeing the clock tick past the hour, he gritted his teeth, parked illegally and put his *Garda Síochána Official Business* sign on the windscreen.

Ignoring the slight cackle that came from the passenger's seat and the grin on Andrews' face, he locked the car and stepped smartly toward the hotel.

32

The conversion of three old Victorian buildings into the Randolph Hotel had been done both sympathetically and expensively. Not far from the law courts, it attracted a mixed clientele who could afford its exorbitant room tariff. In its Michelin-starred restaurant, wealthy criminal types, with and without their legal teams, dined shoulder to shoulder with judges and solicitors.

If the price of eating or drinking within its walls didn't deter the unwelcome, the doorman, who looked down on the undesirables with a supercilious air, certainly did.

West and Andrews ignored him as they ran up the steps to the entrance. He gave them a quick once-over and stood back.

Despite illegally parking, they were five minutes late and Dominic Farrell was anxiously checking his watch as they walked in. He looked up in relief when he saw West approaching, the expression changing to annoyance when he saw he hadn't come alone. He wasn't a fool, however, and acknowledged the presence of Andrews with a considered nod. 'Official it is,' he said. 'Shall we go into the lounge? I could do with a coffee and it will be easier there.'

They found a corner seat, sheltered from others by the convenient placement of large leafy plants. Farrell raised his hand and attracted the attention of a waiter. 'Coffee?' he asked, looking at them.

Both men nodded, Andrews wondering vaguely if he'd have to take out a loan to pay for it.

By unspoken agreement, they didn't discuss what Farrell wanted to tell them until their drinks came. While they waited, solicitor and ex-solicitor discussed mutual acquaintances. Andrews, sitting back, looked on and listened to this insight into the life West lived before he joined the gardaí.

'You've no regrets?' Farrell asked, when the conversation had run its course.

West smiled and shook his head. He might have said more, but their order arrived with great ceremony; a whole palaver of cups and saucers, tiny spoons, sugar lumps with tongs, two pots, one with coffee, one with hot milk and, just in case, a jug of cold milk. The waiter, with great and unnecessary ceremony, poured a cup for each of them, asking each whether they wanted milk and sugar and whether they wanted hot or cold milk, one lump or two. West caught his partner's eye and gave a barely discernible shake of his head.

Andrews winked at him. 'Hot milk, two lumps,' he said, before he was asked his preference.

Finally, the waiter left them to it.

'Was it always like this?' West asked, looking around.

Farrell's brow creased. 'Like what?'

West put his cup down. It wasn't particularly good coffee. 'It doesn't matter,' he said. It was he who had changed, not the Randolph. He couldn't believe, now, that he'd ever liked the place. 'Tell me what you discovered.'

Farrell finished his coffee and sat back with a sigh. He shot a resentful glance at Andrews, before reaching into his pocket to withdraw a folded piece of paper. Unfolding it slowly, he looked around before putting it on the table. It was the email they'd sent him, with the photo attached.

'I didn't have to ask anyone who she was,' he said slowly, 'I recognised her immediately.'

West and Andrews exchanged glances. This was better news than they'd expected.

'Her name is Lesere Osoba. She is, or at least,' he amended with a shake of his head, 'she *was* Nigerian.'

'Was? She's dead?'

'It was tragic,' Farrell said. 'She hung herself, just a few months ago.'

West frowned. Where had he heard something similar? Recently. He closed his eyes briefly. 'Bloody hell,' he swore.

It was such a rare occurrence to hear him swear that Andrews looked at him in surprise. 'What?'

'Enda Careless's wife.' He looked across the table at Farrell. 'I'm right, aren't I?'

Farrell nodded. 'I met her a couple of times at official functions. He absolutely adored her and was devastated when she died. It was worse, of course, because he was the one who found her.' He met West's gaze. 'You didn't say why you were looking for her.'

They hadn't, but they owed him an explanation. West gave him a brief summary, watching as the frown on Farrell's face deepened.

'You think Lesere might have hired this Fearon person to smuggle a child into Ireland?'

'It's our running theory, Dom,' West said. 'Do you know anything about her, where she was from, whether she had children, younger siblings?'

Farrell shook his head. 'I don't, I'm afraid. They weren't married that long, you know. Only a year, maybe less. They met at a conference almost two years ago in Abuja, and I think, although I'm not sure, that's where she was from.'

'Thank you, that is helpful,' West said.

'You'll need to speak to Enda.' Farrell's eyes narrowed at the expression that crossed West's face. 'There's something you're not telling me, isn't there?'

West smiled slightly. 'It's an active investigation, Dom, there's only so much I'm at liberty to discuss.'

'Ah,' Farrell said, his face pinching in annoyance. 'I suppose you'd prefer if I said nothing either?'

'If you please,' West said, with a nod.

Checking his watch, Farrell muttered under his breath, and stood. 'I have to go. I can't say it was good to see you again, Mike, but it was certainly interesting.'

With a wave he was gone.

'You know he's left us the bill, don't you?' Andrews said, taking a quick look around to see if the coast was clear before lifting the pot and filling their cups. 'Hot or cold milk,' he asked in a feigned posh voice before pouring hot into both. He sat back with the cup and saucer in his hand. 'What do you think?'

West sighed. 'That we'd better step carefully for one. I'll contact the Nigerian embassy when we get back and see if they can fill in some details.'

'There are a lot of gaps,' Andrews said. 'If the child is a relation of hers, why didn't she bring her with her when she came over here and married Careless?'

'Maybe it's not her child, maybe it's a younger sibling, or a friend's child. We may be left with no choice but to ask him. I'd prefer to have as many of those gaps filled in as possible first.'

The waiter came to see if they wanted anything else. West shook his head and asked for the bill. When it came, even he was taken aback. He met Andrews' eyes. 'I'll put it down as expenses,' he said, 'don't worry.'

Morrison, who checked all their expense claims with a magnifying glass, would go ballistic at paying almost forty euro for three cups of coffee. West hoped they'd solve the case successfully before the end of the month.

Back in the station, Andrews got on the phone to the Naturalisation and Immigration Service while West attempted to contact someone in the Nigerian embassy who might have the information they wanted.

It took time and patience but eventually he was given a contact name in Abuja who, he was assured, would be more than willing to be of assistance. West hoped so. Investigating by phone was soul-destroying. He looked out to where he could see Andrews with his hand gripped in his hair. It didn't look as though he was faring much better.

He'd no idea what the time difference was between Ireland and Nigeria and spent a few minutes on the internet finding out. People were much more likely to be forthcoming if they weren't contacted at difficult times. To his surprise there was only an hour's time difference between Abuja and Dublin.

'It certainly makes things easier,' he muttered, as he dialled the number he'd been given and asked, hoping his pronunciation was acceptable, for Ginikanwa Obayomi.

'Just hold while I transfer you.'

He waited, tapping the fingers of his other hand on the desk. Enda Careless's face came to him. He'd seen the sadness there. Had it eaten away at him and made him do the unforgivable?

'Hello,' the voice came loud in his ear.

'Hello, my name is Mike West; I'm a police officer here in Dublin, Ireland. I'm trying to find some details on a Nigerian subject, and your efficient staff in the embassy here said you were the person to ask for.'

'Mike West,' the man said, his voice deep and melodic. 'I'm going to ring you back in five minutes, if I may?'

Surprised, West hurriedly agreed, and hung up.

Exactly five minutes later, the phone rang.

'It's Ginikanwa here,' the voice said, 'sorry about that. I just needed to check you were who you said you were.'

Amused, West asked, 'So who did you check with?'

'Our embassy in Dublin to begin with. They confirmed what you'd said. And the Garda Síochána head office were happy to fill me in on your qualifications. Now what can I do for you?'

West told him the details of the case. 'This Nigerian woman, Lesere Osoba, took her own life. There is no doubt with the finding. What we are trying to ascertain, is if she had any connection to a small child who died several months ago, and whose body was discovered recently.'

'A child, you say?'

'Yes, less than three years old. Our theory is that she was the victim of a people trafficker who transported her into Ireland in a large suitcase. She had sickle-cell anaemia and possibly suffocated.'

The Nigerian's *tut tut* was loud. 'Shocking,' he said. 'And the child was not reported missing?'

'No, we did a comprehensive search through various agencies. With so many children displaced because of war and unrest, it is a difficult task and so far, we've had no luck.'

'Indeed. Well, let me see if I can help you put a name to the child.'

'The University of Dundee did a reconstruction of the child's face for us; it may not be accurate but may be of some help so I'll send you the image. And I can send you a photograph of Lesere Osoba, if that would be of assistance?'

'It would all help, certainly. You can fax it to me.' Ginikanwa read out the fax number, said he'd contact him later if there was anything to report, and hung up.

It was back to the waiting game that was often such a large

part of West's working day. He usually managed to fill the wait with something useful. That blasted audit, for instance, he could get finished with that. He stared at the computer screen with little enthusiasm before standing and heading to the general office. Perhaps it was time to check up on the progress of other minor cases the team were dealing with.

There was nothing of any importance; certainly nothing they needed his help with. Andrews was on the phone, West perched on the side of his desk and waited for him to finish.

By the sound of his end of the conversation, he'd learnt something more useful than he had. Andrews, sensing his scrutiny, looked up, nodded and held his thumb up.

West gave an exaggerated sigh of relief that brought a smile to his face. After a few minutes of listening to the repeated uh-huh and a-ha that was Andrews' side of the call, he headed back to his office and sat waiting for his phone to ring.

It would be good to get these two cases closed. He could spend some time with Edel, get away to that spa hotel in Aughrim he'd heard such good things about. Perhaps he should ring and see if they had a vacancy for the following weekend. Or was that tempting fate a bit too much? He could wait.

Resting his elbows on the desk, he linked his fingers and tapped his chin, a position he was still in several minutes later when Andrews appeared in the doorway. 'A penny for them,' he said, 'but from the expression on your face, I guess it's Edel and those damn photographs.'

West smiled. He was sure he'd not always been such an open book, or maybe Andrews just knew him too well.

'You found something interesting,' he said, getting conversation back to the crime in hand.

'I found lots interesting,' Andrews said, plopping into a chair. 'I have a sore ear from the phone. We should have those earpieces that those call-centre people have.'

'Well, hopefully what you found out will make up for it,' West responded, resisting the temptation to say *get on with it.*

Andrews opened the A4 pad he was holding. 'Lesere Osoba. Born in Abuja in 1990. She was a lecturer in politics in the University of Abuja. Two years ago, she met Careless at a conference. He made several visits to Abuja over the following months until, eight months ago, they married and she came to Ireland. There isn't much known about her since she came here. She didn't work. She socialised with him but didn't appear to have any friends of her own. Three months ago, he arrived home to find her hanging from a tree in the garden. There was a typed suicide note, which read, *I'm sorry.*' He stopped and looked at West. 'A sad suicide note. What was she sorry for?'

West frowned thoughtfully. 'I'm sorry for marrying you. I'm sorry I came to Ireland.'

Andrews shook his head. 'How about, *I'm sorry, I can't live without my daughter*?'

33

'Her daughter,' West repeated, stunned.

'Yes, and we have a name. Abasiama. The very knowledgeable Sandra, who I was speaking to in the immigration office, told me it means *blessed by God*. They have a fairly large file on Lesere Osoba.' He flicked through the pages he was holding. 'Since she moved to Ireland, eight months ago, she's made several visits to them. According to Sandra, she was trying to have her daughter brought into the country under family reunification guidelines.'

'There wouldn't have been any issue,' West said with a frown. 'But I'm puzzled, why didn't she bring the child with her in the first place? They'd have had to organise residency for her, so why not include her child?'

Andrews threw the A4 pad on the desk and ran a hand through his hair. 'Because they couldn't find her. Lesere wasn't married to the child's father, a Nigerian called Utibe Omotoso. Just over two years ago, when the child was only a few months old, he went to South Africa to work. He liked it there, and asked Lesere to follow. She refused. He came back to Abuja to beg her to go, when she continued to refuse, he went back without her. She didn't realise until too late that he'd taken the child with him.'

'Ah, now I understand.'

Andrews nodded. 'He left no forwarding address. She tried to contact him, but he hadn't applied for any permit to work there so there was no way she could trace him. She spoke to rental agencies to see if he'd rented somewhere to live. Again, with no luck. Officials she spoke to told her he could be living in any one of a number of townships.' He shook his head. 'Do you know that some of those townships can have up to a million inhabitants, many of them immigrants with no status?'

West nodded. He knew the statistics. 'It sounds like she might have been looking for a needle in a haystack, Pete.'

'Sandra said that Lesere had contacted social workers in several townships.' He reached for the pad and opened it. 'Kayalesha, Zwelihle, Langa and Khayelitsha townships,' he said, pronouncing each phonetically. 'They probably don't pronounce them that way, but I had her spell them out to me.' He tossed the pad back onto the desk. 'She had no luck, obviously. A few months after the child went missing, Lesere attended the conference where she met Careless.'

'She would have told him, and probably asked him for help.'

The phone interrupted them. It was Ginikanwa Obayomi.

'My colleague, Garda Peter Andrews is here with me,' West told him, 'may I put you on speaker?'

'Of course, my friend,' he said, 'it will be good to tell my story to two rather than one.'

'Thank you.' West pushed a button for the speaker option and returned the handset. 'Am I still clear?'

'I can hear you perfectly,' Obayomi said. 'Greetings to you, Garda Andrews.'

Andrews raised his eyes to the ceiling before answering. 'Greetings to you.'

'Well, since the formalities are done with, let me tell you what I've discovered about the poor lady, Lesere Osoba.'

Most of what he had to tell them they already knew, but he had a few interesting pieces of information to add. Lesere had appealed for help to the authorities in Nigeria who in turn had contacted the South African authorities. Nothing worked, simply because they couldn't locate either father or daughter.

'Lesere met one of your countrymen, Enda Careless, at a conference in Abuja. He tried to intercede with the authorities for her before quickly discovering that their hands were tied. How can you do business with a ghost?

'They didn't stop trying to locate the child. Regular emails were received requesting updates on the situation. Then eight months ago, as you know, Lesere and Careless were married, and she relocated to Ireland. I suppose she felt she could do as much there as she could from here.' A loud sigh came down the phone. 'A few weeks later, Utibe Omotoso and his daughter were seen in Khayelitsha township by a social worker who had seen his photograph. Unfortunately, by the time the police arrived, he'd fled.'

'Was the information passed on to Lesere?' West asked, trying to keep the timeline straight in his head. Was this before or after she met with Fearon?

'Yes, of course, Garda West,' the Nigerian said, 'she had a right to know.'

Of course, she did. It was what she did with that information that West was more interested in. 'Can you tell me what date she was told?'

'Of course.'

The date made him close his eyes briefly before he looked

across at Andrews and nodded. A week before she met Ollie Fearon.

There was nothing more to be learned from Ginikanwa Obayomi. West promised to keep him informed of any break in the case.

'The child, Abasiama, she will be buried with Lesere?'

West took a deep breath. It would be a fitting end for the child to be reunited with her mother. 'Yes,' he said, 'I would hope so. At least now, thanks to your assistance, she will be buried with a name.'

'Abasiama,' Obayomi said quietly. '*Blessed by God.* Thank you, Sergeant West.'

West hung up. He and Andrews sat in silence for a moment digesting what they'd heard.

'What do you think happened?' Andrews said.

'She was desperate. Appeals to the authorities had achieved nothing. She was ripe to be milked by someone like Fearon.' He picked up a pen and tapped it on the desk before sliding his finger and thumb down until it fell flat, then sliding it upright and starting again, lost in thought. 'We're missing a step, Pete,' he said before tossing the pen aside with a grunt of frustration.

'What d'you mean?'

'The child... Abasiama... she was smuggled into Ireland in a suitcase, yes?'

On cue, Andrews nodded.

'Gallagher said they'd trafficked people using a camper van. I can't see him driving that all the way from Cape Town to Dublin.'

'Maybe, he came by sea?' Andrews suggested.

'There had to have been some plan,' West said. 'Lesere was an intelligent woman; she'd have wanted to know exactly how he was going to rescue her daughter before she handed over hard cash. We're missing something.'

'I think it's time to speak to Enda Careless. I rang his office; they said he wasn't working today, that we should be able to catch him at home.'

'Yes, you're right, it's time we spoke to him. Hopefully, he'll be able to clarify what happened.'

'He might also be our killer.'

West looked down for a moment, and when he looked back up his face was sombre. 'When I find out who's responsible for destroying Edel's career, I'll want to beat the person to a pulp. If it turns out that Fearon was to blame for Lesere's suicide, can we really blame Careless for killing him?'

Andrews stood. 'You might want to beat the person responsible to a pulp, but you won't. You'll ensure due legal process is followed. Anyway,' he said with a chuckle, 'you're not the *beat-someone-to-a-pulp* type.'

West stood and followed him. 'I am,' he said, slightly aggrieved.

They were still discussing the matter as they drove towards Mount Merrion where Enda Careless had an apartment. If he were there, they'd ask to speak to him. If not, they'd wait.

Careless's apartment was in a three-storied building backing onto Deerpark. They pulled into a designated visitor's parking spot and sat admiring the view.

'This is very nice,' West said.

'I bet he's on the top floor too,' Andrews said, 'he struck me as a penthouse kind of guy.'

'I used to be a penthouse kind of guy,' West offered. 'But it was in the city, always noisy. This is much nicer.'

They got out and walked to a smart front door bracketed on each side by brass plaques and doorbells. 'Just numbers, no names,' West said, 'very discreet.'

'He's in number ten.'

There was no sound when they pressed the bell.

'How do we know if it's even working?' Andrews complained, looking balefully at the doorbell as if it were to blame.

'We don't.' A buzz from the door caused them both to start. 'Well, now we do.'

34

West pushed the door open into a small, bright hallway. 'There we are,' he said, pointing to a directory on the wall beside the lift door, 'number ten. Top floor, just as you guessed.'

They took the stairs rather than the lift and arrived on the top landing minutes later. There were only two doors. 'Big apartments,' Andrews said quietly. Neither door was numbered. West shrugged and went to move toward the nearer one, when the other door opened and Enda Careless appeared. 'Come on in,' he said and disappeared again.

With an exchange of glances, both men shrugged and followed him.

The apartment was open-planned and light-filled, two floor-to-ceiling windows looking out over the park. It was impeccably furnished, matching tables, chairs, just the right pictures and ornaments. West guessed it had been a show flat and bought fully furnished. It said nothing about the personality of the pale-faced man who stood looking at them.

'You were expecting us,' West said with a slight smile. 'Dominic?'

Careless shrugged. 'We go back a long way.' Turning, he walked to the window and stared out. 'You'd better read me my rights, hadn't you?'

Andrews did the necessary formalities, while West's eyes drifted around the room. There were photographs of his wife in a number of places. She was even more beautiful than he'd thought or maybe it was the setting. He saw another photograph and moved to pick it up. Abasiama. Dundee had done a good job, the likeness was amazing, the professor would be pleased.

'You saw the poster pinned to the noticeboard at the station, didn't you?' West said, turning with the photograph in his hands, and holding it out to show Andrews who raised an eyebrow in response.

Careless turned to face him. 'Do you know what Lesere said to me weeks before she killed herself?' He walked across and sat into one of the armchairs. 'Sit down, please, this might take a while.' When they sat, he continued. 'She said it would be easier if she knew Abasiama were dead, she could grieve for her and try to move on. It was the thought that she was somewhere, maybe in pain or distress that ate away at her day and night.'

He rubbed his face hard with both hands, leaving his cheeks red. 'The poster on the noticeboard caught my eye immediately. I'd never met the girl, of course, but the likeness to that photograph' – he nodded at the one West continued to hold – 'was inescapable. I made some enquiries about the child and found out that she'd died months before Lesere's suicide.' He closed his eyes briefly, and when he opened them, they were bleak. 'I'd never felt such rage. It consumed me.

'Fearon killed her as surely as if he'd tightened that belt around her neck. It was only right that he pay with his own life.'

'So, you killed him?'

Careless's eyes grew cold. 'You think killing him would make up for the loss of my wife and her daughter? His miserable, squalid life equating to both of theirs.' He shrugged. 'I did, however, arrange to meet him.'

'He wasn't suspicious?'

'Suspicious?' he said with a sneer. 'Why would he be? He'd never met me. I rang him, told him I needed someone brought over from Calais and heard he was the man to go to. You know the way it is, flatter their ego, and they'll believe anything. I stressed we needed to be discreet and arranged the meeting place and the time.'

Standing abruptly, he walked over to the kitchen. 'Would you like a drink?'

'Coffee would be good,' West said, and seeing Andrews nod, he added, 'For both of us. Lots of sugar in his, milk in both.'

Several minutes later, Careless handed them each a mug, returning to the kitchen to pick up a wine glass he'd filled nearly to the brim. 'Now, where was I?' he said, sitting back into the sofa. 'Ah yes, my meeting with Oliver Fearon. There isn't much to say really. He obviously didn't see me as any sort of threat.' He laughed. 'Well, look at me, weedy is one of the kinder epithets that have been applied to me. The laneway was perfect, once I emphasised the need for discretion, he followed me in without question.'

He emptied half the glass of wine in one mouthful and put it down. 'I don't think he even knew what hit him,' he said conversationally. 'One minute, he was telling me how clever he was at getting people through border security, the next he was lying at my feet groaning.'

West's lips compressed into a grim line. Anger and violence, he found easy to deal with, but this cold, calculated and surprisingly detached account of Fearon's murder chilled him to the bone.

Careless swilled wine around in his glass before taking another gulp. 'I bent down beside him, my face close enough to smell his fear, then I looked him straight in the eye and said, *this is for Lesere and Abasiama*.' He wiped a hand over his mouth and brushed tears away with his knuckles. 'Fearon's grey, sweaty face looked puzzled, so I repeated the names.' He looked down at his glass. 'Do you know what he said?' A tear, alone and unnoticed, trickled from the corner of his left eye. He didn't brush it away and it continued, gathering momentum, falling to his shirt where it caused a round dark spot on the pale-blue fabric.

West watched as Careless's lower lip trembled. He pictured him, bending over the dying man, his hand still gripping the knife as he waited for some words of apology or justification, for some trace of sorrow for what Fearon had done to his wife and her child.

'Do you know what he said?' Careless asked again, his voice barely more than a whisper. He raised his face and looked at them. 'He said, *Who?*'

The final insult. West shut his eyes on the swell of emotion that swept over him.

'I stood and watched him die,' Careless said, draining his glass in one jerky movement. 'He did it without any fuss, then I left him there in the gutter where he belonged, got into my car and drove away.'

The silence that followed was heavy with emotion. West could see Andrews from the corner of his eye, his face set. He'd be wondering, West knew, if he would do the same to someone who hurt his son, his wife. Careless's action wasn't an easy one to sit in judgment of. Luckily, that wasn't their role. Theirs was to take him in for a crime he'd confessed to.

'We'll need you to come to the station and make a statement,' West said. 'But would you mind answering a few questions first?'

Careless shrugged. 'Why not?'

'Did Lesere meet Fearon at the South African Embassy?'

'Yes, her ex-partner, Utibe Omotoso, had taken Abasiama to Cape Town; Lesere never gave up hope of finding her and hoped the embassy would be able to help.'

West frowned. This was the part that didn't make sense. 'Fearon couldn't have taken the child from Cape Town to Ireland in a suitcase.'

Careless laughed. 'You're missing a bit of the story, I'm afraid. Fearon approached my wife outside the embassy. She was understandably distraught at her ongoing failure to find her daughter. Fearon... his type... are expert at finding those who are ready to be exploited. When she told him that Abasiama was probably in Cape Town, he shook his head and told her his area of expertise was getting people over from France.' His lips twisted in a grimace. 'She said he actually phrased it that way, *area of expertise*. He gave her his card and told her to give him a ring if things changed.'

West's eyes narrowed. 'But then the child was spotted in Cape Town.'

'Yes, however, the police arrived too late and Utibe and the child vanished. Lesere was distraught to have been so close to being reunited with her. Over the next couple of weeks, we did everything we could to try to locate them but it was impossible, there were just too many places they could have gone. Lesere spent a lot of time on Facebook and Instagram, monitoring contacts, peering at photographs, looking for something... anything... that might give us a clue. Her vigilance eventually paid off when a cousin of Utibe posted a photograph of a party on Facebook. In the background, almost unnoticed, was Abasiama.'

'Lesere wouldn't have missed her child,' Andrews commented.

'Actually, at first I thought she was imagining it. It was just a profile shot of a very small child, but, as you say, a mother wouldn't miss her own child.' He blew out a weary sigh. 'After that, it didn't take long to find out where they were. A small village in the south of France.'

West nodded as all the pieces started to fall into place. 'You sent Fearon over to snatch her?'

Careless looked at him with tear-filled eyes. 'Outside the embassy, he'd mentioned the sum of twenty grand. When we rang him, he must have sensed the desperation; he said it was a more complex case and would cost fifty.' His face clouded at the memory. 'Lesere would have given anything to get her daughter back, so we agreed. The plan was simple. He would go to the village and find out where she lived. When it was safe to do so, he would snatch her, then hide her in the suitcase and take her over on the ferry. Two weeks later, we had a call from him to say that Utibe and Abasiama had left the area, and he couldn't find out where they'd gone. We never heard from him again.'

He stood, walked to the kitchen and refilled his drink. 'Three months later, Lesere killed herself.'

'You'll need to come with us,' Andrews said, eyeing the full glass of wine.

Careless walked unsteadily back to his seat and sat. 'I'll go into the station tomorrow and make a statement,' he said, holding his glass cupped in both hands.

Andrews shot West a puzzled look. The man was a solicitor, he'd know how it went. He was being charged with murder, waiting until the next day wasn't an option.

'What Garda Andrews is trying to say, Mr Careless,' West said quietly, 'is that you'll need to come with us *now*. You'll be charged with Ollie Fearon's murder.'

Careless lifted his glass and took a deep drink before looking at West. He laughed, startling both men.

'Murder. Oh dear, Sergeant West, you have it wrong. *I* didn't murder him.'

35

'What?' Andrews said, looking bewildered. 'You've just told us you killed him.'

West shook his head. 'No,' he said thoughtfully, 'he didn't. He said he watched him die.'

Careless nodded. 'I heard you were a good solicitor, Sergeant West. You listened well, that's exactly it. I watched him die. You could, of course, charge me with failure to report a crime, but I think that's probably it.'

Andrews scowled. 'You admitted you lured him into the laneway where he was killed. That would get accessory to murder, if nothing else.'

'I told you, it was necessary to be discreet,' Careless said. 'Being seen with a well-known criminal would not be good for my reputation. I just wanted to ask him about Abasiama and Lesere.'

He was good, West acknowledged. There was no point in pursuing the matter. 'Okay,' he said, reaching to put his empty mug on the table before standing. 'Let's go, Garda Andrews, we've wasted enough time here.' He looked down on Careless who was smiling slightly. 'We'll get proof of your involvement,' West said, 'and we'll be back.'

Careless's smile grew wider. He finished the wine in one long gulp and handed the empty glass to him. 'Fingerprints,' he said, 'just in case you've any to compare them to.'

West took the glass by the stem. 'Thank you,' he said, 'that will save a lot of time.' He glanced at Andrews who, true to form, reached into his pocket and pulled out an evidence bag. West dropped the glass inside. 'We will need you to come down to the station and make a statement about what happened,' he said firmly. 'There will be questions asked as to why you didn't report the crime. Even if you had nothing to do with Fearon's murder, which I don't for a minute believe, your career is over, Mr Careless.'

There was no reaction to his comment. Careless stared straight ahead, ignoring them both.

'Bloody hell,' Andrews said when they sat back into the car. 'I feel like my brain has been scrambled.'

'Direction and misdirection,' West said, starting the engine and reversing out of the parking space. 'He's playing with us.'

'Why?'

'He didn't kill Fearon, but he knows who did.'

Andrews yawned and stretched. 'This blasted case is exhausting, why are you so sure he didn't kill him?'

West pointed to the glass he was holding. 'There are finger-prints on the knife. Clear ones, forensics said, so they must belong to the killer. Careless knows that, that's why he gave us the glass. There won't be a match, and he'll be in the clear. For murder anyway.'

'Gloves?'

West indicated to turn onto the Stillorgan dual carriageway. 'Had the prints been smudged, maybe, but they said *clear prints*.'

Andrews nodded and sighed loudly. 'Should have guessed it wasn't going to be that damn simple.'

'We'll get him as an accessory. Tomorrow, have one of the lads take a selection of photographs down to Kilkenny; see if that young lad, Bud, can pick him out.'

'Buzz, not Bud. Yes, I'll get someone to go down. If he can pick him out, it would be a start.'

West said nothing. It would be a start but Careless's presence in the shop could be discounted for any number of reasons. Even if Buzz could positively identify him, it wasn't illegal to buy a knife, and probably impossible to prove that the knife bought there was the murder weapon. Any good solicitor would have it dismissed as circumstantial in seconds.

'We'll just chip away,' he said, more for his own benefit than the solid man sitting beside him for whom chipping away was almost an art form. It was irritating to be played for a fool. His sympathy for the man's predicament was fast disappearing. Careless may not have killed Fearon but West was positive he was instrumental in his death.

They didn't speak until West pulled into the station car park.

'I'll get the glass to the fingerprint lads,' Andrews said, getting out of the car.

The two men wore determined expressions on their faces as they went inside. Andrews headed to the Fingerprint Division, prepared to argue that his case deserved precedence over whatever robbery case they were working on. He knew they'd be happy to oblige and would take inordinate pleasure in telling Sergeant Clark that something more important had come up.

Back in his office, West contacted forensics and asked for Fiona Wilson. Dealing with her would help to speed things up.

'Mike,' she said, when his call was eventually put through. 'How good to hear from you.'

He smiled and relaxed into his chair. 'Good to speak to you

too, Fiona,' he said. 'I wish I could say it was purely a social call, but unfortunately, it isn't.'

'But not *purely* business either,' she said, picking him up on the word and laughing lightly.

'How about we settle for business tinged with pleasure?'

'That'll do,' she agreed. 'Now what can I do for you?'

It took just a couple of minutes to fill her in. 'Our fingerprint team are taking the prints from the glass. When they upload them, will you check them against the ones you have on file that were taken from the murder weapon? We don't think they'll be a match, but we need to make certain.'

'Of course,' she said. 'I'll get back to you as soon as I've done it.'

West thanked her and hung up.

He ruffled his hair. This case was irritating him. He wanted to be shot of it. How much of that was due to his desire to concentrate on his relationship problem, he wasn't willing to guess. Relationship problem. It was the first time he'd acknowledged that they had one. He brushed it aside to think about later.

First things first. Who the hell killed Ollie Fearon? He rested his chin in one hand, and tapped the desk with the other, mentally reviewing everything they knew, putting what Careless had told them together with what they already knew about Lesere.

A frown on his forehead grew deeper as he worked his way through the data. There was something there.

When Andrews appeared in the doorway, he waved him in. 'Sit down and listen for a minute, will you?' He waited until he'd sat obediently into the empty chair before continuing. 'We know Careless had something to do with Fearon's death, yes?'

Andrews nodded.

'It's a pretty safe bet that he didn't wield the murder weapon himself, but if he'd hired a professional, why would he have left such clear fingerprints as evidence.'

'Not a professional killer, then,' Andrews muttered.

West shook his head. 'No, it was someone who didn't care that their fingerprints were identifiable.' He sat back in his chair; his eyes suddenly sharp. 'Abasiama's mother was dead, but what about the father, Utibe Omotoso? Wouldn't he have wanted revenge for what Fearon did?'

Andrews nodded. 'You think Careless managed to contact him?'

'Careless said they'd discovered where Abasiama was from a cousin's Facebook page. Fearon told him that they'd left the area, but we know that was a lie; he took Abasiama and fled with her. Maybe Careless contacted Omotoso on the same Facebook page.'

Andrews pursed his lips thoughtfully. 'He must have loved the child very much; he took her with him, kept her with him even when he had to flee from Cape Town. He must have been devastated when she was snatched.'

'And more devastated to know she was dead. That's a pretty good motive for murder.' He slapped his hand down on the desk. 'Contact the Immigration Service, Pete, and see if a visa was issued for him. If we are right, he'd never have risked trying to come in illegally. I'll contact our friend in Nigeria; see, if by any chance, they have his fingerprints on file.'

West wasn't in luck. His contact in Abuja wasn't available, and he spent several fruitless minutes trying to explain to the official the information he was looking for. After being told a number of times that he would have to speak to Mr Obayomi, he gave up.

'I hope you had better luck than I had,' he said when Andrews came through the door a few minutes later.

'I have.' He smiled. 'Utibe Omotoso came to Ireland on a

tourist visa two days before Fearon was killed.' His smiled widened. 'He's still here.'

West clenched a fist. Finally. 'The visa application had to have said where he intended to stay.'

'It did. It said he was staying in the Ambassador Hotel.'

'But he isn't,' West guessed.

'Afraid not,' Andrews said. 'But thanks to the Immigration Service, we now have his photograph. I've set Baxter and Edwards onto the delightful task of emailing every hotel in Dublin and sending his photograph. Jarvis and Allen are starting the even less delightful job of working through the B & Bs. We'll find him.'

When Andrews headed back out to give them a hand, West tried the Abuja office again with the same lack of luck.

He'd just replaced the phone when it rang. 'West,' he said.

'It's your friendly forensic scientist,' the cheerful voice said.

'Fiona, please tell me you have some good news for me.'

'Hmm,' she said with a short laugh, 'I could, but I'd be lying. There's no match, I'm afraid. Unless of course, that is good news.'

Even though it was what they'd expected, he was still disappointed. He brushed the feeling away. 'Thanks for putting a rush on it,' he said. 'I owe you a drink.'

Her laugh gurgled down the line. 'A drink? I'll expect more than that.' She hung up before he could answer.

He checked the time. Six. He wondered if his Nigerian contact kept late hours and rang the number again. This time it rang unanswered, not even an answering machine where he could leave a message. He hung up.

Home, he decided. 'Come on, Pete,' he said when he was out in the main office. 'They don't need your help, do you lads?'

Four heads shook on demand, as he knew they would. They'd much prefer if he and Andrews left, they'd relax, turn the radio up loud and laugh and joke through the boring job they'd been tasked with. 'How far have you got,' he asked, directing his question towards Baxter.

'Almost finished contacting the hotels and have already had responses from some. In the negative, I'm afraid,' he said.

'We've a long way to go before we cover all the B & Bs,' Jarvis said with a yawn.

'We also sent an email to a few hostels,' Allen piped up, 'funds may be tight.'

'And every Garda station has a copy. If he's visible, we'll get him,' Andrews added, standing and pulling on his jacket.

With a final request that West be contacted if they located the man, he and Andrews left the station together.

36

The rain had been falling heavily all day and as a result the traffic was heavier than usual, and West's journey home slow and frustrating. Enda Careless's face kept coming into his head. There was an emptiness in the man's eyes that worried him. He hadn't killed Fearon, but he'd been instrumental in leading him to his death and had stood by while another had done the deed. Contrary to what Careless believed, a charge of accessory to murder would hold. He exhaled loudly. It would be easier if they caught the man who wielded the knife. It had to have been Omotoso. They needed to find him.

Of course, he may have already left the country. His visa was valid for a month but there was no reason for him to stay. He could have caught a ferry to the UK and another ferry or even the train to France. By now, he could be anywhere and extradition would be impossible. After all, he had experience in staying beneath the radar.

He pulled up outside his house and raced through the pelting rain to the front door. In the hallway, he took off his jacket and shook it before throwing it over the newel.

The house was quiet. 'Hello,' he called up the stairs before picking up his post from the hall table and heading into the kitchen. He sniffed the air appreciatively. Something smelt good. Peering into the eye-level oven, he tried to make out what it was. Something in a casserole. He was hungry, whatever it was, it would be good.

Then he noticed the bottle of champagne sitting on the dining table, beads of moisture indicating it hadn't been out of the fridge long.

'What are we celebrating?' he asked, turning as he heard footsteps in the hall.

Edel almost bounced into the room, her face beaming. She put the laptop she was holding down on the countertop and pointed to the screen. 'This,' she said, 'look.'

It was her novel. *A Family Affair*. Live on Amazon.

'Wow,' he said, impressed, 'it looks really good. The cover is very eye-catching.' He grabbed her in a bear hug and kissed her. 'Well done,' he said, kissing her again.

She couldn't stop grinning. 'It's so great to see it there, Mike. I know there's a lot of hard work ahead on the marketing side of it, but at least it's out there and people can read it.'

Shutting the laptop, she handed him the champagne and took two glasses from the cupboard. 'Let's drink to our success,' she said. 'I'll be a bestselling author, and you'll be the best bad-guy catcher.'

The pop of the cork made them smile. West filled the glasses, handed her one and lifted the other. 'To our success,' he said, touching her glass with his.

Edel sipped her champagne, chatted about her book and explained her marketing strategy; he nodded encouragingly without really knowing what she was talking about. He guessed, by the fervour in her voice, that situation was likely to change but tonight his mind was elsewhere.

Bad-guy catcher. Enda Careless, Utibe Omotoso and Ollie

Fearon. All bad guys? Or were there degrees of badness? It was the kind of philosophical question that Andrews would enjoy over a pint. He'd keep it for him.

They finished the champagne before the casserole was ready. 'It's beef bourguignon,' Edel said, taking the dish from the oven, 'there's a bottle of red in the cupboard, will you open it, please?'

He busied himself with rinsing the champagne flutes, taking out red wine glasses and opening the wine. They didn't speak, each lost in what they were doing until he sat at the table and looked across at her as she dished up the meal.

He loved her; his life was immeasurably better when she was around. The ordeal with the photographs appeared, strangely, to have brought them closer as if together they could get through anything. And, thankfully, there was no more talk of her moving back to her Blackrock apartment.

'I've listed the apartment with a rental agent,' she said, as she placed the plate in front of him, surprised when he started to laugh. 'What?'

'I was just thinking you hadn't mentioned the apartment in a while,' he said, waiting until she sat down before picking up his fork and starting to eat. 'Very good,' he said, swallowing the first mouthful and tucking into the rest with gusto.

'It seemed a shame to leave the apartment empty,' she said. 'It was tempting to sell it, but they don't come up for sale very often so I thought it would be a good long-term investment.' She watched as his fork stayed motionless for a minute and smiled across the table. 'No, Mike,' she said, 'I'm not keeping it as a bolt-hole in case things go wrong. I love you, we're good together.'

He nodded and continued his meal. It had crossed his mind that was the reason but only briefly. They *were* good together. He picked up his wine glass. 'To us,' he said.

'To us,' she replied, picking up hers.

. . .

Next morning, Edel was still asleep when West came up to say goodbye. He dressed in the spare bedroom but he never left the house without speaking to her.

She rolled over and smiled when he left. Things were good. Despite those damn photographs. Throwing back the covers, she stood and went to the bathroom. Twenty minutes later, showered, dressed and bare-footed, she headed downstairs for breakfast. Since the photographs, she viewed every postal delivery with a feeling of dread. West had insisted on waiting until it had come for a few mornings, but at her urging he'd resumed leaving at his usual time.

'I'll be fine,' she'd assured him. It was getting easier, but the slight feeling of panic when she saw the post lying on the hallway floor hadn't gone.

She scooped the few letters up, took them with her while she put the kettle on and slipped two slices of bread into the toaster. It wasn't until she sat down with her breakfast that she sorted through them, dividing them quickly into his and hers.

Two were for her. The first was from the estate agent she'd contacted about renting the apartment. A quick glance through the letter and an even briefer glance at the included contract had her putting it aside with a sigh. It was definitely something to go through after several cups of coffee.

The second letter made her take a deep breath. She should have left it, called the gardaí, or at least called Mike, but instead, she picked it up. Using both hands, she flexed it. Firm. Photographs again? But this time addressed to her, not Mike. Holding her breath, she slipped a finger under the edge of the flap, eased the envelope open and emptied the contents onto the table.

Four photographs landed face up, fanning out to tell their

tale in full colour. Edel felt a wave of nausea hit her. She sat back, taking deep breaths, waiting for it to pass, hoping it would. Her heart was beating a rapid *thump thump,* her vision blurring. Afraid she was going to pass out, she pushed away from the table and leaned over to drop her head between her knees.

It was a few minutes before she felt able to straighten, several more before the nausea eased and her heart rate returned to something near normal. With a final deep breath, she turned to look at the photographs. They were good. She was no expert, but they didn't look like composites this time.

Ignoring the subject of the photographs as well as she could, she concentrated on the surrounding details. Within seconds, her eyes narrowed and with a grim smile, she reached for the phone.

37

As soon as West arrived in the station that morning, he rang the Nigerian office and asked to speak to Ginikanwa Obayomi. This time he was in luck and was put through straight away. Keeping it brief, he filled him in on the progress of their case. 'We're looking for Utibe Omotoso now,' he said, 'he gave the name of a hotel on his tourist visa application but he's not staying there.'

'So how can I be of assistance?' Obayomi asked.

'Would you be able to find out if he has relatives here, someone he may be staying with?' The sound that came down the line was definitely non-committal, so he rushed on with the other matter. 'I've no idea what Omotoso did in Nigeria, or whether he has been involved in any criminal activity. Could you check and see if his fingerprints are on file anywhere?'

'I can have a look, of course,' he said, his voice not relaying any enthusiasm. 'I'll ring you if I find anything helpful.'

Thanking him, West hung up. He'd not hear from him, he guessed, giving an irritated grunt just as Andrews appeared in the doorway.

'Bad night, or is it already a bad day?'

'Our Nigerian friend isn't feeling too helpful this morning,' West said, running a hand through his hair. 'Did the lads have any luck with the search?'

Andrews shook his head and perched on the side of the desk. 'Not so far anyway, but they haven't heard back from everybody yet. I did hear from the Kilkenny gardaí. I sent them a copy of Enda Careless's and Omotoso's photographs and asked them to do a line-up of both for that young lad, Buzz. No luck.'

West shrugged. 'There was never much hope there, was there? Right,' he said wearily. 'I'm going to get this blasted audit out of the way before Mother decides to come looking for it.'

Two hours later, he entered the last piece of data before saving and closing the programme. Then with perfect timing, the phone rang. To his surprise, it was the Nigerian.

'I have some news for you,' he said without any preliminaries. 'Utibe Omotoso has a cousin who lives in Dublin, in a place called Rathmines. Would you like the address?'

A bit of luck at last. 'That would be good,' West said, trying not to indicate just how helpful this piece of information was.

'It is number twenty-five, Saddler's Court, and the cousin's name is Dayo Lawal. He has lived there for a number of years and is married to an Irish woman. I have no name for her.'

'That's great,' West said, writing the name and address down. 'Thank you for your assistance. I will be sure to inform you how the case is resolved.' Hanging up, he quickly used Google maps to check the address. 'Just off the Lower Rathmines Road.' He stood and headed out to the main office.

Allen, he noticed, was still working on the list of B & Bs. 'I think you can call a halt to that,' West said with a rueful smile. 'It turns out Omotoso has a cousin living in Rathmines. I'm hoping we'll find him staying there.'

Andrews, who had been busy refilling the coffee pot, heard the end of what he'd said. 'You've found him?'

West explained that his Nigerian contact had come through. 'With a bit of luck, he is either staying there, or they know where he is.' He looked around the room. 'Where are the others?' he asked.

'Baxter and Edwards were called to an assault, and Jarvis is helping Foley with a robbery since Clark is taking personal time,' Allen said.

'Again,' West growled at him. 'Who told Jarvis to assist?'

Allen's mouth hung slightly open.

'I did,' Andrews said quickly, 'you were buried in your audit; I didn't want to disturb you.'

West knew he was lying but shook his head. There was no point in complaining, he'd have agreed if he'd been asked. Sometimes he wondered if he weren't just a little too easy-going. Pushing the idea away, he looked at Allen. 'Well, you may as well come with us,' he said, 'we may need someone young and fit if this Omotoso tries to do a runner.'

Allen laughed at Andrews' look of outrage and the three made their way to West's car, Andrews muttering under his breath about easily being able to run a marathon if necessary. West inputted the address into the car's satnav and thirty minutes later they turned onto Ardee Road.

The road was a mix of older semi-detached and newer town houses. Halfway down they found Saddler's Court. Unfortunately, it turned out to be a gated cul-de-sac. They couldn't drive up, but West was relieved to see an open pedestrian gate.

'We'll park where we can, and walk to it,' he said, looking ahead to find a space.

'It's resident's permit parking only,' Andrews told him, pointing to a prominent sign with a knowing grin. 'We could go and park in the Swan Centre, if you like.'

West had no intention of parking in the nearby shopping centre. He was just about to say so when Allen stretched forward from the back seat. 'Not up there,' he said, pointing ahead. 'That's a pay-and-display sign.'

West drove on and found a space. He paid the parking fee, guessing an hour would be more than enough, and stuck the ticket on the windscreen.

The town houses that comprised Saddler's Court were large and modern. Very nice, West thought, looking around before spying directional signs pointing them to number twenty-five, toward the back of the development. They walked and stopped outside the house.

Hanging baskets rocked gently in the breeze on either side of the uPVC door. They squeaked with every sway, providing background music as the three detectives stood with narrowed eyes assessing entrance and egress; a quick risk assessment none were aware of doing.

West took the lead up to the front door, the other two keeping a few steps back, their eyes constantly moving, their stance on high alert.

He pressed the doorbell once and waited. The swaying baskets caught his eye. They'd probably been a riot of colour in the summer, now they bore straggly ends of dead plants. A passing thought that winter pansies would look good in them was swept away as he heard the distinct sound of approaching footsteps.

The door was opened without hesitation, a pleasant-faced woman holding it open with one hand, as she held fast to the arm of a mischievous-looking child of indeterminate sex with the other. 'Yes?' she said.

West held up his identification card. 'My name is Detective Garda Sergeant West,' he said, watching as her pleasant open face quickly shut down. He indicated the two men behind him. 'Garda Andrews and Garda Allen.'

'What do you want?' Not precisely rude, definitely not welcoming. She bent and scooped the toddler up.

'May we come inside, please, Mrs... Lawel, is it?'

She nodded to the name, stood her ground for a moment as if to make a point and, with a grunt of dissatisfaction, stood back to allow them in. The hallway was too small to accommodate three tall men comfortably, so she reluctantly indicated an open doorway. 'Go on in,' she said, following them into the sunny kitchen-diner that stretched across the back of the house.

The toddler, released from her arms, immediately scampered toward the men, grabbing hold of one leg after the next, beaming up at them, unafraid.

'He's a cute lad,' Allen said, watching as a sticky hand left an imprint on his trouser leg.

'Her name is Halima,' the woman said, taking the child by the hand and walking her over to a small sofa in front of a television. She switched it on and put on a DVD. 'She'll be happy for a while,' she said. 'Now, what is it you want?'

She didn't waste her time on polite chit-chat. That made their job easier. 'We're looking for Utibe Omotoso,' West said, 'we've been told he is a cousin of your husband.'

'A very distant cousin, as it happens,' she said grudgingly, 'and what of it? Utibe is here legally on a tourist visa.'

'We'd like to speak to him,' he said without elaborating.

'Why?'

West smiled. She didn't look to be a stupid woman. She'd know that if three detectives arrived looking for Omotoso, there was likely to be a good reason.

'For goodness sake,' she said, when the silence stretched out. 'Utibe has been through enough. He's lost the daughter he adored. All he wants to do is find out who killed her. That's not a crime surely?' The look on West's face made her catch her breath and reach out to the back of a chair for support. 'Oh God,' she said, 'what's happened?'

'May we sit down,' West said.

All the fight seemed to have left the woman. She nodded and sat in the chair she'd been holding, body slumped, eyes looking down at clasped hands.

West wished that breaking bad news got easier with time. 'We believe that someone contacted Omotoso and told him that Abasiama's body had been found. The man we think was responsible for her death was found dead a few days ago.' She didn't move. 'Two days after Omotoso arrived in Ireland, Mrs Lawel.'

She ran a hand over her face and sat up. 'Dayo didn't have much to do with his relatives in Nigeria. He knew Utibe by name, that was all, so he was surprised to hear from him.' She frowned. 'I don't remember exactly when, maybe a couple of weeks ago. Anyway,' she went on, 'he asked if he could stay for a day or two. Dayo asked me and I agreed. Our child is half-Nigerian, I thought it was important to keep up connections.

'When he arrived, it was obvious there was something wrong. He was gaunt, his eyes red, and he barely spoke until Halima came running in.' She looked across the room to where her daughter was watching a children's movie, a smile on her face, her eyes glued to the screen. 'He cried when he saw her, frightened her actually, it took a while to calm her down. When she was asleep, he told us about Abasiama's death. He sobbed as he told us what a perfect, beautiful child she was and how much he'd loved her. He'd have done anything to make her happy, he said, but one day she vanished.'

'Why didn't he contact the child's mother?' West asked. 'He must have known that she was trying to get custody of Abasiama, and that it was likely she'd taken her.'

'He tried,' she said, 'he rang her number, only to find it had been disconnected. He sent letters that came back unopened, and when he rang her old job in Nigeria, he was told she'd left. They wouldn't give him her new address, or even a contact number. In France, he did what he could.' She shrugged. 'He's not a rich man; there was only so much he could do. After a while, he said he'd started to accept he'd never see his daughter again. Then he had a call from someone here in Ireland to tell him that both Lesere and Abasiama were dead.'

Her eyes were tear-filled when she looked around. 'I don't know if you have children, but I know how I'd feel if someone took Halima, and then to find out she was dead. I don't think life would be worth living.'

There was no arguing with this point. Those of the three who were childless looked across at the giggling child on the sofa, and Andrews thought of his son, Petey. But they still had a job to do.

'Where can we find him?' West asked her.

She sighed. 'He had a phone call earlier this morning and said he had to go out.'

West bit back the groan of frustration. So damn close. 'Did he say who he was speaking to?'

She shook her head. 'No, but it was someone local.'

'How do you know?'

'I heard him say he'd be there in about twenty minutes.'

West frowned. 'Did he know many people here?'

'I don't think so,' she said, 'but he didn't stay here every night so he must know some.'

Andrews leaned forward. 'The night of the twenty-first of November, did he stay here then?'

Mrs Lawel stood and walked to a wall calendar pinned on the back of the kitchen door. 'He was very considerate, he told me the nights he would be away so that I wouldn't have to cook for him. I've marked them on here,' she said with a smile before looking at it. She turned back to them. 'No, that was one of the nights he was staying elsewhere.'

The three men exchanged glances. The night in question was the night of Fearon's murder. At least now, when they found him, he couldn't claim the Lawels as his alibi.

There was nothing else to be learned from her. West stood and handed her his card. 'When he returns, tell him to contact me, Mrs Lawel.'

She took it but said nothing.

Outside, they stood for a moment.

'What now?' Allen said impatiently.

'Let's go back to the station,' West said. They fell into step, but nothing was said until they were in the car. He started the engine, but instead of moving off, he sat staring out the window.

Andrews looked at him. 'What?'

'Just thinking of what she said. How much Omotoso had loved his daughter, his devastation at her disappearance. He probably felt justified in taking the life of the man responsible.'

'Probably,' Andrews agreed.

West turned to him. 'But Fearon wasn't the only man responsible, was he?' He took his mobile from his jacket pocket and tossed it to Andrews. 'Ring Careless, his number is there under C.' Starting the engine, he did a U-turn on the narrow street.

38

'There's no answer,' Andrews said, the phone pressed to his ear. 'You think he might be in danger?'

'If it hadn't been for Lesere and Careless's attempts to get custody of the girl, she'd still be alive. Lesere is already dead, that leaves the solicitor. You could argue he's as much to blame for Abasiama's death as Ollie Fearon.'

They pulled up outside Careless's apartment fifteen minutes later and got out. West pushed the doorbell, pushing it again when there was no answer. After a few seconds, he pressed every doorbell and finally got an irate answer through the intercom.

'It's the gardaí,' he said without preamble, holding his identification up to the camera, 'can you let us in please?'

The door buzzed almost immediately and the three men sped up the stairs. On the landing they stopped, eyes drawn to the open door of Careless's apartment. West nodded at the other two and they drew their weapons.

West pushed the door fully open and waited. 'Armed gardaí,' West shouted loud and clear. And then again, 'Armed gardaí.'

When there was no sound, he moved in, SIG held in both hands pointing toward the floor. He moved to one side as

Andrews moved to the other, Allen following close behind. They stayed there for a moment, their backs to the wall as they surveyed the open-plan apartment. Only Careless was there, slouched on the sofa, and he wasn't moving.

From where they stood, they could see where arterial spray had peppered a wide area around him. West, with Andrews covering him, darted across the room. It was useless. Careless's upper torso was sodden with blood, his eyes wide and staring. West carefully felt for a jugular pulse. There was none.

They searched the rest of the apartment, room by room, checking any possible hiding place, covering one another, grunting as each door opened.

'We just missed him,' Andrews said, when they'd cleared the last room.

Back in the living room, they holstered their weapons. West looked down at Careless with a sudden feeling of helplessness. With a shake of his head, he turned to Allen. 'Phone for an ambulance, and get a...'

A groan made him stop and turn around, his hand grasping the holstered SIG. It wasn't until the sound came again that they pinpointed the direction. It was coming from the balcony, the door to it hidden behind full-length curtains.

Pushing them back, they saw the man they were looking for propped against the balcony wall, his face ashen. He held a knife in one hand, the blade pressed to his wrist, blood dripping from the wound to the balcony floor.

His SIG drawn, West slid back the door. 'Utibe Omotoso,' he said, stepping outside. It was bitterly cold, but the sky was blue and winter sun shone through the trees in the park. Looking down on him, seeing the shallow breathing and the waxy sheen of his skin, he knew the man had chosen this place to die.

Squatting down, he said, 'You are Utibe Omotoso?'

The man nodded.

'Tell me what happened,' West asked. Holstering his SIG, he shuffled closer and saw that the blood was oozing, not spurting from the self-inflicted wound. There was still hope.

Turning, he shouted through the open door behind him. 'Get an ambulance.'

'That won't be necessary,' Omotoso said.

West looked back to him. 'Tell me what happened,' he said again.

It seemed for a second that he would ignore him, but then, in a barely audible voice he said, 'Lesere was never interested in Abasiama. It was I who rose during the night to feed her, who changed her when she was wet, washed her when she was dirty. My friends laughed at me; told me I was turning into a woman. I told them they didn't understand. She was the light in my life. That's why I wanted to move to Cape Town. There she had a better chance. But Lesere wouldn't move, her career was too important, so I went without her.'

'But she wanted Abasiama back?'

Omotoso smiled. 'Lesere was beautiful, but she only cared for herself and what people thought of her. She'd no real interest in Abasiama; the role of the grief-stricken mother, however, was one she enjoyed playing. It would have gained her a lot of sympathy and attention.'

In the distance, the sound of a siren grew louder.

'Careless contacted you?'

'He told me Abasiama had been found, tossed away like garbage and he told me about Lesere.' He lifted the knife for a moment and looked at it as if wondering why he was holding it before looking back at West. 'I don't know why she killed herself,' he said, 'but I doubt it was because of Abasiama.'

The siren grew louder, it would soon be outside.

'Did you kill Oliver Fearon?' West asked.

The Nigerian looked puzzled for a moment, then his face

cleared. 'The man who carried my daughter over in the suitcase, yes, I killed him.' He held the knife up. 'I had a very sharp knife; it went in easily. This one,' he waved it gently, 'is not so good.'

'And Enda Careless,' West asked, hearing the ambulance siren switch off as it arrived outside the apartment block.

'It was his money that allowed that man to take my daughter. But for him, we would still be in France. Abasiama would still be alive.' With a quick movement, he brought the knife back to his wrist, pressed down hard and drew it across. The blood spurt was immediate and dramatic. 'Stay back,' he said, as he saw West move. 'You would do me no favours if you succeeded in saving me, and justice is better served in letting me die.'

West drew a ragged breath before sitting back on his heels and watching as the spurt quickly reduced to a bubble. Omotoso gave him a faint smile and his lips moved. From where he crouched, West could hear *Abasiama*, whispered like a prayer.

Raised voices in the apartment alerted him to the arrival of the ambulance crew. He threw a last assessing glance over the man. There was no sign of life. Paramedics pushed him aside with no ceremony, their attention on saving the man, his story unknown to them. Within seconds, as West watched from the doorway, monitors were attached, his wrist bound, and intravenous fluids pumped in to save a man who didn't want saving.

He turned away from the indignity of the scene and stepped back into the apartment. Andrews, seeing his pale face, caught his upper arm in a tight, reassuring and brief grip. 'A garda tech team and the pathologist are on their way,' he said, releasing him and nodding toward the balcony. 'We're giving them a two for one offer, are we?'

West shook his head at the man's grim sense of humour. 'I'm not sure,' he said. He turned to watch the crew through the glass door. 'I hope so,' he murmured, as Andrews moved away to join

Allen who was standing over Careless's body, examining it dispassionately.

'He's almost decapitated him,' Allen said.

'Well, I'm damn glad he didn't,' Andrews said, bluntly. He'd seen a decapitation once; he wasn't sure he could face another.

One of the ambulance crew came in from the balcony. 'It's brass monkeys out there,' he said, rubbing his hands together and blowing on them.

'Well?' West asked.

He shook his head. 'If we'd been a few minutes earlier, he might have had a chance.' The other paramedic came in, and without another word they gathered their equipment and left.

Andrews and Allen went out to put a face on the man they had been looking for, returning seconds later, both faces sombre.

'It doesn't get easier,' Allen said. 'But at least he's with his daughter now.'

'They're all together,' Andrews commented. 'Lesere and Careless. Abasiama and Omotoso.'

Remembering what the man had told him about Lesere, West frowned. The truth or a different version of the truth. They'd never know.

The pathologist arrived shortly afterward, raising his eyebrows when he was informed of the second death. 'Enda Careless and...?'

'Utibe Omotoso, a Nigerian. He was the father of the child we found in the suitcase,' West explained, and pointed to the photographs of Abasiama and Lesere. 'Careless was married to her mother.'

Niall Kennedy picked up the photograph of each, his face unusually grave. 'You'll have to give me the details when you have time,' he said, replacing the photographs and turning to look at the body of Careless. He shook his head. 'The landlord isn't going to be happy, is he?'

West frowned. 'Landlord? I was under the impression he owned it.'

'No, it's a rental,' Kennedy said with an authority that didn't invite doubt. He saw the puzzled look on West's face. 'I thought you knew his story.'

'So did I. We were told he sold his house in Cork and bought this when he moved to Dublin.'

'That's partially correct,' Kennedy said. 'He sold his house all right, but he'd taken out a huge mortgage to fund the search for the child. Private detectives, it seems, don't come cheap. When Lesere came to Dublin, which she did frequently, she stayed in the Shelbourne Hotel and spent her time shopping. The staff in Brown Thomas knew her well.'

'How do you know all this?' West asked.

The pathologist grinned. 'The missus, Fern, she works as a legal secretary in the law courts, didn't you know?'

West shook his head.

He nodded toward the dead man. 'When they married first, he brought Lesere to a few official functions in Dublin. She made quite an impression.' He glanced around before leaning closer and dropping his voice. 'The gossip goes that she wasn't always alone when she stayed in the Shelbourne, Mike.'

West ran a hand over his face. 'To Careless she was a distraught mother who couldn't live without her child, to Omotoso, a manipulative woman who only cared for herself, now you're giving me a third version of her.'

Kennedy shrugged. 'Does it matter? She's dead.'

West opened his mouth to explain. Only the first of the three versions gelled with her suicide. Maybe Careless learned about her dalliances in Dublin. Maybe he'd realised he was being taken for a fool. West closed his mouth without saying a word.

The pathologist was right. It didn't matter. All concerned were dead.

They waited until he'd finished and until the garda technical team arrived and then with a nod to them, and a final look at the dead bodies, they left.

Outside, it was bitterly cold, but when West suggested they walk around the park, Allen and Andrews nodded agreement. An icy breeze buffeted them as they took the path up the hill to where, even in the winter light, the view over the city was lovely. For a moment, they stood lost in thought and then, without a word, they turned and walked back to the car.

39

Edel was in a different part of the city, outside a different apartment block. Her first instinct to ring West had been brief, and she'd hung up before he answered. This was something she could handle herself.

He'd mentioned where the apartment was, and if she had to ring every apartment in each of the four blocks, she'd find the right one. As it turned out, it wasn't that difficult in the end. She knew it had views over both the river and the Park, and it was a penthouse. So, she quickly narrowed it down to four.

A sleepy, annoyed voice responded after several rings on the doorbell of the second apartment she tried. 'Who the hell is that?'

Edel breathed a sigh of relief. 'It's Edel Johnson,' she said. She didn't have to say anything more. The front door buzzed seconds later; she pushed through into the foyer and headed up the stairs to the top floor.

Fiona Wilson, a thin robe covering her obviously naked form, stood in the doorway of the apartment waiting for her. Her eyes swept over Edel dismissively. With a shrug, she stood back and gestured for her to come in.

Passing her without a glance, Edel strode across the open-plan room and headed to the small dining area. She pulled out a chair and sat, her handbag on the table in front of her.

Fiona took a chair on the other side of the table, her eyes sharp and assessing. 'It's a long way from Clare Island,' she said, as if there had been nothing between them since that meeting.

Both women knew better.

Edel looked at the petite, attractive woman opposite and shook her head. 'Why?' she asked.

Fiona laughed and ran a hand through her hair, tucking it behind her ears. 'Shouldn't that be my question?'

Edel's smile was forced. 'I think we both know why I'm here.'

'Perhaps you'll enlighten me?'

'I've heard about predatory females like you,' Edel said, her eyes sweeping over Fiona as if at an unattractive specimen in a laboratory. 'Women who are only interested in men who belong to other women–'

'Belong?' Fiona interrupted with a sneer.

'For want of a better word,' Edel continued. 'Your kind aren't interested in a relationship; the thrill is in the conquest. The more difficult it is, the greater the buzz you get.'

'I've no idea what you're talking about,' Fiona said, standing and walking to the kitchen where she busied herself putting on the kettle. 'Tea?' she asked, as though this were a perfectly normal social meeting.

Edel shook her head. She waited until Fiona came back with a mug of tea in her hand and resumed her seat, before placing the photograph she'd brought with her on the table.

It was a photograph of West in the act of taking off his shirt, his torso lean and smooth, the angle flattering.

'Women like you,' Edel said in a steely voice, 'don't understand the nature of honest, decent relationships. You probably thought he wouldn't mention being encouraged to take off his wet shirt, but he told me all about it. He's too decent a man to have been suspicious, but women like you have motives for everything you do, nothing is inspired by philanthropy.'

'Women like me,' Fiona sneered. 'What about women like you?' She smiled at Edel's look of surprise. 'Oh yes, I know all about you, Miss Poor Little Victim. He deserves a more worthy, equal match than a spineless woman like you.'

Edel laughed. It was a laugh so unexpectedly full of humour that Fiona, who obviously expected to see her reduced to tears, was taken aback. 'Miss Poor Little Victim,' Edel repeated. 'Yes, for a while I was exactly that, but d'y'know something, Fiona? I'm not that woman anymore. Now,' she said, picking up the photograph and standing, 'I want letters of explanation written to my editor, Hugh Todd, and to Elliot Mannion, the managing director of Books Ireland Inc., to inform them that it was you who made and sent those photographs, and that I was entirely innocent of any wrongdoing. If I've not had confirmation that the letters have been received within two days, I will take further action, and expose you for the nasty piece of work that you are.'

Fiona laughed, but for the first time she looked slightly less self-assured. 'Who'd believe such a ridiculous story?'

Edel shrugged and picked up her bag. 'If there's one thing I've learned over the last few days, Fiona, it's that it doesn't matter whether there's truth in the story or not, it just matters how forcibly it's told.' Her eyes hardened. 'With Mike on my side, we can make sure it's told very forcibly indeed.'

She left the apartment with her bag swinging from her hand, feeling lighter than she'd felt in a long, long time. Outside, she stood a moment taking deep breaths. And then, from the corner of her eye, she saw West getting out of his car.

He ran towards her, stopped inches away and looked at her. Whatever he saw in her face must have satisfied him because he nodded and smiled. 'I was going to take you for a celebratory lunch,' he said, 'so I went home early. The photographs were on the table.'

'She won't be bothering us again, Mike,' she said.

'You're damn right she won't,' he said, fire in his eyes at the thought of what Fiona had done. 'I'll have her charged. This will be the end of her career.'

'No,' Edel said, reaching for his hand. 'She's going to write letters of explanation to Todd and Mannion, it won't remove the damage, but it will lessen it. She'll leave us alone now, that's all I want.'

Seeing his hesitation, she squeezed his arm. 'Please, this is the best way. Not dragging it all through the courts and reliving it again.'

'Okay,' he said, bending to place a kiss on her lips. 'We'll do it your way.'

Edel reached a hand up to caress his cheek. 'Thank you. Now,' she said, linking her arm in his and walking toward her car, 'you mentioned celebrating. Does that mean you've solved the case?'

'It does. Let's go somewhere and I'll tell you all about it.'

'And we can talk about that hotel in Aughrim you want to take me to. Let's go soon before something else happens.'

'Don't worry,' he said, with a reassuring smile. 'Foxrock will be quiet for a while.'

And with that promise, he saw Edel to her car before returning to his. He stood for a moment before getting in and looked back to the apartment block where Fiona lived. He hoped he was doing the right thing in not bringing charges. After all, if he'd brought charges against Denise Blundell, Ken would still be alive.

But Edel was right. It would be a messy case, the

photographs purporting to be Edel would have to be submitted in evidence and Fiona would probably get off with a suspended sentence.

He climbed into the car, switched on his engine and drummed his fingers on the steering wheel. She'd mentioned being recently promoted. He wondered if that entailed a new contract. And a probationary period? His eyes narrowed, and he pulled out his mobile. Her boss, Stephen Doyle, was a decent sort; he'd have a quiet word. If she were on probation, he would make sure it wasn't extended.

Fiona Wilson would be advised to look abroad. He'd make sure of it.

He'd get it done and he'd take Edel to Aughrim.

And Foxrock *would* be quiet for a while.

ACKNOWLEDGEMENTS

Grateful thanks to the wonderful team at Bloodhound Books, especially, Betsy Reavley, Tara Lyons, Heather Fitt, Ashley Capaldi and Ian Skewis.

A huge thank you to all the readers, reviewers and bloggers who read, review and share – it makes it all worthwhile.

Ongoing thanks to my brother-in-law, retired Detective Garda Gerry Doyle, for answering my questions so patiently – as ever, errors are mine alone.

Thanks to my writing buddies who help keep me sane – especially Jenny O'Brien and Leslie Bratspis.

And, of course, thanks as always to my wonderful family and friends.

I love to hear from readers – you can contact me here:
https://www.facebook.com/valeriekeoghnovels/
Twitter: @ValerieKeogh1
Instagram: valeriekeogh2

Printed in Great Britain
by Amazon

44169995R00168